The Wantland Files

THE WANTLAND FILES

by
Lara Bernhardt

ADMISSION PRESS

Prologue

Danielle awoke, the bedroom pitch black. Silent. The glowing numbers on her alarm clock read 1:42 a.m. Her abdomen shook, rumbling slowly at first, then building in intensity like an earthquake. Her unborn baby, once awake, would play for an hour at least, jostling her insides and making sleep impossible. The little guy had no concept of night and day. How could he? She didn't remember this much nighttime activity during her first pregnancy.

A foot or maybe a fist pressed against the inside of her belly, stretching her skin until she could almost perceive the outline of the tiny appendage. She ran her fingers over it in circles and decided it must be a fist. The little guy jerked away, then gently pressed his fist against her fingers. She pressed back. He jerked away again. When he punched her waiting fingers, she smiled. He seemed very inquisitive already. And playful.

He tired of that game and dug his toes into her rib cage. So, no sleep for a while. Her stomach growled. Cheese and pretzels sounded so good her mouth watered. Or cheese and crackers. Or both. She hefted her weight into a sitting position, careful not to disturb her sleeping husband, Stephen. On the way out of the room, she ran a hand over the crib in the corner, which was all set up and waiting for the baby's arrival.

She waddled down the hallway, sacroiliac joints aching. She was eager to meet her feisty baby. Her due date was only a few weeks away, and she didn't have much longer to wait. But these last few weeks had been brutal. He woke up in the middle of the night habitually and was so big and active, she could no longer sleep through his waking times.

And he squeezed her stomach to the point she could eat only small portions before indigestion kicked in. She swung constantly between uncomfortably full and starving.

She paused to check on her sleeping three-year-old, Drew, as she passed his room. He'd been suffering terrible nightmares since they'd moved into this house. She'd thought he would love having his own room. Instead, now that he slept by himself, he cried out most nights, sobbing about not liking "the dark" as she consoled him. She hoped he adapted before the new baby arrived. Two little ones screaming in the night would be exhausting. Reassured to see him sleeping peacefully, she continued to the kitchen.

She opened the refrigerator and removed a block of sharp cheddar, then stood in front of the pantry and deliberated between crackers and pretzels. She grabbed both. After slicing half the block of cheese, she settled at the dining table with her plate of cheddar, the box of crackers, and the bag of pretzels. She stabbed a pretzel stick into a piece of cheese and popped it in her mouth. *Delicious.* Possibly the best cheddar ever made. Or her pregnancy made it taste that way.

A rustling noise outside interrupted her snack. She stopped crunching and listened. Did she imagine it? Probably just the wind.

She resumed chewing.

There it was again.

She swallowed and sat completely still. Again she heard a sound—a whispery noise she couldn't identify. She listened intently but heard nothing except the chirping of a single cricket overwintering in the house.

She impaled another bite of cheese with a pretzel and chewed cautiously.

When the plate sat empty, her thoughts turned to peanut butter. But her stomach already churned with early indigestion. She decided water would be a better choice.

She pressed her glass to the refrigerator dispenser and heard something. A different sound.

She froze. No sound assaulted her ears but her own ragged breathing.

Her abdomen tightened, clamping down on her distended belly. She put a hand to her stomach and noticed the baby had stopped moving. He remained still as her muscles continued to contract. When the pain kicked in, she leaned forward and moaned.

She looked at the clock to time both the contraction and the baby's still episode: 1:57. Even though this was probably only a Braxton-Hicks contraction, she wanted to make certain. She attempted to remember Lamaze breathing. At 1:58 it relented. She stood straight and resumed regular breathing.

Five minutes passed uneventfully. No contractions. No noises. And the baby shifted only once. He seemed to have gone back to sleep. Which sounded like a fantastic idea to her. She turned to leave the kitchen and switched off the lights.

She heard crying in the backyard.

She flipped the lights back on. That was definitely not the wind or her imagination. That sounded like someone needed help.

Heart hammering, she turned to the back door. She heard it again. Closer this time. Scarcely able to breathe, she forced her feet to carry her forward.

Whatever waited in her backyard cried out again. Wailing.

No human could make that sound.

3

Drew slept just a room away. She had to find out what was out there and make sure it posed no threat to her son.

So why did her feet refuse to move? She waited, hoping the sound would repeat and she could determine the source without looking outside.

A sense of dread enveloped her. She didn't want to know.

The minutes ticked by. Maybe she should wake her husband. She hated to disturb him. He had to get up and go to work in the morning. She could nap in the afternoon with Drew, but he couldn't. Besides, what if it turned out she was spooked over nothing?

She moved to the back door and placed her hand on the knob. *Don't be silly. There's nothing out there. Just open it and see the backyard is empty and go back to bed.*

Another cry. She dropped her hand. She'd heard that sound before, though not for many years.

She pushed aside the curtain and peered out the window.

Nothing.

Then movement.

Something neared the porch a step at a time.

The light spilling from the kitchen and dining room windows cast enough illumination for her to make out the figure. And his familiar features.

She opened her mouth but produced no sound. Her throat constricted. She gulped for air, unable to draw a breath.

The figure reached the porch and stared directly at her. He opened his mouth and wailed again. She screamed.

1

Kimberly Wantland rubbed her temples. "I hate this. I don't like to say no to any of them."

Michael Thompson, her director, laughed. "You have it easy. The website receives over a thousand submissions daily. We've weeded through the junk and the cranks and the trolls and the guys who just want to hit on you. You only see the good ones."

She shuffled through the folders. "Any of these would work. The hotel in Eureka Springs . . . the lawyer's wife in Oklahoma City. I don't know."

"It needs to be good. Season finale and all."

"I know that. I've been doing this show for three years."

Her lead researcher, Elise, weighed in. "Try winnowing them down to your favorites. Any cases we don't select for the finale, we'll put on next season's slate. I've researched every one of these. They're all excellent candidates."

Kimberly dropped her face into her hands and moaned. "I don't know. Someone else decide."

"No can do, sweetie," Michael said. "You're co–executive producer now."

She looked away from the manila folders and watched the rest of her crew, headphoned and staring at monitors, selecting

5

footage from last week's investigation to send to the production company. Once they finished the episode, they would distribute it to the network.

She never could have predicted her little research project would come so far.

She covered her eyes with one hand and held the other over the file folders, index finger pointed down. "Eeenie, meanie, miney—"

The sound of a crying baby interrupted her. She dropped her hand from her eyes.

The secretary's voice carried from the lobby. "Ma'am? Ma'am! You can't go in there."

A young woman pushed her way into the room, gaze darting over every face until landing on hers. "Ms. Wantland!"

Kimberly jumped from her seat as the woman crossed the room, crying baby cradled in one arm and a toddler in tow.

Michael stepped in front of her. "Can we help you?" He held up a hand to the secretary following the woman.

The woman stopped in the middle of the room, eyes wild. "I just want to talk to Ms. Wantland."

"About?"

The woman looked around the room. The crew watched warily. "I need your help. Please. I don't know what else to do."

Michael moved closer to the woman. "You need our help with a case? You can submit your request online, ma'am. You really shouldn't come barging in here—"

"I did that! I did apply online. My case wasn't accepted. And I've called and called. No one will let me talk to Ms. Wantland. So I had to come. I drove three hours to get here. Help me. Please."

Kimberly stepped from behind Michael to get a better look at the woman, whose demeanor relaxed somewhat at the sight of her. The infant continued to cry while the toddler slurped two fingers and stared at her. "What do you need my help with? Tell me about your case, Ms . . . ?"

The woman took two more steps into the room, releasing the toddler and shifting the infant to her shoulder. "Williams. Danielle Williams. I see a ghost. At my house. We moved in while I was pregnant, and everything was great until I started seeing the ghost."

"That sounds awful. Visible manifestations can be quite alarming. Does the apparition stand over you while you sleep? Does it attempt to communicate? Has it—"

"It's the ghost of my grandmother's cat. I'm sure of it."

Michael groaned. "It's the ghost-cat lady. Ma'am, I'm sorry. We declined your case because it simply isn't scary. Just . . . shoo the cat away."

"A cat?" Kimberly turned to Michael. "We've never investigated a disturbance that revolves around the spiritual entity of an animal."

"For a reason. Because it isn't that interesting."

"I disagree. I'm intrigued."

Danielle stepped closer. "He is scary. Very scary. Please. I haven't slept in months. Taking care of these two is challenging enough, but now I have a horrifying demon cat waking me up at night, too. It's ruining my life. My husband is beside himself. He thinks I'm crazy."

Kimberly shook her head. "That's terrible. Nothing worse than being called crazy for seeing something others don't see. Some of us—"

Michael rested a hand on her arm. "You can't possibly be considering this. We need to focus on an amazeballs finale right now that will blow viewers out of the water and have them psyched for next season. If this was a good option, I would've brought it to you."

7

"I don't know what he means," Danielle said. "All I know is I need your help. Please, Ms. Wantland. My husband says you're a fraud, but I knew if I could talk to you—if you could see how much we need your help—I knew you'd come. I watch your show every week. You're the only one who can help me. I don't know what else to do."

She crossed her arms. "A fraud, huh?"

"We declined for a reason. Focus on the selected shows."

"How often do you see the apparition?" she asked.

"Almost every night."

"Every night, Michael. How often do we have an entity that manifests that regularly? We're guaranteed activity. That never happens."

Elise spoke up. "Maybe we could work this into next season?"

Danielle shook her head. "Next season? How long will that take? This has been going on for months. I need help now."

Kimberly grasped the quartz crystal around her neck and crossed to stand beside the distraught woman. Closing her eyes, she allowed Danielle's energy to wash over her. Reading the woman's spiritual spectrum, she detected fear and desperation but also strong compassion and sturdy strength. And hope. The heart chakra radiated stronger than all the others, with flares of the survival chakra, deep red. This woman told the truth. Danielle truly feared for her family's safety and wanted only help.

Michael was right. This could be a ratings disaster. But this was a good woman and a good mother who feared for her family's safety. And Kimberly knew the pain and frustration of asking for help only to be laughed at and ostracized.

She opened her eyes. "Okay. We will take your case." The relief rolling off the woman nearly knocked her over. The one-armed hug, baby squashed between them, did knock her off balance.

"Thank you! Thank you so much!"

"Whoa," Michael said. "You can't just—"

"You told me to choose, and I have. The ghost cat is now our season finale. Let's start the case file. Elise, can you take her information?"

"Sure thing." Elise led Danielle back to the lobby.

Michael crossed his arms. "What was that?"

She returned to her desk and gathered the file folders. "Here. You and Elise can start scheduling these cases for next season's open slots. I suggest we start in Eureka Springs. The hotel sounds complex. It's been investigated before, but they want me to come now."

"Don't change the subject. You just accepted a case we turned down."

"A case *you* turned down. This was the first I heard of it."

"I get it. That woman twisted your bleeding heart. But this case isn't finale material. It's boring. Probably nothing."

"It's not nothing. I could feel it. She needs help."

"I agree she needs help. From a psychiatrist."

"Michael! Rule one. We never call anyone crazy."

He pinched the bridge of his nose. "Fine. Take the case. But push it to next season. We can bury it during a holiday week."

"This woman needs help *now*. You didn't feel what I felt. This is real. Something is haunting her family."

"And you just played the sixth-sense card. You know I hate that."

"Well, now I'm playing the co–executive producer card. Only Randall Hoffmeier can overrule me. And he won't."

"Why do you think that?"

9

"Because you're going to back me on this and tell him it's an amazing case."

"Why would I do that?"

"Because I know you miss the old days just like I do. When we first formed APS and no one had heard of Kimberly Wantland. When our only focus was helping people no one else believed. Not ratings and viewers and sponsors and ads and Internet gossip and which talk show wants to interview me. Just . . . helping people."

Michael blew out a deep breath. "You're right. I do. But we're not the Albuquerque Paranormal Society anymore. Now we're *The Wantland Files*."

"We'll always be APS in my mind."

"That's sweet. But I also really love my Manhattan flat and being able to pay my rent."

"I don't know why you even keep that place in New York. You're almost never there."

"Because I can. And because I want a place to stay when I see Broadway shows. It's an investment. You know that. What makes no sense is that you stay here in Albuquerque. In the house you grew up in. You could live anywhere."

"I waited years for that house to come back on the market. And you know why I wanted it."

"I know, sweetie."

She squirmed at the pity in his expression. "So. Are we doing this?"

"Looks like we are. A ghost cat for a season finale. I'll pitch Hoffmeier. And you better deliver." He reached for his phone, then paused before dialing. "Can I tell him the cat holds a dagger in its mouth? Or speaks Latin backward? Or carries its head in its paws?"

"No."

2

Kimberly passed a tissue across the table to Danielle. Years of experience taught her to come prepared for tears. She knew the cameraman would zoom in for a close-up. Stan was a pro. She covered the woman's hand with her own and squeezed. "What happened next?"

"It's just so difficult to talk about, you know?"

"Absolutely. But we're here to help, Danielle. We need to know what we're dealing with."

Danielle nodded and dabbed the tears from her cheeks. "I started seeing him while I was pregnant."

Now they were getting somewhere. Even though she already knew what happened, they needed it on camera. Getting people to share while the cameras rolled was the hard part. But that was why she got paid the big bucks. She nodded, encouraging Danielle to keep talking.

"I couldn't sleep toward the end, you know? I was so big and uncomfortable, and Joshua was so active at night. I thought he was throwing a party in there." Danielle offered a watery smile through her tears. "The first night I saw him, I got up 'cause I craved cheese. A midnight snack, you know? So rather than thrashing around wide-awake in bed, I got up to get something to eat."

"The first time you saw the apparition, you mean?" She needed to keep the woman focused. Her one-hour time slot didn't allow for extraneous chatter. And she didn't pull in top ratings by discussing midnight snacks. They would edit that out.

"Yes." Danielle's eyes widened. "People are going to think I'm crazy, but I know what I saw."

"Danielle, tell us what happened that night." She leaned forward to allow Stan to get some wide-angle shots of both of them.

"I fixed a plate of cheese and pretzels and crackers. It just sounded so good, you know? And I sat down at the dining table to eat."

"This table, Danielle? Where we're sitting now?" Kimberly placed both hands on the table.

Danielle nodded, her eyes even wider. "Yes. Right here where we are. And I heard a weird noise in the backyard." The woman gestured to the door behind her.

Kimberly watched Stan motion to the other, younger cameraman, TJ, who zoomed in on the door.

"What did you do when you heard the noise?"

"At first, nothing. I thought it was my imagination or the wind or something. But it kept getting louder. Sounded like it was coming closer."

"What did it sound like?"

"Kind of like a whisper or a rustle. I don't know. Then there was an awful sound. Almost like a howl or a scream. A wailing noise. It got louder and louder. I could hardly breathe I was so scared. I almost yelled for Stephen, but I didn't want to wake up Drew. Once a toddler wakes up in the night, you can't get them back to sleep, you know?"

"Of course." She didn't know the first thing about toddler sleep patterns but nodded anyway. "So what did you do?"

"I told myself I was being silly. I went to the door to open the blinds so I could see out. And that's when I saw him." Danielle choked up again, covering her eyes with the tissue.

"Him?"

Danielle nodded, the tissue pressed to her eyes, and whispered, "Felix."

Kimberly's brow furrowed briefly. None of her research or interviews mentioned that name. Mindful of the cameras, she hid her confusion, smoothing her features. "Felix?"

"I flipped on the back light, and there he sat on the porch, staring right at me. Just like he used to when I was a little girl. Those eyes . . . I knew he hated me. He arched his back and hissed. Just like he used to."

"Danielle, tell us who Felix is."

"He's . . . he was . . . my grandmother's cat. But he died when I was twelve."

"Most people might think you're getting worked up over nothing. It's just a cat, right? Why not just ignore it?"

Danielle's head snapped up. "You don't understand. You didn't know this cat. He was vicious. Creepy. Weird yellow eyes, razor-sharp teeth, and long claws. Like the *Pet Sematary* cat."

"How so? Why were you so scared of him?"

The young woman shuddered. "He scratched me and hissed at me. He hid under the couch and pounced on my feet when I walked by. I hated him. And I knew he hated me. One night, he crept into the bedroom where I slept at Grandma's house, sat on my chest, and pushed his nose against my mouth. I think he wanted to smother me. And no one believed me. Not my mom and definitely not my grandmother. That cat terrified me when I was little. I couldn't stand going to my grandmother's house because of Felix."

13

She nodded. "Folklore surrounding cats goes back centuries. People once believed cats sucked the breath from sleeping children. And, of course, cats were used as familiars by women practicing witchcraft." She made a mental note to have her researcher look into any history of witchcraft in the area. The thought crossed her mind that perhaps Danielle's grandmother had been a witch. One look at the weeping young mother told her this was not the time to ask.

"I was . . . I was glad when he died, even though my grandmother cried for weeks."

"And why do you think you saw a vision of your grandmother's deceased cat instead of, say, a stray that wandered into your yard?"

"No, it was Felix. I knew that without a doubt. The color of the fur, the markings, the gleaming yellow eyes. And the way he acted. After all these years, he's back to terrorize me again." The woman broke down into another fit of sobs.

"I'm so sorry." Kimberly offered another tissue to replace the damp, wadded mass in Danielle's hand.

"Thank you." The woman blew her nose and took a deep, shuddering breath. "When I saw Felix on the back porch, I couldn't move. I couldn't speak or call for Stephen. Something paralyzed me. I blinked a few times, trying to make the image disappear. But it didn't. Then he turned and walked back toward the yard . . . and disappeared. Just faded away."

"What did you do then?"

"I screamed, which woke up Stephen." Danielle gestured to her husband, who stood on the other side of the room, waiting for his turn in front of the camera. He shifted from one foot to the other and ran a hand through his hair. "I couldn't sleep after that—I was so shaken, you know? He thought I dreamed it."

"How can you be sure you didn't?"

14

Danielle took another deep breath. "I saw him again. He keeps coming back."

"How often have you seen him?"

"Gosh, I've lost count now. Almost every night. Every time I get up, I'm terrified I'll see him. I hear him wailing and hissing." Tears dripped from her eyes, spilling onto her cheeks.

"What is it you're hoping for by inviting me to your home? How do you want me to help?"

Danielle leaned forward and grabbed her hand. "I've watched your show for years. I've seen you clear houses of all sorts of entities. I hope . . . I hope you can make him go away. I want him to leave me alone. I never want to see that cat again."

"And moving isn't an option?"

"No. We haven't even been here a year. We lived in an apartment but decided to get a house when we found out Josh was on the way. It took everything we had to move in here. We can't possibly afford to move again."

Kimberly nodded, allowing the cameras to zoom in on her comforting smile before bringing the husband in.

"Stephen, won't you join us?"

TJ spun his camera around, focusing on the husband, who looked as if he'd rather be anywhere but here. He rested a hand on his wife's shoulder before he sat. *Good.* He'd remembered the instructions Michael had given him earlier. Appear supportive and reassuring, whether he believed his wife or not.

"Stephen, have you seen the apparition that's scaring your wife?"

"No, ma'am. She doesn't see it when I get up with her. I've tried. For weeks I got up almost every night. But nothing happened."

"Do you believe your wife is seeing the ghost of her grandmother's cat?"

He took a deep breath, running his fingers through his hair. He glanced at his wife, who still dabbed at her eyes with a soggy tissue. "Before, her doctor said it could be a pregnancy-related psychosis. But she still sees it."

Danielle cried softly. Stephen wrapped an arm around her and tugged her close, holding her head against him.

"And you believe I can help?"

"My wife sees something that scares her. I don't know what it is, but she sees something. Please figure out what's going on. I just want my wife to find peace again."

She stood and spoke directly to the camera. "What caused Danielle's nightmare from her childhood to haunt her in the present? Is the spirit of her grandmother's cat still wandering the earth, drawn to the descendent of his former owner? Or is something more menacing and dangerous prompting these nighttime visits? Stay with me as I unravel the mystery of the prowling ghost cat and bring peace back to this family. Tonight on *The Wantland Files*."

3

Kimberly allowed herself a glance at Michael after the scene cut. Normally he flashed a thumbs-up and a huge smile after a successful scene. But he wasn't even looking at her. Back turned, he seemed deep in conversation with someone she couldn't see. What was so important he couldn't even acknowledge her? *Rude.*

Stan's voice drew her attention from Michael. "Hey, Kimberly. You want to try to squeeze in the walk-through before lunch?"

She threw a glance at Danielle, who was drying her eyes while Stephen sat beside her. Michael still focused on the other person. When he threw his head back and laughed, she made her decision. "After lunch. We all need a break." And she needed to learn who Michael found so delightful.

"Ms. Wantland?" Danielle called from the table.

She stopped in her tracks and turned away from Michael and his visitor, forcing a smile on her face. "Yes?"

"You don't think I'm crazy, do you?"

"Not at all."

"What do you think is happening?"

She sank into a chair. "Hard to say without some investigation. Any number of things could cause it. I've seen residual and active hauntings where the entity is attached to the house. Instances where the spiritual energy is tied to a particular object. This case intrigues me for two reasons. First, the disturbance appears to be fixated on you personally. And second, the arrival of the apparition seems to correlate with the birth of your second child."

Danielle's eyes widened. "So you think Felix is out to get Josh?"

"I didn't say that. We need to take some readings, investigate, and spend time in the house before we can formulate any hypothesis about what's happening here."

She stood up, looking for Michael, but he was gone. "Let's break, have lunch, and I'll start preparing for our walk-through with the crew. Okay?"

She walked away before Danielle could respond. This time Stephen intercepted her.

"Ms. Wantland?" He crossed the few steps she'd managed to put between them.

He leaned close and spoke in a hushed tone, keeping his back to the dining table where his wife sat. "You don't need to encourage her. In fact, I prefer you didn't."

She noticed the deep concern in his eyes. A skeptic. She curled her hand around the quartz crystal hanging around her neck and took a deep breath. "I'll bear that in mind as we move forward with the investigation. But I'm here to discern the truth. Whatever that may be. I advise you to bear *that* in mind. You may not like what I find."

"Kimmy?"

She gritted her teeth, fighting the urge to reply, "Yes, Mikey?" Only Michael called her by the detested nickname. Anyone else dumb enough to try it never repeated it a second time.

She contemplated going straight to her trailer, pretending she hadn't heard him. Instead she set her long, gauzy skirt twirling yet again.

"Kimmy, come say hi."

Someone tall and wiry, dressed completely in black, stood beside Michael. Dark eyes stared at her from beneath a shock of unruly and equally dark hair. Recognition sparked somewhere in her mind. How did she know that face?

Three steps closer, he came into focus. The insolent smirk enabled her to dredge the proper name from the proper file.

What was *he* doing here?

"Come here, Kimmy." Michael waved her forward. Her feet plodded one after another until she stood beside him. "Kimmy, this is Sterling Wakefield."

"I know who he is."

"And everyone knows who you are." His smirk blossomed into a full smile as he grabbed her hand and shook it. "I'm flattered you know me. Always happy to meet a fellow entertainer."

She disengaged her hand, glaring at Michael. Why had he brought this man here? "I'm sorry, you're mistaken. I'm not an entertainer. I'm a serious paranormal investigator—"

Sterling threw his head back and laughed. *Laughed* at her. "Fastest flip from smile to frown I've ever seen."

"You got that right." Michael threw an arm around her shoulders. "Don't make our Kimmy mad. She's got an open line to call down vengeful spirits."

"Right. Sure." Sterling winked.

"Hey, Michael. We need your opinion on camera angle." Stan motioned down the hall.

"Okay, you two. Let me see what they need to get set up, and we can have lunch together." He gave her a look that

19

clearly told her to behave, squeezed both of their arms, and left them alone.

"Sorry," Sterling said. "Didn't mean to call you an entertainer in front of your latest marks." He jerked his head to indicate Danielle and Stephen. "You need to maintain the illusion for them."

The man had no tact. She curled her hand around her crystal and breathed deeply. "I'm not maintaining an illusion. And please don't insult these nice people with such a crass term as *marks*. As if I'm pulling a fast one on them."

"Come on. You can't kid a kidder."

"I'm not trying to kid anyone."

"Right. Not in front of the clients. I gotcha." He winked again. "So. Have you seen my show?"

"Yes, Mr. Wakefield. I'm familiar with your show. I've also seen your video calling me a fraud and challenging me to let you come on my show."

"Please call me Sterling, Kimmy." His eyes danced as he drew the word out, almost as if he knew it would set her off.

She gritted her teeth. She didn't think anything could irritate her more than calling her Kimmy, but that smirk came close. "It's Kimberly, thank you." She focused on deep, calming breaths. *In. Out. Unclench the jaw.*

"And yet Michael gets away with Kimmy. Hmm, I sense a story there." He wiggled his eyebrows and propped his chin on a fist, shifting from one foot to another. He seemed to be waiting for her to fill him in. As if she would share anything with this sensationalist slime.

"No story. Now, if you don't mind, I'd like to relax in my trailer and prepare for this afternoon." No way could she endure an entire meal with this cretin. Michael would just have to understand.

Michael rounded the corner of the hall as she made her way to the front door. He wrapped an arm around her waist, lifted her off the ground, and swung her back toward Sterling.

"Michael! Put me down!"

Sterling laughed. "I need to remember that trick." He clapped his hands while his eyes took her in. "The perils of weighing a hundred pounds. Dripping wet. With rocks in your pockets."

"I told you—lunch today with Sterling and me." He pointed a finger and gave her a look. Then he turned to the crew. "Okay, everybody. Lunch. Walk-through this afternoon."

TJ sidled close to Sterling. "Excuse me, Mr. Wakefield? Could I have an autograph?"

"Of course."

She attempted to edge away as the crew dispersed, and Sterling went with TJ to find a pen. "Really, Michael, I just want to relax—"

"Nope. Lunch."

"Michael—"

"No whining. I'd hoped you would cooperate. Since you won't, you force me to tell you. This lunch is mandated by top brass. Network. Actually, the meeting is mandated. I just thought food might make it more palatable." The corners of his lips twitched as he watched her face. "Get it? Palatable?"

Network? Some suit insisted she meet with Sterling? *No.* That could only mean one thing. *Surely not.*

"Come on," Michael said, bumping her with an elbow. "You haven't heard the news yet. Don't go all pale and deflated on me. How long have we known each other? Would I let anyone hurt my Kimmy?"

The edges of her crystal dug into her palm and fingers. She didn't even remember wrapping her hand around it.

21

Michael chucked her under the chin. "I thought we'd go off-site. I saw a quiet little sandwich place on Main Street I'm dying to try. Maybe we can sneak in and out before anyone recognizes you. And I hear the food is fabulous."

"I'll let Rosie know I'll be back in an hour or so for touch-ups and relaxation."

"That's my girl. And smile. It's not that bad. I promise."

4

K imberly nodded her thanks to the waitress who placed a house salad in front her. She would've preferred a spinach salad with strawberries and pecans tossed in olive oil and balsamic vinaigrette, but this would do. Especially since it was the only salad on the menu.

"And dressing on the side," the waitress added, setting a plastic cup of low-fat Italian next to her plate. The young woman hovered a moment, twisting her fingers together and beaming at her. "I'm a huge fan, Ms. Wantland. I watch your show every week. I can't believe you're here."

"Thank you. Always nice to meet a fan of the show."

"Can you tell me what building you're investigating?"

"I prefer to respect my clients' privacy. But you'll see your city on television when the episode airs. This is our season finale."

The girl squealed. "I can't wait. Could I . . . could I have your autograph?"

"Sure." She pulled a napkin from the dispenser and her autograph pen from her purse and wrote her name.

"Thank you. Thank you so much." The young woman tucked it carefully into a pocket.

"Just a salad? Bor-ing." Sterling wrinkled his nose. "No wonder you're so tiny. You should order some real food."

The waitress slid his plate in front of him—a sizzling hamburger glistening with grease, surrounded by a mountain of golden fries. A plate of carbs and fat rather than a bowl of vitamins and phytochemicals? *Never.*

"Anything else?" the waitress asked, eyes on her.

"I think we're good. Thanks."

Sterling bit into his burger. "Mmm-mmm. Nirvana. That's a good burger." Between bites he gestured to her. "Please tell me you're not a vegetarian."

She drizzled dressing over her salad and gritted her teeth. Why did he think her diet preferences were any of his business? She ignored the comment and stabbed her salad. "Michael, I believe you brought us to lunch for a reason?"

Michael nodded as he swallowed his toasted club on whole wheat. "I have some great news."

His overenthusiastic tone suggested he knew she wouldn't like it at all.

Sterling looked back and forth between the two of them, a slight frown crinkling his brow.

"Sterling's show already wrapped for the season. So he's been invited to cohost this episode of *Wantland Files* with you."

Sterling returned his burger to the plate and leaned forward. "I'm sorry. I thought she knew. No one told her? No one told you? You said you saw the video. You didn't accept my challenge?"

Her stomach lurched. She nearly dropped her fork in the salad she shouldn't have bothered ordering. She couldn't eat now. This guy was here to crash her show—and she was last to know.

Of course she'd seen his video. Everyone had asked her about it. It had trended everywhere. Practically viral. He'd called her a fraud and suggested she allow him to come on her show and prove it. "Proof. That's all we're asking for. You've never once captured quantifiable evidence of the existence of ghosts. I've never met an illusionist whose tricks I couldn't unravel. I challenge you to a showdown. Let's match wits. Either you prove you can talk to spirits, or I prove you're a fraud."

She'd ignored it, of course. Why let an obnoxious ass like that on her show? She didn't need to prove anything. Not to herself and not to her fans. This guy just wanted attention.

"I'm an executive producer on the show. I have approval authority. And I didn't approve this."

Michael shook his head. "You're co-exec, Kimmy. And this comes down from RandMeier himself."

Sterling jumped back in. "RandMeier? You mean Randall Hoffmeier? Top exec of the network? He invited me?"

"Yes, RandMeier is our nickname for him. Inside joke—goes back to our early days. He saw the video and how much attention it's drawing and thought it was a good idea to capitalize on it to boost ratings."

She stared at the dressing oozing from the lettuce leaves and collecting on the plate. "My show brings in good ratings, especially for the seven o'clock Thursday slot."

"You're trending down this season, sweetie. We want to shake things up a bit. Keep you on top. I think it's a good idea." Michael's soft voice, intended to soothe, almost brought tears to her eyes.

Do not cry. Not in front of Sterling.

"We don't need to resort to a cheap trick."

"Hey, now," Sterling said. "I'm not a cheap trick." He leaned forward, attempting to make eye contact. "My show may have a cheap budget and air on a cheap network. And I know a lot of cheap tricks. For example . . ."

He held his open, empty hand in front of her face, then reached behind her ear and flourished a penny. "See that? Not even a quarter. Cheap."

She reached behind her ear. "How did you—"

"But I, myself, am not a cheap trick." He smirked again.

She struggled to compose herself. "So you think a guest cohost will boost ratings?"

"This guest cohost, yes," Michael answered. "It'll be a crossover from our subsidiary network. His fans will follow him to your show. Not to mention all the people who are clamoring for the challenge."

"Or he may simply alienate my fans. *SpookBusters* isn't remotely similar to *Wantland Files*."

"I disagree," Sterling said. "We both dabble in the art of trickery. You pretend to solve ghost problems. I debunk alleged hauntings, manifestations, and cons seeking to prey on the innocent."

Her pulse hammered. "I am not a con artist. I communicate with trapped spiritual energy. My show isn't a hoax. And I don't need to be busted by you."

Sterling's eyebrows shot up and that insolent grin twisted across his face again. "I didn't intend to bust you yourself, but—"

"Relax, Kimmy. RandMeier loves the idea of you two working together. Sort of a Mulder and Scully thing. Sterling will be the skeptic to your believer."

"It is rather brilliant," Sterling agreed.

"And I'm last to know. It's my show, but I'm last to know. Why?"

"Well, they checked with Sterling to see if the scheduling would work before they told me about it. And then RandMeier said he'd let me tell you the good news. He doesn't know you as well as I do and actually thought you'd be excited about this." Michael tilted his head. "Or maybe he knows you better than I think. Maybe he said, 'I'll let you tell her the good news,' and then ran to take cover."

Sterling laughed. "Of course, I jumped at it. I'd work out the scheduling no matter what I had to do. But *SpookBusters* already wrapped for the season. And we haven't been renewed yet for next season. We're on the maybe list. This is just the boost I need. If we get some good publicity, I should be good to go."

Terrific. He had no interest in helping solve her case. All he wanted to do was save his show. "How exactly do you see this working? While I clean the house of negative entities and spiritual residue, you'll be trying to make me look like a fool?"

"Not at all. I'll just be finding the real causes of the imagined ghostly flickers and thumps in the night. There's always an explanation. I've never seen a ghost."

"That's because you aren't in tune with them. You're too loud and don't listen. And it does, in fact, sound like you intend to make me look like a fool."

"Me? Too loud? What?" Sterling made wounded faces at her until she cracked a smile. "It'll be fun. I'm a fun guy."

Michael nodded. "It will be fun. And Kimmy will come around. She's the best. You'll see. Okay, Kimmy?"

"Seems like I don't have any choice."

5

Kimberly flopped down in her makeup chair. One glance in the mirror at her furrowed brow confirmed she needed to calm down and relax. She would need all her energy focused for the walk-through, when she would take her initial readings of the house. With Sterling breathing down her neck, waiting for any reason to call her a fraud, she hoped to find at least one hot spot.

"Uh-oh," Rosie said. "I can see the lunch didn't go well. What happened? What do I need to do?" Her makeup artist darted about the tight space, lighting candles and incense.

She dropped her head in her hands and massaged her temples, breathing deeply, in through her nose, out through her mouth. "It's awful, Rosie. I can't believe they'd spring this on me. No notice or anything."

"Here. Have some chamomile." Rosie pressed a steaming mug into her hands. "What's the awful news?"

"Sterling Wakefield is cohosting the show with me this week. Hoffmeier's idea, so I have no say in it. I need lavender."

Rosie did a double take. "Sterling Wakefield? From *SpookBusters?*"

She nodded.

"Oh, girl, you don't need lavender." Rosie scurried to the collection of essential oils on her makeup table and lifted bottles to read their labels. "You need some sandalwood, vanilla, and . . . cedar. The aromatic equivalent of the come-hither gaze." Leaving the bottles on the counter, Rosie whirled the makeup chair to face her. "I'll get a little more of a sloe-eyed smokiness going up here on your eyes. And let's find you something a little lower-cut. Revealing, even."

"Can you please stop trying to pimp me out and help me prepare for the show? I need to focus. And this is not a good thing."

"You get to spend a week working with a hot guy. Doesn't sound too horrible to me." Rosie picked up a powder brush.

"Your ex-husband maxed out all your credit cards, emptied your bank account and your house, and took off with another woman. You last boyfriend dropped you off at work and stole your car. I'd think you'd give up on men at this point." She turned her head as Rosie touched up her makeup.

"I'm just saying I wouldn't mind putting a little lipstick on the guy. And I don't mean in the makeup chair, if you know what I mean."

"You're incorrigible."

Rosie lifted a lock of hair and twirled it around a curling wand. "What about you? When was your last date?"

"You know how I feel about relationships. They're too entangling. Nothing good ever comes from tying yourself to a guy. I need to keep my emotional and spiritual centers open and free. Not all clogged up with relationship mess."

"But that can clog you up, too. You must be so constricted and repressed. A good romp would take care of that for you. Free you right up. You'd be good and relaxed after."

"If that were true—"

"It is."

"I don't agree. But even if I did, Sterling Wakefield is the complete opposite of my type. He's crass and glib and noisy."

"Bet he makes some noise in bed."

"Would you stop? Have you seen *SpookBusters*?"

"Of course. And I follow him on Facebook, Twitter, Instagram. I could look at that man's face all day."

"If you follow him that closely, then you should realize he's not here to help. He's here to debunk everything I do. Everything I've built my career on." Her voice cracked.

"Okay. I get it. Deep breaths." Rosie rubbed her shoulders. "Oh, girl. Your muscles are like steel cables. Relax."

The trailer door opened, and Sterling stepped inside.

"Is this the makeup trailer?"

"It's *my* trailer," she corrected him.

"Oh. Michael told me to see if someone named Rosie could get me some makeup. I'll take a massage, too."

He grinned at Rosie, who flushed a deep crimson. *He's good,* Kimberly thought, *if he can fluster Rosie.*

"I need to finish getting ready."

Instead of taking the polite cue to leave, he closed the door behind him. "This is quite the setup. Candles, incense. Not your typical makeup trailer. Guess you get whatever you want."

She bristled at the implication she was spoiled. "Perhaps I wasn't clear. 'I need to finish getting ready' means I need to relax and focus. Which means I need to be alone. I'll let you know when Rosie is free."

He held up his hands. "Whoa. Didn't mean to offend. I'll leave you alone."

"Thank you."

He grabbed the door handle, then paused. "You know, I've been looking forward to working with you. I think this will be fun. I can tell you don't, but I hope you'll change your mind." He left, closing the door with a soft click.

Rosie resumed freshening up Kimberly's long, loose curls.

She closed her eyes and breathed deeply, in and out, in slow, measured breaths. The lavender soothed her as she focused on relaxing each muscle in her body and freeing her spiritual center to perceive whatever entity had disturbed Danielle.

"There. You're ready." Rosie's tone was off.

And now that she thought about it, she realized her makeup artist had been unusually silent since Sterling had left.

She opened her eyes. Rosie gave her "the look."

"What? Why are you upset?"

"You were kinda rude to Sterling."

"I was honest with Sterling," Kimberly corrected her.

"I think you hurt his feelings. You could at least try."

"Try what? Try to pretend I'm happy he's invading my show and making fun of me?"

"Try to be a little gracious. He was invited here. You probably ought to try to pull it off if for no other reason than to keep your boss happy. And seriously, you can't tell me your pulse doesn't race a little bit when he smiles," Rosie said.

"It definitely does not."

"Sure. And your cheeks are turning pink right now because . . . ?"

"I need to go inside. Might as well get this over with."

"Good. Send Sterling in. It'll be just the two of us."

"Looks like you get to put some lipstick on him after all. Be gentle," Kimberly said.

"I don't have a shot. He's dating some supermodel right now. Pics of them are everywhere."

"And you wanted to tart me up for him?"

"Duh. You're much better than some model. You help so many people. And you two would be adorable together," Rosie told her.

"He's not my type. But thank you." She smiled and hugged Rosie. The woman always knew when she needed a boost. Even when she didn't realize it herself. The compliment eased her mind far more than the candles and incense. "You know how much I rely on you, don't you?"

Rosie beamed. "I got your back, girl. Send that hottie in here, and go do your thing."

6

"How do you want to handle this?" Kimberly asked Michael. "Since we already recorded the opening sequence without Sterling?"

"I did that on purpose. I want to let him make an entrance during the initial walk-through."

"Right. Big, splashy entrance." She rolled her eyes. *Typical.*

"And you're going to smile and look thrilled to accept his challenge when you announce he's joining you."

Her stomach churned. "I'm a clairvoyant and a clairaudient. I am not an actor."

"You're a what?" Sterling's grating laughter hurt her ears.

"Mr. Wakefield." He didn't look flushed or embarrassed. Rosie must have decided not to pounce yet. "I see you decided against lipstick."

"Just a little powder. To tone down my natural brilliance." He flashed a grin. "And please, call me Sterling. We're cohosts now. No need to be so formal."

"You're a guest on my show for one week. Not a cohost."

Michael spoke before Sterling could respond. "We were discussing your introduction. Kimmy will introduce you—"

"You mean Kimberly."

Her eyes nearly popped out of their sockets. She coughed a few times and attempted to signal the buffoon to shut his face. He didn't look.

"Well, she's Kimmy to me." Michael looked at Sterling like a parent indulging a precocious child.

Could she get close enough to Idiot Wakefield to kick him squarely in the shins—repeatedly, if necessary—before he caused irreparable damage? Not without Michael noticing.

"Michael was just explaining I get to announce you and bring you in during—"

"Seriously, Michael, she hates it. She hates being called Kimmy."

Silence descended. She felt the eyes of the crew on her.

She took a deep breath to calm her thumping heart. *What a jackass.* Why did this second-class hack think he could waltz in here from his low-rated, crappy show on a two-bit station and butt into her business?

Michael's head swiveled in her direction, his brow furrowed, eyes questioning.

She arranged her face in what she hoped resembled confusion. She shrugged and shook her head.

"Tell him the truth. Or were you lying to me when you instructed me to call you Kimberly because you hate Kimmy? You're lying to one of us. That's what you are—a liar."

She gaped at him. What provoked this?

Michael's face fell. The right side of his mouth drooped. *Great.* The lopsided half frown typically preceded tears. She did not need this drama when she was about to perform an initial reading.

"Kimmy?" Michael's voice quivered.

Sure enough. Here came the tears. *Terrific.* They needed to shoot, and her director was about to lock himself in a room and cry his heart out. She had to put a stop to this.

"Michael, this is nonsense."

"No one else calls you Kimmy, though," he choked out.

"Exactly. No one else calls me Kimmy. It's *our* special thing. Why would I let this . . . this . . . interloper call me by your pet name?"

Michael's features relaxed. "Yeah?"

"Heck, yeah. Yes. Absolutely."

Sterling clapped. "That's the story you're going with? Well, you nearly convinced me. My apologies, Michael. But just wait until the cameras are rolling. I'll prove she's a liar."

Michael shook his head. "Given how long we've known each other, I'd like to think you could be honest with me. How much have we been through? Let's just start the walk-through." He looked over his shoulder, then the other shoulder, then spun in a circle. "Stan? Where's Stan? Anybody seen Stan?"

When she was certain Michael was out of earshot, she whirled on the traitor. "How could you do that?"

"Do what?"

"Crush his feelings like that."

"I think honesty is important. Obviously you don't."

"I want you off this show."

"Afraid of a little competition?"

That stupid, annoying smirk. She shook, attempting to control her fury, and spoke through clenched teeth. "You are not competition. You are nothing."

He squared off in front of her and crossed his arms. "We'll let the audience decide who's nothing . . . but a liar." He cocked an eyebrow.

"What is wrong with you? What about everything you just said in my trailer? Did you not mean any of it?"

"Shhhh." He covered her mouth with his hand, glancing about as if she'd said something scandalous. "Don't let anyone know we were alone in your trailer."

She tried to remind him they weren't alone, but his hand muffled her words into a garbled mess. She jerked away from him, hot words bubbling to her lips.

"Is the guy who asked for my autograph called TJ?" He stepped away, thrust his hands in his pockets, and scanned the crew.

She struggled to make sense of this lunatic's behavior. "Are you having a stroke? What is wrong with you?"

"I hope he got all that. Brilliant. That bit about us in your trailer. I never would've thought of that. Not yet at least. Hope TJ kept recording after Michael broke away."

"What are you blathering about? We're not shooting."

"And you said there was no story behind Kimmy. Nothing between you and Michael, either, I bet." He winked at her.

At what point was winking considered a reasonable motivation for poking someone in the eye? She clenched her fists. "No, there's not. And never has been, you—"

"There's TJ." Sterling pointed to TJ before cocking his thumb up and down. He raised his eyebrows. TJ flashed a thumbs-up.

Sterling beamed. "He got it all. *Yes.*" He pumped his fist. "Good job."

She stared at him.

"Come on. Don't I get some knuckles? That was a great scene."

She watched TJ scurry from the room. He cast a single guilty glance her way.

Everything clicked all at once. The crew was recording while they fought. Sterling had baited her, and she'd walked right into the trap. She scowled. "Let me guess. You're miked."

"Yep. Rosie fixed me up. Hid it great. Girl knows her stuff. Of course, Kimberly Wantland gets only the best."

"Once again, everyone is in on it but me. You're already making me look like a fool, and you haven't even been introduced on the show."

"Rosie didn't know anything about my plan to record a squabble. Neither did Michael."

"So you tricked me and hurt his feelings for what? That'll never make it into the show. We have a specific format. It doesn't vary."

"This wasn't for the show. This is to leak to the Internet. We'll tag you and get millions of views."

"You can't do that. Your appearance is supposed to be a surprise for the viewers."

"A surprise? No, we want people to tune in to watch. Lots of people. Your fans, my fans, new fans. We need to let people know what's coming. And the best way to get attention is to leak something to the Internet. Preferably something entertaining like people fighting. We stir up a little controversy, no one will be able to resist."

"Did you run this past Michael? This needs to be okayed by top brass."

"Run what past him? I don't know what you're referring to. I can't help it if the crew recorded us arguing and someone leaked it." He smirked again.

"Did you tell TJ to leak it? Or pay him? I do not appreciate this type of low behavior."

"You will when your ratings skyrocket."

"Don't pretend this is about me. What happens when Hoffmeier hears about your stunt and demands to know the source of the leak? What happens to TJ when he's caught?"

"Nothing. Hoffmeier cares only about ratings. He'll be thrilled when he realizes how good this is for the show and wish he'd thought of it himself. No one will know TJ was involved any more than they'll know I arranged it."

"I know you arranged it. And I will protect my crew. They've been with me from the beginning." Maybe this was the way to get rid of him. If she told Michael right now, maybe they could keep the footage from reaching the public.

"You're going to tattle? Really? Is this middle school?"

"You're the one who started this nonsense."

"I'll deny it all. And then say you're just jealous and trying to get rid of me."

"I'm not jealous of you in any way." The man was infuriating. But Michael knew she didn't like him or want him on her show. Sterling probably could spin this to his advantage. She would have to keep quiet. She didn't have anything to take to Michael now anyway. "Go ahead and post the video. I think it's disgusting how you're attempting to leech off my success. I don't think you'll accomplish a thing, but by all means, knock yourself out."

Head high, she stalked down the hall, hoping she appeared more confident than she felt. His video painted her in a bad light. All she could do was hope he didn't cause any damage in his quest for ratings and celebrity status.

She needed something she could use against him. Some leverage to shut down his obnoxious antics. And maybe get him booted from the show.

7

Kimberly stood in Danielle and Stephen's living room, surrounded by toys. She could do this. Despite Sterling's behavior and insistence she was a fraud. She would show him. Her show drew higher ratings for a reason.

Danielle clutched her baby, rocking gently and bouncing the blanketed bundle. The woman glanced at her, fear in her tired eyes. Kimberly offered her a reassuring smile. Never once had she failed to solve a haunting, and she didn't intend to break her record now.

The couple's toddler—Drew, was it?—sat nearby, engrossed with running a train along a wooden track. He chugged and puffed and choo-choo'ed until the train crashed into a truck abandoned on the track and derailed in a clatter of train cars, complete with explosion noises provided by the toddler. He raised both fists over his head and yelled, "Crash," before collapsing in a giggling heap.

She looked at Michael. They couldn't shoot like this.

As always, he came to her rescue. "Maybe Mr. Drew could draw a picture for us?"

Stephen scooped up the giggling heap. "Let's draw, buddy." He situated the boy at the dining table, where Danielle hovered beside him.

"Okay, Kimmy . . . Kimberly." Michael shook his head, a slight frown on his face. "Ready?"

She nodded. Stan and TJ took their places. Rosie dashed in for a final powder touch-up and pushed a lock of hair back into place.

She mentally took note of the train track and crash site lest she trip and ruin a take.

Michael counted her in and pointed, indicating she should start when ready.

She looked directly into Stan's camera. TJ would capture Sterling's entrance. "We need to determine the areas in the home to focus on by taking an initial reading. But before I check for activity, I have some news."

Michael stood behind Stan, a huge grin plastered on his face, mouthing, "Smile." He held rabbit ears over Stan's head, danced the Robot, and made goofy faces—all in the span of five seconds. He really would do anything for the show. And for her.

One week. One show. She could do this. She relaxed and smiled. "Sterling Wakefield is here to help figure out what's happening at the Williams home. Sterling?"

Sterling bounded from the kitchen. They shook hands as though meeting for the first time as Michael had suggested.

"Thank you, Kimberly. Pleasure to be here. Glad you accepted my challenge. So excited to be on your show. Thanks for having me."

"Glad you could join us." Now he could truly call her a liar. No truth in that statement at all. "Danielle believes she's seeing the ghost of her grandmother's cat. The presence disrupts her sleep and causes a sense of dread. I'm about to—"

The Wantland Files

"Sense of dread, huh?"

Her head snapped in his direction. He wasn't supposed to say anything yet, let alone interrupt her.

"From a cat? You're here to investigate a ghost cat? What will you call this episode? 'The Case of the Killer Kitty'?"

She stared at him. She hadn't even started the investigation, and he was already making fun of her. "Yes. A ghost cat."

"Did you run out of real ghosts to investigate? What do we do first? Set out a bowl of Fancy Ectoplasmic Feast? A dish of ghost-white milk?"

She saw Danielle shift from foot to foot. The young woman scowled. Probably wondering why she couldn't keep control on her own show.

Flustered, she stared at Sterling, unable to speak. Michael gestured for her to keep going.

"I . . . no, of course not. Ghosts don't eat." *Ghosts don't eat?* What was wrong with her? She wasn't handling this well. No one on her show challenged her before.

He laughed. "Oh. My bad. Ghosts don't eat. I thought this challenge would be a real test of my abilities but looks like you're going to make it easy for me. This will be a cakewalk. Scariest thing to watch out for will be spectral hair balls."

What if Hoffmeier felt the same way? What if he'd brought Sterling here for the season finale because he'd heard she planned to investigate a ghost cat and thought the episode would fizzle? Had her producer lost all faith in her?

She straightened and took a deep breath, returning Sterling's stare with a glare of her own. She'd show him. She'd show them all. This was her show, and she wouldn't let him ruin it. "I'll conduct my initial walk-through to locate the paranormal hot spots in the house."

41

"Hot spots. Right. Lead the way." His lips twitched as he gestured her forward.

If this episode failed, it wouldn't be her fault. His presence and his galling behavior made focusing difficult. He was throwing her off already. How could she survive a week with this cretin? She couldn't let him get to her.

She walked down the hall, clutching her crystal, braced for more skeptical comments. She took deep breaths and tried to clear her mind. She had to ignore him.

The first bedroom belonged to the toddler. *Jeez.* And she thought the living room was littered with toys. She stepped over a jumble of blocks and picked her way around miniature cars. Smiling trains stared at her from the bed sheets. The closet door gaped open, action figures, wadded clothing, and shoes spilling out of the space.

She centered herself in the room and closed her eyes. Her crew remained silent as she concentrated. All she could do was relax and open herself to possible input. She couldn't force anything to happen—only be receptive to what was there.

A hand on her shoulder startled her. She jumped. Sterling grinned at her. "Sorry. Just me. Not a ghost. Feline or otherwise."

"Please, Mr. Wakefield. I need quiet to concentrate."

"Gotcha. I thought maybe I should know what's happening. Since I'm here, too."

"For the moment, I just need quiet."

"What exactly are you doing? What do you think you detect during these sessions?"

She bristled. *What do you "think" you detect?* "I'm listening to the room and opening my extrasensory perception to disturbances. If you're familiar with the show, you'll know presences can be detected in numerous ways."

"Sure, but couldn't this all just be your imagination?"

She couldn't believe Michael hadn't cut the scene and told the guy off for interfering. She nearly instructed Stan to stop the cameras herself but remembered how Sterling had baited her earlier. Allowing him to get the better of her only made her look bad. She had to remain calm and take the high road.

"I understand we have different methods, Mr. Wakefield. You'll have to trust that I do experience phenomena in ways others may not. You may not be able to measure these experiences with equipment and may not experience them yourself. But they're still real. Please, allow me to do my job."

He held out his hands. "By all means."

She heard the cynicism and thought she saw disappointment in his eyes. He'd hoped she would lose her cool again. She focused on untangling her frustrated emotions. *Breathe in and out.*

Nothing reached out to her. Which in all honesty was to be expected. The toddler never reported seeing a cat, and Danielle hadn't reported seeing the cat in this room. It should be free of ionic energy.

But she would not give Sterling the satisfaction of hearing her say she got nothing. "Let's move on."

"Nothing, huh?" His glib tone told her his insolent smirk graced his face.

"I'll save my report until the end of the reading, as I always do."

She passed from room to room, growing increasingly concerned as nothing set off any of her senses. No visions or voices, no eerie presence, no hot or cold spots. Nothing. Why this week? Why did this have to happen while Sterling was here? In three seasons, she'd classified only two locations as "no manifestation," indicating the cause of whatever scared the owners wasn't supernatural. Sometimes people's imaginations

43

did, in fact, get the better of them. But she had a feeling that Danielle had experienced something out of the ordinary.

Just as she was about to enter the master bedroom, raised voices in the front of the house interrupted. *Now what?*

"What is that?" This reading incurred more interruptions than she'd ever encountered.

Michael shrugged, so she retraced her steps down the hall, cameras and crew trailing behind. As she turned the corner into the kitchen, she heard Danielle and knew something had upset the woman.

". . . means he's seen it, too. This is proof!" Danielle held a piece of paper and shook it at her husband.

Stephen took the paper and set it on the table, rocking the seat the infant slept in. "Danielle, please, you're scaring Drew. And you'll wake Josh."

Drew stared up at his mother, two fingers thrust in his mouth.

Stan and TJ moved to either side of the room.

"What happened?"

Danielle snatched up the paper and dashed to her side. "Look what Drew drew."

Stan swung his camera behind her, no doubt focusing on the paper. She suspected TJ would focus on her reaction.

She stared at the paper, covered mostly with incomprehensible scribbles. But no one could mistake the central image—a scowling, red-eyed, arch-backed cat, mouth drawn back in a hiss, complete with razor-sharp fangs.

"That's Felix," Danielle said. "He drew a picture of Felix."

8

Kimberly attempted to hide her shock. This episode threw her one unexpected curve after another.

Sterling took advantage of her hesitation. "Felix the cat? Wasn't that a cartoon?" He hummed a few notes and sang, "Felix the cat, the wonderful, wonderful cat—"

Danielle's eyes blazed. "I don't want to hear that song. My grandmother sang it to that horrible cat all the time. He was anything but a wonderful cat. But she rescued him from a shelter and thought he'd been abused. She wanted him to be a wonderful cat."

"Okay, no singing. My bad." Sterling stepped forward and took the paper. "Let's see. Clearly it's a cat. But why do you think this is Felix?"

Danielle took the page from him and gave Sterling a "butt out" look.

"The coloration matches Felix's exactly. See these stripes? Drew captured the pattern perfectly, right down to this one with an unusual jag on the side."

"So Felix had red eyes? I thought I heard they were yellow." Sterling cocked an eyebrow at her and offered his smirk.

Though he'd managed to throw Rosie off balance with his charms, Danielle was not similarly affected. "Obviously he gave Felix red eyes because that's the way Felix looks now. Right, Kimberly?"

Sterling persisted. "You claim you've seen the apparition. Did you note red eyes when you saw the so-called ghost cat? Have they changed from yellow to red?"

"I don't remember. I was scared. Maybe he didn't have red eyes when I saw him. So what? This could mean he's getting angry. Right, Kimberly?"

Sterling crossed his arms. "Is that the conclusion you immediately jump to, Kimberly?" Sarcasm dripped from his words.

She loved that Danielle gave him the cold shoulder. And thank goodness she'd left the cameras rolling. In all honesty, she would normally hype something like this big-time. But she needed to remain professional. For now. She could gloat later, when the cameras were off.

She situated the paper flat between both palms and closed her eyes. The silent minutes as all eyes were undoubtedly riveted on her were a balm to her soul. Her spiritual energy recharged, feeding off the hope that hinged on her abilities. But she didn't need to exaggerate or skirt the question. She did sense something.

"I'm getting something from the paper. But I believe it's residual rather than active."

"Residual what, exactly?" Sterling asked.

"Don't interrupt." Danielle hushed him. "Is it Felix?"

"I'll review all the evidence after I complete the initial reading."

"Evidence?" Sterling scoffed.

His interruption couldn't throw her off her game now. "Could I read Drew's spectrum? Would that be okay?"

"His spectrum? What does that mean? Is this related to Felix being here?" Danielle's voice rose.

Stephen interrupted. "I don't want my kids dragged into this." He pulled Drew to his side.

"If it helps, let her." Danielle looked frantic.

"How does this help? I don't like how worked up you're getting. I don't want Drew freaking out, too."

"I agree," Sterling said. "This is getting out of hand. And over what? A child's drawing."

Danielle whirled on him. "What do you know? You haven't been here, sleepless and terrified. I don't know what's causing these things to happen, but I know Kimberly can figure it out for me. This isn't your show, and I didn't invite you here. I waited months to even get in touch with Kimberly, and then we had to wait for them to work us into their schedule. I only have a few days for her to figure out what's happening here. So no offense, but I don't want you interfering. All you do is make fun of people. You probably want to make me look crazy."

Sterling actually looked taken aback. And for once had no quick reply. She pressed her lips together to keep from smiling. *Thank you, Danielle.*

She placed a hand on the woman's arm. "No one thinks you're crazy. But I don't want to upset anyone, either." She faced Stephen. "I won't hurt or antagonize your son in any way. I promise. And, no, I don't think he's causing or provoking the apparitions. I'm just curious about a feeling I have."

Stan and TJ shifted around the room as Danielle pleaded with her husband. "Stephen, let her. Please."

He shrugged and released the boy.

She squatted to toddler level, admiring the picture. "Did you really draw this all by yourself?"

47

Still slurping two fingers, the boy nodded.

"Wow. You are a very good artist."

Drew grinned around his soggy fingers and moved close enough to lean against her. He released his fingers with a wet smack. "Tat!" He pointed to his drawing.

"It's a pretty cat. Do you like cats?"

He nodded again.

She placed a hand on his back and immediately felt all the vibrant, spinning energy sources he produced. Just as she suspected. One of them outshone all the others.

"I like cats, too. This is a terrific drawing." She smiled at the boy. He tipped his head onto her shoulder. *Please, Stan, catch every second of this.*

She handed the drawing back to Drew. "I hope you'll color more pictures for us."

Stephen held his arms out, and Drew returned to his embrace.

She stood up and met Danielle's anxious gaze. "He's not only a great artist. He's also an Indigo child."

Sterling and Stephen exchanged a look. She knew what it meant. She'd once investigated a home where the woman's friends refused to believe anything unusual might be happening, even when they experienced strange occurrences themselves. That woman had offered a bit of advice: Skeptics be skeptics.

"What does that mean?" Danielle asked. "Is that good?"

"Depends on how you look at it, like most everything in life. Indigo children are empathetic. He may be quite emotional and affected by the emotions of others around him. Some days he may feel moody and not know why. Indigo children are more in tune with their sixth sense. The indigo chakra at the top of the spectrum is the dominant energy in these individuals. Thus, the name. The fact that he's open to and aware of other entities around him leads me to believe he may, in fact, have seen the manifestation that's been disturbing you."

Danielle ran her fingers through Drew's hair. "I knew he was special. I knew it."

Sterling clicked his tongue and shook his head. "I feel like you're using the word *fact* rather loosely, Kimberly." He turned his attention to Danielle. "No offense, ma'am, but there is absolutely no proof that chakras or Indigo children exist. Your son doesn't need a label to be special."

Kimberly gritted her teeth. "I'm an Indigo myself, Mr. Wakefield. I know what I'm talking about. And I know it exists. He may not grow up to manifest clairsensory abilities, but he will be empathetic, have strong instincts, may dream things before they happen—"

"There is no proof of any of that," Sterling said. "You can say anything, but that doesn't make it true."

"My proof is that it happens to me. I experience these things. Just because you don't—"

Michael cut her off. "Why don't we return to the master bedroom to finish the reading? You can talk to Danielle about this later." He put an arm around her, leading her out of the kitchen and down the hall. He leaned in to whisper in her ear. "Don't bother wasting time arguing with him. Danielle believes in you. Getting anything in the reading yet?"

She shook her head. "Not yet," she mumbled.

"That's unusual. You said you had a good feeling about this one. Were you wrong?"

"Don't doubt me, Michael. I know there's something here. I just haven't found it."

"I hope so. And I hope you find it quick. The episodes where we don't find anything are the least popular. And I don't want a nothing episode for a season finale."

"Believe me, no one feels more strongly about that than I do."

Stan maneuvered into the master bedroom before her and recorded her entering the room, while TJ stayed behind and focused on Sterling.

She felt it immediately. "I'm getting something."

She scanned the room, not sure what she sought, but certain she'd know if she saw it.

Or if it saw her.

Static, fog, shadows, bright flashes of light or color. Anything out of the ordinary could signal something attempting to communicate. She took a few more steps into the bedroom, watching for any shift. Nothing grabbed her attention.

She closed her eyes. Input could reach her in many forms. She tuned out the world and opened her senses to whatever might be attempting to communicate. She strained her ears, listening for whispers. No words formed around her. She didn't feel any hot or cold spots. This was elusive, a twinge she couldn't quite explain, drawing her forward. She put her hands out to prevent stumbling into anything and allowed herself to be pulled.

She bumped into the bed and ran her hands over the cover, groping along the edge. Nothing from the bed.

"Oh, boy. Here comes the Helen Keller routine. My favorite." Sterling's voice shattered her concentration.

Half a dozen voices shushed him. She also thought she heard Michael's low whisper. Probably telling Sterling to zip it.

She refocused and allowed the unknown force to lead her. The twinge grabbed her again, but stronger this time, as though someone held a firm grip on her shirt and pulled her forward. She opened herself to the sensation, encouraged it. The other energy drew strength from hers, growing more powerful.

Beads of sweat collected on her brow as she inched forward. She gulped lungsful of air. In the few steps she took crossing the room, the force left her drained, as though she'd just run ten miles.

Where are you? What are you? Talk to me.

She couldn't maintain the connection much longer.

The pulling sensation stopped. Whatever pulled her dropped its grip.

Heat. Something hot stood in her path. She opened her eyes.

The crib.

Nothing appeared out of the ordinary, but heat waves rolled off the baby bed as if she stood in front of an open oven. Sweat dripped from her chin. She held her hands over the crib.

Barely aware of murmuring voices behind her, she lowered her hands, gripping the rail. Heat hot enough to blister seared her palms, but she held fast. It wasn't real. The heat was in her mind, triggered by whatever sought to communicate with her. She couldn't stop now.

Hazy images appeared in the crib—soft, wavy edges at first that sharpened into focus. What she saw made her physically ill. She didn't want to see. She jerked her hands away and turned from the baby bed, severing the connection to the unknown entity to end the vision. Exhausted, she nearly fell to her knees but managed to stay upright, though she gasped for breath.

Michael hurried to her side with a handkerchief to blot the sweat, but she held up a hand. She was fine. In the first season, she would accept his help and take breaks after draining encounters like this one. Not anymore. She could handle it.

Michael still worried. "You were right. There's something here. And it looked pretty powerful."

She looked for Stan. Her top cameraman, who had probably been right beside her the entire time, already focused on her as she recovered. Hopefully, he'd taken plenty of crib footage. That bed was the key to this mystery.

Sterling watched her, arms crossed, brow furrowed.

Danielle stood just inside the doorway, wringing her hands. She didn't want to scare the woman, but she had to tell her the truth.

"Danielle, I had a vision."

"What was it?" Danielle asked.

"In the crib, I saw a baby . . . very still." She didn't admit the word *lifeless* had crossed her mind. "A cat stood over the infant, hissing, red eyes boring into me."

Danielle moaned and fell against Stephen. "It's Felix. He's after Joshua. I thought he was here to scare me. Not my baby."

TJ swooped in on the couple as Danielle dissolved into tears.

Sterling cleared his throat. "You're lending entirely too much credence to a so-called vision. Let's not get carried away."

Stan kept his camera trained on her face.

She spoke directly into the camera. "Tonight we will attempt to communicate with the entity and determine what it wants. And how to stop it."

9

Kimberly sat at a table with Michael and Rosie in the hotel restaurant nursing a virgin daiquiri. The drink held more sugar than she normally put in her body, even though she'd ordered the "skinny" option. She never drank during a shoot. Alcohol dulled the senses, and she needed hers honed. But this had been a long day. She wanted a drink badly and hoped the placebo effect would calm her.

Las Cruces boasted plenty of fine dining options, but they'd opted to grab something at the hotel restaurant. It attempted to offer a classy experience but fell short in her opinion. Mostly owing to the television set to a sports channel droning about impending drafts.

But also because of the food choices. Or lack of choices. While Michael and Rosie went for a plate of loaded nachos, she searched the menu for baked salmon and grilled asparagus. The closest she could find were roast chicken and steamed broccoli, which she'd instructed the waiter to prepare dry steamed. It would suffice.

She loved her show and the opportunities it gave her to help people. But the constant traveling got old. So did the sleepless nights. The nature of the business required nighttime investigations. The show shot one week, then they edited the following week. But she slept so little during shoot weeks, she didn't fully recover during edit weeks. She never complained aloud, lest someone think her ungrateful. Hosting a popular show was a fantastic opportunity many people sought but few achieved.

Like Sterling. His show never took off like hers did. Maybe he should take a hint and realize people just didn't like him. She couldn't wait to see how he handled sleep deprivation. He wanted recognition and celebrity, but could he put in the effort?

Most of their fellow diners stared at her and whispered. One even pointed. They seemed to be attempting to determine if she was the celebrity they suspected she might be. This was typical. When her show had first become popular and people began recognizing her, she'd found it disconcerting. But she'd grown accustomed to it. Mostly.

"Anyone know how Sterling reacted to the crib encounter?"

"He stayed pretty quiet," Michael said, glancing around the restaurant. "Where is he, anyway? I told him we were eating here. Thought he might join us."

"If he shows up, I'll share my seat with him." Rosie shifted to one side of her chair. "His tight little butt will fit here."

Michael shook his head and held out a palm. "Or we can pull up another chair."

"Another option. But way less fun for me."

"I'm okay eating dinner without him. I already endured one meal with him today." Kimberly slurped her daiquiri.

"I'm excited about tonight," Michael said. "What exactly happened with the crib, Kimmy?"

"Pretty much what I said. I held back a bit so I wouldn't scare Danielle. Something drew me to the crib. The crib gave off enough heat to burn."

Michael checked her palms again. "Still no marks. Good. I saw you sweating pretty good, and it worried me. And you looked exhausted. You gonna be okay tonight?"

"Of course. I have to be. This is a powerful force we're dealing with. And seeing the cat from the drawing standing over what appeared to be a lifeless baby . . ." She shuddered. She didn't want to admit how she felt. "Whatever is threatening them, we need to get rid of it soon. The part I don't understand is why I didn't feel anything malevolent in the house."

Michael rubbed his hands together. "This could actually be a fantastic season finale." He held up a hand. "Don't say a word."

"I wasn't going to." She couldn't help smiling, though.

"So tonight we should focus on the crib, don't you think?"

"Yes. It's pretty worn. More than you'd expect from one baby sleeping in it. Maybe it has some history."

"It looks old," Rosie agreed. "Not something you'd walk into a store and buy today. Worth looking into."

"Am I awful because I hope the ghost cat shows?" Michael asked.

"Not at all. Of course we want to catch it while we're here. And I can protect the family."

"I'm thinking we should set up cameras in the backyard and the bedroom."

"Yes, both places. And I'd also like to record in the kitchen and living room areas. I'll attempt to communicate, see if we can get some EVP activity." Electronic voice phenomenon often offered clues to the spirit's identity, and she had an excellent track record of convincing ghosts to talk to her.

"No problem. We've arranged for the family to stay at the hotel tonight. So we'll have the run of the house and won't disturb them."

She nodded. "Good."

"There's my crew." Sterling approached their table, a pale, willowy woman in four-inch stilettos on his arm.

She groaned. No amount of alcohol could help her cope with him. And she wasn't even drinking. Michael kicked her under the table. Rosie sat up straight, smoothed her hair, and wiped the lipstick off her glass with her thumb. As if anyone would believe that fire-engine red, patent-leather lips occurred naturally.

"Hi, guys." He placed a hand on the woman's back and pushed her toward the table. "I'd like you to meet my girlfriend. This is Amber. She drove down here to meet me for dinner tonight. Barely had any time in her busy schedule. But you guys know that already."

She glanced up from her daiquiri to discover that though he addressed the table, his eyes remained fixed on her. He looked quite pleased with himself. But then, he always did.

Offering a hand and a smile, she studied the woman. "Kimberly Wantland. Nice to meet you. What is it that keeps you so busy?"

The young woman, whose odd shade of platinum hair no doubt came from a bottle, blinked once before squeezing her hand with fingertips and thumb.

What sort of handshake was that? It sent shivers down her spine.

Amber blinked her blank eyes once more before turning them on Sterling.

"She's a model, as everyone knows." His eyes took in Kimberly's clothing. "That is, everyone with knowledge of the current fashion trends."

She expected Amber to giggle, but the woman's bovine, empty expression remained unchanged.

Strange.

"Yes, your black denim, black T-shirt, and black jacket are undoubtedly on every Parisian runway this season." She gulped her drink before she said anything ruder.

"Boozing it up before tonight, huh? That's gotta help with your focus. Or do you already realize we aren't going to find anything?"

"It's a virgin daiquiri. There is no alcohol in it, you—"

"Won't you two join us?" Michael jumped to his feet. "We can pull up some more chairs."

"Yes," Rosie said, scooting her chair over. "Sit by me, Sterling. Amber, I love your nails. That color is amazing. Kimberly, we should try purple on you sometime."

Sterling grinned. "You should. It'll bring out your natural 'Indigo' highlights. Thank you for the invitation, but Amber is only here for the night. I asked for a table for two. For some . . . alone time." He winked at Michael before leading Amber to their table.

She stifled a gag. "That'll be some earth-shattering 'alone time' considering we have to shoot in an hour."

Rosie bit a fingernail and watched them cross the restaurant. "I'd settle for fifteen minutes with him."

Michael nodded. "And I think I'd take fifteen minutes with her. Which makes absolutely no sense. Since she's, um, not at all my type."

"What has gotten into you two?" She looked around the room. All the men who stared at her earlier now fixated on

Amber. Not just their eyes, either. Their bodies oriented themselves to her, as if they had no control.

Granted, the woman was attractive. But not enough to account for this response. She'd only seen this type of reaction once before. Could it be? If so, Sterling was in way out of his league and had no idea. This was almost too good to be true.

The waiter delivered their meals, smiling at her as he passed the plates to them. As she feared, the "roast" chicken breast, bloated and almost as pale as Amber, appeared poached or boiled, and the broccoli dripped with oil, limp and overcooked.

"Is everything okay?" the young waiter asked, hovering at her side. He looked so eager to please, she assured him they were fine.

She clutched her quartz in one hand and downed the last swallow of daiquiri, still, sadly, alcohol-free. No way would she send her food back to the kitchen. If she did, tomorrow's top news story would be "Kimberly Wantland Rude to Waiter, Sends Food Back to Kitchen." Commentators would postulate on whether celebrity had gone to her head, if she was out of touch with reality, and whether something should be done about it. Never mind the food wasn't prepared as she'd ordered it.

The drone of sports commentators ended midsentence. The momentary silence caught her by surprise.

Then her own voice startled her. She looked at the television she'd been working hard to ignore. Her face stared back.

The waiter stood by the television, giving her two thumbs-up. "Marathon," he mouthed at her. He'd turned on reruns of her show playing in syndication. An episode from season one. The scene cut away and shifted to the opening sequence. Theme music played beneath her introduction.

"Dark figures. Flickering lights. Moving objects. Noises in the night. The feeling something isn't quite right. Is it your imagination? Or something reaching out from beyond? I'm Kimberly Wantland, and these are *The Wantland Files*."

She decided this place wasn't so bad after all and picked up her knife and fork. She'd tip the waiter well. Unlikely that would show up online anywhere. But he deserved it. And her face on the screen managed to win back some of the whispering patrons. Always good to remind people they wanted to watch her show. Now they'd watch for a glimpse of their hometown and maybe a neighbor. And they'd tell all their friends they saw her at the restaurant.

The rerun had not escaped the notice of Sterling and Amber. He shot a dirty look her way over the rim of his beer. She made mental note of his unprofessional behavior. They were practically on the clock.

Amber stared over a shoulder, apparently putting two and two together. Finally. The woman raised a hand to wave.

Something about the look on Amber's face set off another red flag. The woman slanted her eyes and appeared almost predatory. She needed to get closer and verify her suspicions. Or dismiss them if she was wrong.

She choked down the bland, rubbery chicken and soggy broccoli as quickly as she could.

Michael noticed. "Ready to get back and set up?" he asked. When she nodded, he and Rosie dived into their meals.

While Michael settled the check on the expense account, she palmed the waiter a twenty-dollar bill on top of the generous gratuity she knew Michael would give him. Waiters appreciated the cash they could slide directly into their pockets. She remembered that from her college years spent scraping by waiting tables. She also remembered the difference an extra twenty could make at the grocery store.

The young man lit up when he realized she'd double tipped him. "Wow. Thanks, Ms. Wantland. Our manager told everyone not to ask for your autograph, but—"

"You'd better not ask, then," she said, sliding her autograph pen out of her purse. The restaurant used cloth napkins, so she retrieved an old business card, as well. After signing it, she pressed it into his hand. "We can both honestly say that you didn't ask for anything."

She detoured to Sterling's table on the way to the exit. "I'm headed back to set up for tonight. You two enjoy your alone time. See you back in thirty minutes. So nice to meet you, Amber."

Laying a hand on the woman's back, she grasped her crystal and read what she could of the woman's spectrum. Dominant red chakra. Significantly dominant. Something else . . .

Amber pulled away from her hand, brows knitting together in a tense scowl. "Nice to meet you, too." The woman's brittle tone didn't support her statement.

She shuddered at the ancient residue she detected on Amber's soul. The woman looked so young and vapid. But that appeared to be a false front for a malevolent being. Sterling Wakefield was in serious danger. And she couldn't bring herself to care.

10

Kimberly sat on the floor of her makeup trailer, breathing deeply, while the sound of ocean waves washed over her. Rosie had already touched up her makeup and hair. She needed to relax and allow her senses to focus before she headed into the house.

Sterling barged into the trailer carrying a drink tray. "Oh, good. You're out of the makeup chair. My turn."

Breathe in—one week. Breathe out—let it go.

He handed Rosie one of the cups from the tray. "I brought you coffee. Thought you could use a shot of caffeine before we start tonight." He lifted the second cup from the tray and slurped.

"Thank you!" Rosie took the cup and drank deeply. Then her eyes darted to the empty tray.

Kimberly opened her mouth to comment on the fact that he'd brought two instead of three. She would've gladly taken a cappuccino. But she suspected he wanted to irritate her. She wouldn't give him the satisfaction of knowing it worked.

"I would've brought you one, too, Kimberly, but I wasn't sure if coffee falls into your healthy choices. Besides, I didn't know how you'd take it. You're the mind reader."

"I'm not a mind reader. I'm a clairvoyant, and I am able to interact with discarnate entities." She could tell by the look on his face he felt quite pleased with himself. Didn't need to be a mind reader to see that.

Sterling squatted next to her and leaned in, speaking directly into her ear. "Saying sciencey-sounding things doesn't make them true."

A shiver ran up her spine in response to his breath on her skin. She ignored both that and his attempt to goad her. "Coffee is quite good for you. It has many beneficial health properties. I notice you didn't feel the need to read minds to bring Rosie coffee."

"Nope. I knew she'd appreciate whatever I brought her. I went with mocha to match her gorgeous complexion." He threw a grin at her.

Rosie, taking a swallow of her mocha, nearly choked.

Kimberly breathed in and out, determined to rise above it. "For future reference, I take mine with just a little skim milk and no sugar."

He lifted his cup as if to toast her as he moved to the makeup chair. "Just a little powder, Rosie. Can't see how I need anything more when we're shooting in the dark. I've noticed nobody looks particularly good through night vision." He looked directly at her as he said it.

She ignored her inner voice, the one telling her to stay quiet. "So how was dinner? Have some good alone time?"

"So good. I'm really glad Amber made the visit. I notice your boyfriend didn't come for dinner. Does he ever meet you?"

She bristled. He'd managed to turn the conversation back on her. She didn't want to share personal information with him. But now she was stuck. "I'm not currently dating anyone.

My busy schedule doesn't allow for relationships. It works better this way."

"It works if both people are willing to make the effort. Like Amber and I are."

"And how long have you known Amber?"

Rosie answered. "They just started dating a couple of weeks ago." She flushed. "Sorry."

"No problem. I know we're making a big splash. I'm fine with it. People think we look good together. We're a good match."

"And you think a couple of weeks is long enough to know she's willing to work for a relationship?"

"I think she demonstrated it tonight. You saw. She came all this way to see me."

"Or to be seen with you."

"What are you implying?"

Don't do it, she told herself. She'd already talked to him more than she wanted to. He'd made his bed, let him lie in it. He wouldn't take her advice anyway. Once again, she ignored her own advice. "Have you slept with her yet?"

He choked on his coffee. "Excuse me?"

"If you haven't, I advise you not to. You don't know what you're dealing with. She's bordering on dangerous. It would be the best sex you've ever had, but for your own well-being, you should break it off and stay away from her."

"Don't be preposterous. She's very sweet."

"Is she? Be honest with yourself."

"Why would I stay with someone who wasn't nice to me? I mean, I'm not exactly desperate."

"You must be giving her lots of presents, then."

"I like to spoil my girlfriends—I won't deny it."

"I suspect she's asking for more than you're gifting. Try not giving her what she asks for and see what happens."

"So you think she's just after my money?"

She noticed a tinge of concern cross his eyes. She'd struck a nerve. "No, not just your money. Your celebrity, too."

"No, she's not." He didn't sound quite as confident as he probably wanted to.

"If you're that sure, try it once."

"Let's get you powdered and ready," Rosie said, lifting the brush to his face.

Touch-ups complete, Sterling took his coffee and headed for the door. He paused on his way out. "I think it's obvious you're jealous because I'm in a relationship and you're not."

She laughed. "No, not the slightest bit true. I told you—my relationship status is a choice."

"Sure." He left before she could answer.

"That man!" she seethed to the closed door. This would never do. He riled her up continually. She couldn't work like this.

Rosie held her cup out. "Want some?"

"No, thanks. I'm wide awake now."

"I think he kinda likes you," Rosie said before sipping her mocha again.

"You must be joking. He insults me every chance he gets. Goes out of his way to antagonize me. Hasn't said one nice thing to me since he got here."

"Exactly. Just like a little boy with a crush who will pull a girl's hair or insult her in front of the class. Because he wants her attention, however he can get it. Sterling is attracted to you—"

"No—"

"And he doesn't know what to do about it. Especially since he's dating another woman."

"First of all, though I do agree his mentality and emotional level seem to be about that of a little boy, I don't believe that theory. I think he dislikes me and my profession. Which he wouldn't even call a profession."

"I'm telling you, I know what I'm talking about. Remember Angelo? He trash-talked me right up until we went to bed."

"Your last boyfriend? The one who stole your car? That guy is a psychopath."

"Yeah. But he sent me to the moon in bed."

"I'm going to pretend I didn't hear that. Secondly, Sterling isn't dating another woman. He's dating a succubus."

Rosie nearly dropped her mocha. "Are you sure?"

"Pretty sure."

"That's why you asked him if he'd slept with her yet."

"Right."

"You have to tell him."

"You saw his reaction. He's God's gift to women. And he wouldn't listen even if I did tell him."

"But he's in danger," Rosie insisted.

"Eventual danger. Not immediate. And after this week, he's not my problem anymore. Let him snark all he wants. I know what I'm talking about. And I'll be the one saying 'told you so' when that succubus destroys his soul."

11

Kimberly spotted Sterling as soon as she entered the house. He stood in a corner alone, TJ's camera recording whatever he said. Her curiosity got the best of her, and she edged close enough to hear. She heard her name almost immediately.

"I'll admit Kimberly's vision at the crib took me by surprise. We've seen these fits before, where she seems to go into a trance, sweats or babbles, and later reports a vision or voices. I fully expected the camera to cut away while her makeup artist sprayed her with fake sweat. In this regard, I was incorrect. Kimberly did flush red and sweat of her own volition. This does not, of course, prove she saw a vision of a baby and a cat in the crib. A red face and excessive sweating are not proof of supernatural activity. Frankly, the simplest cause of these symptoms would be ingestion of high amounts of capsicum extract, available at any health food store. Even if she didn't take supplements, the symptoms could be completely self-caused. We see similar physical responses in individuals who report religious fervors and purport to speak in tongues or believe they've seen angels or demons. They want so badly to experience these things that their bodies produce the desired symptoms. But the origin is psychogenic, similar to how somatic illnesses can occur—"

She'd heard enough. She stepped into the shot. "Saying sciencey-sounding things doesn't make them true, Mr. Wakefield."

"Damn it. That was going so well. Can you edit her out?"

She smiled back. *Finally.* She'd managed to get under his skin. And by using his own words.

TJ nodded. "Just repeat the last couple of lines."

Sterling grabbed her arm as she stalked away. "I'm not saying sciencey-sounding things. I'm discussing actual science with research, statistics, and brain scans to back it up."

"That is your belief."

"No. That is the scientific community's belief. Not one person's opinion based on aberrant personal experiences."

She jerked her arm free and stormed away. Why did someone so thick he didn't even realize he was dating a succubus irritate her so much? She had to learn to control herself around him.

She found Michael in the bedroom.

"There's my girl. Just double-checking camera angles, battery packs, all the usual stuff." He peered through a camera mounted on a tripod. "This one will be dedicated to the crib all night."

"Good. What is Sterling doing?"

"Is he standing in the corner talking while TJ records him?"

"Yes."

"He's shooting a Confidential Camera Corner. New segment we're adding for him."

"What? We don't have time for that. My show follows a carefully planned sequence. Each minute accounted for."

"I know, sweetie. It's just this week. I'll figure it out in editing. This is to allow him time to present his feedback and theories without disturbing your work. I asked him not to interfere so much."

"You did?"

"Yes. So let him have his Camera Corners. And return the courtesy. Don't interrupt him."

Oops. Too late. Well, she wouldn't interrupt him again.

Elise, her researcher, entered the bedroom. "Kimberly, there you are. I spoke with Danielle about the crib after your vision."

Michael stopped adjusting the camera. "I've said it before, but I'm saying it again. We have the best people on this show. Kimmy and I were just talking about the crib over dinner. Find out anything useful?"

"It does have some history. The crib belonged to her grandmother and was handmade by her grandfather. Their children all slept in it, including Danielle's mom, who inherited it after her mom's passing. Danielle also slept in it, and her mom gave it to her when she was pregnant with Drew. So at this point she considers it a family heirloom."

"Wow. You don't hear stories like that much anymore," Kimberly said. "So some definite history. But nothing negative associated with it?"

"Nothing Danielle knows about," Elise answered. "I'm also looking into the history of the house and property. So far no red flags. No tragedies or murders. The previous owners lived here for decades. Not much history before that."

"Anything about cats?"

Elise laughed. "That's tough to detect. Not much in the records about previous owners' pets. But I'll keep digging."

"Danielle is convinced this is a specific cat anyway. I wouldn't expect to find anything about pets. One more thing.

Can you quietly determine if Danielle's grandmother dabbled in witchcraft?"

"I actually started looking into that. Haven't made any progress yet. But I'll let you know when I know something."

"Thank you. You're awesome."

"I'm good here," Michael said. "Let's round everybody up and get started."

A few minutes later, she stood in front of the crib. Stan's camera focused on her. The rest of the crew crowded into the room. Sterling stood beside her. Michael counted her in.

"We will keep a camera on the crib and the area around it throughout the investigation tonight, since it seems to be the biggest hot spot in the home. I've also learned the crib has been passed down through the family to Danielle and could carry some strong residual energy from the many years it has been in use."

The group shifted to the backyard. This transition would be edited to an instant cutaway.

"I'm standing on the exact spot Danielle says Felix originally appeared. His steps carried him along this path." Glow-in-the-dark tape lit her marks. She knew the six-step trajectory from rehearsal. "Then he disappeared. We will have a dedicated camera in the backyard, as well, in case the spirit always approaches the same way as before."

They moved back into the house, settling at the dining room table.

"I'll start in the dining room and kitchen area and attempt to establish contact with the entity. If we do not succeed with direct contact, perhaps we will hear some EVP on the recordings. Meanwhile, I've asked TJ to carry the FLIR tonight and make continual sweeps through the home, hoping he will catch some helpful thermal imaging. Let's turn out the lights, go dark, and start tonight's investigation."

The crew flipped off all the lights. Stan took several shots of switches being flipped and fixtures going dark.

She placed the digital voice recorder on the table and arranged the multidirectional external microphone beside it.

"What exactly do you expect to hear on these recordings?" Sterling asked.

"Good question. Dealing with an animal spirit, there's no telling."

"No, I mean, generally speaking. What do you think you hear on the recordings you make?"

"You've seen the show. The recordings often capture the voices of entities who wish to communicate with us. We've heard voices plenty of times. Season two, episode eight, we heard a female voice clearly say hello. The owner of the house identified the voice as his mother's. Sometimes we record messages from previous home owners. For example, we heard a voice saying, 'Helen,' and determined it was the voice of an elderly man who'd died in the home. His wife's name was Helen, and he seemed to be calling out, looking for her. Rather heartbreaking. But I helped him move along."

"What does that even mean?"

"I encouraged him to leave the house and cross over to the spiritual plane instead of staying in his old home. He was scared to move on, afraid to leave his wife behind. But, in fact, she had passed away and was probably waiting for him. I convinced him to go find her in the next life."

"You have a fantastic imagination—I'll give you that."

"This isn't fantasy. The home owners had no more problems afterward. His spirit moved on."

"But that could be due to the power of suggestion. You told them their 'spirit' was gone, and they believed you. Whatever noises or disturbances they attributed to a ghost before your visit they dismissed after. As they should have done all along."

"We clearly heard the man say his wife's name. How do you explain that?"

"I doubt these voices are as 'clear' as you insist. I look forward to reviewing the recordings."

"That's why you're here this week. To offer your two cents. There are Stan and TJ. Let's get started." Stan moved to her side and recorded her. "We're ready to begin our EVP session. TJ will remain here with the FLIR, to detect any potential attempts to materialize while I engage the entity."

Sterling leaned back and crossed his arms, humming the theme song to *Felix the Cat*.

She depressed the "Record" button and grasped her crystal, focusing all her energy on creating a connection with ethereal beings. "Hi. My name is Kimberly. I won't hurt you. I'm not angry. I'd like to talk to you."

She paused and listened. No one expected to hear anything right away. Spiritual entities rarely responded on command. A poltergeist or a demon might, but she didn't sense those. *Thank goodness.*

"You might be aware of the man with me. His name is Sterling. He won't hurt you, either. The negative energy you feel from him is only skepticism. He doesn't believe you exist."

Sterling sat forward. "But I'd love to be proved wrong. So, please, come play with us."

"Play? That's actually a good idea."

"What idea?"

"Michael, can someone get a ball of yarn and some newspaper?"

Elise answered her request. "Danielle crotchets. She has lots of yarn. I'll see if I can find some paper." Her researcher left to gather the items.

She turned her attention back to the camera. "We're putting the EVP session on hold to explore Sterling's idea. That was actually quite clever. Thank you."

Her cohost furrowed his brow. "I'll never disagree when someone says I'm clever, but what idea?"

She faced the camera. "We're attempting to engage a cat spirit. Verbal stimuli may not be the most effective tool. Let's try approaching Felix as we would any cat."

Sterling straightened. "I didn't suggest anything about trying to contact a cat spirit." He shoved his face in front of the camera. "For the record, I did not say I thought this would help us contact a cat spirit. Whatever she's about to do is her idea."

"Don't be so humble. I never would have thought of it without you." She reveled in his apoplectic expression. So maybe she shouldn't enjoy goading him. Felt good to get back at him, though.

Elise returned with a skein of yarn and some newspaper. "I didn't find a ball of yarn, but here's this."

"Perfect. That will work fine." She ripped a rectangle of newspaper and squished it in the center to make a bow. Then she pulled the loose end of the yarn from the skein and tied it around the bow. She tossed it into the kitchen and dragged it slowly back to the kitchen table. "Let's see if we can get him to play."

"I do not in any way believe this will establish a connection with a ghost cat. I don't even believe there is a ghost cat. This might be the most ridiculous thing I've ever seen on your show."

"Aren't you glad you're here to see it? Relax and enjoy."

She continued to toss and drag her bow, the paper scratching along the tile floor the only sound in the home. "Here, kitty, kitty, kitty," she called.

"Really?" Sterling shook his head.

"This was your idea."

"This ludicrous display of nonsense was not—"

The skein of yarn fell from the table to the floor.

She froze. She'd been poised to toss the paper again.

Silence. Stan and TJ both moved in closer.

She kept her eyes glued to the yarn on the floor. "Have you come to play, Felix? Do you want the yarn? Good kitty. You can have it."

"Come on," Sterling said. "The yarn is still attached. This is so transparent I'm not even going to call it a trick. You pulled the yarn so the whole thing would fall."

"I didn't pull the yarn at all. I was about to throw the paper again."

"Right. And while everyone watched the paper, you tugged the yarn. Sorry. I see right through this one."

"I wasn't even exerting pressure on it."

"Not buying it."

The yarn moved an inch to the side.

"There! See? Good kitty. Play with the yarn."

"This is complete BS. You're manipulating that yarn."

Glaring at him, she held both arms out and dropped the yarn to the floor. "There you go, Felix. It's all yours."

She watched the yarn intently in the ensuing quiet. "TJ, keep the FLIR focused on the area around the yarn." He probably already was, but she wanted to make sure. The younger cameraman wasn't as experienced as Stan.

She lapsed into silence, listening for any indication of a presence—paper rustling, soft scraping, anything that might indicate something attempting to gain visibility. She heard nothing. The yarn didn't move again, either.

Sterling leaned forward. "As predicted, the yarn didn't move after you let go of it."

She couldn't see his features clearly in the dim light, but she didn't need to. She could hear the gloating smirk. "You can go stand in the corner, Mr. Wakefield, if you have anything further to contribute." She turned to the camera. "I think we spooked the spirit. Or perhaps he exhausted his energy. I'm going to resume the EVP session and encourage him to come back if he can."

She recorded silence for several minutes before she spoke. "EVP session, Williams house, immediately following noted movements of yarn. Good kitty, Felix. You can play with the yarn again if you want to. Is someone here with you, Felix? You can answer any way you like. You can talk directly to me. My recorder will hear you. You can make any noise you like. Or move the yarn again. Or move something else."

She left quiet gaps between each sentence. Spiritual sounds were easier to hear and analyze against a background of silence.

The yarn remained still, and no further noises encouraged her. Spirits could never be forced. They responded as they chose or perhaps as they were able. She wished this one had cooperated tonight, though. Now Sterling would remain convinced he was right and she was nothing but a fraud. Then again, would he believe anything? He saw the spirit manipulate the yarn and refused to accept it was anything but sleight of hand. He probably wouldn't believe in ghosts if one appeared right next to him and bit him on the arm.

She checked the time. "I think we have as much as we're going to get here. I hope we hear something when we review the recording. Perhaps someone will communicate with us that way. I think we're ready to move to another room. I do want to leave the yarn out with a camera on it and see if Felix may just be a little shy. Maybe he'll come play when it's quiet."

By the time her shows aired, they were edited and streamlined to include only the most exciting moments from her investigations. Most people had no idea how many boring hours she and her crew sat around waiting while nothing happened.

She stepped out back and shivered. Late-March nights in New Mexico were cold. Should've grabbed a coat or something. No sooner did the thought cross her mind than Rosie appeared and helped her into her jacket. And straightened her hair before scurrying back into the house.

"You are so spoiled." Sterling joined her, blowing on his hands.

"I have an excellent team."

"What exactly do we do out here?"

"More of the same. Shooting this show isn't as glamorous as you seem to think. Nothing happens on cue because it isn't scripted. It's real. I don't know what it will take to convince you of that."

"What will convince me is seeing something I can't explain."

"Remember, even doubting Thomas declined the offer to dip his fingers into Christ's wounds."

"You can't honestly be likening yourself to—"

"Kimberly!" Michael beckoned from the back door. "Come inside. TJ got something on the thermal camera in the toddler's bedroom."

"The toddler's bedroom? Danielle didn't report any disturbances in there." She grabbed Sterling's arm and pulled him along. "Change of plans."

12

Kimberly rewound the FLIR footage and hit "Play" for the sixth time.

TJ hovered at her shoulder, biting his thumbnail and shuffling from foot to foot. "What do you think?"

"I think I'm really glad you happened to be walking by and caught this." She turned a smile on her cameraman.

He stared at his feet, a shy grin on his face. "I thought I'd do a quick sweep while everyone moved out back and the house was quiet."

"Smart. You have good instincts."

Stan recorded the exchange, then moved in tighter to capture the FLIR footage review.

"As you can see, a shadow appears in the middle of the room. The shape does indicate a four-legged animal about the size of a house cat. This could be a tail. A moment later, the image disappears and reappears near the bed."

"See what it does there?" TJ pointed to the screen. "It rises on the toddler bed."

"What *is* it doing?" She rewound the last few seconds. The red haze appeared to elongate as though stretching to peer over the bed. "I think you're right. The image seems to be rising on the side of the bed. Is it looking in the bed? This is great footage, TJ. Keep recording, please."

She stepped into the room, closed her eyes, and reached out, hoping the entity TJ caught on the FLIR remained nearby. "Are you trying to tell us something? Are you warning us? Is someone else in the house with us right now?"

"Someone needs to be the voice of reason here," Sterling said. "You realize you're turning nothing into something, right? I see nothing. I don't even know what you're talking about."

She opened her eyes, weary of interruptions. "And because you're unable to read and interpret data properly, you just dismiss it?"

"Dude, it's right there." TJ pointed at the red blur on the screen.

"That could be anything. Or nothing. Point the FLIR at the bed right now and see if any color discrepancies produce the same results."

TJ looked to her.

"Go ahead. Pan the room."

TJ aimed the camera. Afraid to look, afraid Sterling would once again feel vindicated, she watched the screen. No anomalies appeared.

"You were saying, Mr. Wakefield?"

"There." Sterling pointed to the screen. "That's what I was saying. A shadow most likely caused by some of the toys in here."

"That doesn't look anything like what TJ caught earlier."

"Different distortion, same idea. Logical idea. Not fantasy."

"How can you not see that your interpretation is only your opinion?" Kimberly asked.

"You honestly think the best, most logical explanation is that your cameraman recorded a ghost cat? Think about that. Ghost. Cat."

"I think there is far more to this world than you want to believe. And since you don't want to believe it, you refuse to see what's right in front of you."

"No, I just refuse to be duped."

Sterling's red chakra flared, indicating he felt the need to protect himself. At the same time, she sensed a wave of remorse and shame. He'd been duped before. Hurt. He covered it well, but someone had hurt him deeply.

She stepped back, shaken by the depth of pain. She rested a hand on his arm, and spoke as gently as she could. "We aren't here to dupe anyone. We only want to help."

He opened his mouth to speak, closed it, and blinked a few times. His furrowed brow smoothed.

"Right. Okay. Just . . . go ahead." He waved a hand at her, then walked away.

"I really thought I got something," TJ said. "That guy is kinda rude. And after I helped him, too. What a jerk."

She couldn't bear the crestfallen look on the young man's face. "You did catch something. Don't let him bring you down. Wait until we review footage tomorrow. I'll bet the team goes crazy over this. Keep up the good work."

"Okay. Thanks."

She turned to Michael. "You were surprisingly quiet during that."

He held up his hands in surrender. "Hey, RandMeier expects some drama from this mash-up. A little bang for his buck."

"I don't think you need to worry about that. Sterling and I don't seem to be able to do anything but drama. He sets me off so easily."

"You handled him well just now. I'm proud of you. The audience will get to see your tender side. Surprised Sterling brought that out."

"You and me both. Okay, Great and Powerful Director. What next? Backyard again?"

Michael swiveled his head toward the master bedroom and mulled the options. "Sure. Backyard for a while. We can finish in the master bedroom."

Thirty minutes in the backyard yielded nothing but numb fingers and toes. Rosie pressed a cup of hot tea into her hands the moment she stepped back inside. Michael sat her at the dining table. "Stay here until you've warmed up a bit."

The crew shifted to the master bedroom for what she hoped would produce the best footage of the night.

Sterling slid into the chair beside her. "Good grief. You're shivering." He lifted her hand from the table and pressed it between his own.

"It's cold outside." She couldn't bring herself to pull her hand away. His warmth felt so good.

"Not that cold. Another peril of weighing next to nothing. You can't regulate your body temperature."

"How can you be so warm already?" She offered her other hand and luxuriated in the heat that spread through her.

"What can I say? Hot-blooded male."

The accompanying spark in his eyes produced a flush of warmth she wasn't as comfortable with. She withdrew her hands. "Much better. Thank you."

Michael leaned around the corner from the hallway. "Ready, Kimmy? Sterling? We're all set up." He disappeared again.

"Seriously, why don't you tell him how much you dislike that? I see it on your face every time he says it."

"And then try to explain why I said nothing all these years? No, thanks."

"You owe him the truth."

"I can't. He'd be upset. You saw."

"Then let me tell him for you."

"No. That's even worse. Please drop it."

"Why did he start calling you Kimmy? You so clearly detest it. What prompted the nickname in the first place?"

"It's a long story. Something I prefer to forget. Which I think he's done. If he remembered where the nickname came from, he'd never say it again the rest of his life." She swallowed the last of her tea and stood.

Sterling grabbed her arm. "You can't leave me hanging like that."

"Sorry. We have a show to shoot."

"You tease."

She flipped off the kitchen light, plunging the room into darkness.

He bumped into her in the hallway and murmured an apology. But remained close behind her.

As she entered Danielle and Stephen's bedroom, eyes on the crib, her emotions churned. She felt too scattered to hone her own energies, much less captivate and direct another. She gripped her crystal and breathed deeply, determined to calm her heartbeat. She pushed Sterling from her thoughts. This was exactly why she preferred to helm the show alone. And why she held most people at a distance. Too many complications directly affected her abilities, her show—her livelihood.

She imagined pushing all the stress out of her body through her fingers and toes. When she felt lighter and freer, she imagined a golden light in the center of her chest and allowed it to grow and expand until it filled her and radiated into the spirit world around her. She sent out the beacon and waited, hoping something would accept her invitation.

She heard murmurs in the silence. Her crew, well trained, spoke only when necessary and only in soft whispers.

Then she heard another sound. Not her crew. It drifted from elsewhere in the house. She turned from the crib and followed the sounds. Down the hall. A wordless sound, a calling. Distress. Concern. Fear. Almost frantic. From the toddler's room.

She stood in the doorway. Two shadowy figures struggled to resolve into recognizable images.

She clenched her crystal and focused with all her might. *Come on. What are you trying to tell me?* Finally, a clear image burst through the haze—a hissing cat, claws unsheathed, sitting on the toddler bed.

What is it? What do you want?

She stepped closer and felt another presence. The other shadow. It hovered near the cat, dark and dreadful. She attempted to reach out to the hazy entity. For a moment, she connected partially. *Cold. Empty.* She shivered.

The entity pushed her away. It didn't want her here. Was this cold, empty thing behind the cat apparitions? She moved closer. The darkness didn't leave, yet she felt it recede from her. The cat arched and hissed.

What are you? Why are you here?

"Do you guys hear that?" Sterling's voice jolted her from the vision. The shadowy figure dissipated.

Drained, she nearly collapsed, sweat dripping from her forehead. She gasped to fill her lungs before turning on Sterling.

"What is wrong with you? I made a connection. I was making progress. You blew it."

"Listen."

81

A cat meowed.

She blinked. Nothing remained of the cat or the dark entity from her vision. "You can hear that?"

"Of course."

He turned to follow the sound. TJ kept a camera on him.

Kimberly spoke into Stan's camera. "If Sterling and the crew hear that meowing, then the cause isn't supernatural. He's only going to find a cat."

She breathed deeply, attempting to feel any residual energy from the entities she'd connected with. Nothing. They were both completely gone. She hurried after Sterling and discovered the back door open.

Sterling crouched in the backyard, coaxing a kitten.

Shaking her head, she turned to Michael. "This is why I work alone. I made a connection with Felix. And there was something else. Another entity of some sort. I was determining exactly what we're dealing with here. And then Idiot Wakefield interrupted. And we both know exactly what he's going to say next."

Michael pinched the bridge of his nose, eyes closed. "I know."

"He's a menace. I want him gone."

"I can't do that. This is exactly the sort of thing RandMeier hoped he would stir up."

"He's hindering my investigation. For crying out loud, if I could've determined what this entity is, what it wants, how the cat figures in, we might have cleared this house tonight. This could have been a one-nighter, Michael."

The Wantland Files never left a home until the disturbance resolved. Her track record remained 100 percent. A one-night clearing was her Holy Grail—in and out, as little disruption as possible to the family. Although she'd come close, so far she hadn't achieved it.

The Wantland Files

"We don't know that. Don't get carried away."

"Now we'll never know. He scared Felix away, disrupted my connection, and blew my chance."

"Everybody can relax." Sterling sauntered into the dining room, cradling a kitten, which continued to mew in distress, eyes enormous. "Warm this little guy up, feed him, and *voilà!* The Felix problem is gone." He stared her down, eyes glowing with victory, a huge grin plastered from ear to ear.

She held her hands up and shook her head. "That's it. I'm done for the night. I'm too drained to attempt another session."

As she turned on her heal and stormed to her trailer, she heard Michael say, "Okay, guys, let's wrap for the night. Footage review in the morning. Shooting will resume tomorrow night, so get as much sleep as you can."

13

Kimberly woke fuzzy-headed and with a splitting pain pounding against her temples. She dragged the extra pillow over her eyes and willed herself back to sleep.

She'd drawn the blackout drapes before she tumbled into bed at 3:00 a.m. Even the near darkness couldn't convince her body it was still nighttime. After tossing and turning, she peeled one eye open to peek at the clock: 8:00 a.m. *Great. Five hours of sleep.* Her average. At least this hotel served breakfast until nine. She needed coffee. About four cups.

She showered and dressed, then shambled to the dining area. The aroma of coffee soothed her. Coffee kept her going on her worst days.

But the sight of Sterling at one of the tables ruined it. He'd already spotted her and waved her over. She continued to the urn of coffee, adding two splashes of skim milk to the cup she poured.

Resigned to sitting with him, she dropped into the seat he patted. One look at his plate turned her stomach. Rubbery scrambled eggs, a biscuit smothered in what she assumed was supposed to be gravy, a dried-out sausage patty, and a pile of glistening bacon secreting a pool of grease.

She shuddered and sipped her coffee.

"Man, I'm tired," Sterling said between forkfuls of eggs. "How do you ever adjust to these hours?"

"You don't." She took a more substantial gulp.

"You must recover when you're not taping."

"Nope." More coffee. "The network upped my season to twenty-two episodes. We're on location about a week per episode, editing while traveling and researching the next site during the weeks in between. That's forty-four out of fifty-two weeks of the year. My 'downtime' is spent jetting across the country for mandatory promotional interviews, radio shows, guest appearances, conventions, and anything else they throw at me. Or throw me at." She drained the cup.

"So you've just adapted to going without sleep?"

"No, I'm just chronically fatigued and have a constant headache."

"Explains your crankiness, too. The price of fame these days. Frankly, I'd trade you. Waiting for a contract renewal is the worst. I'd rather be sleep deprived by job security. Can I bring you some food?"

Cranky? He didn't even seem to realize he'd insulted her. And then he'd offered to wait on her. She'd never understand this guy. "No, thanks. I need more coffee first. Then I'll see if they have anything I'll eat." She crossed the room and refilled her mug. When she returned, an orange rested at her place.

"Bet that's on your diet." He flashed a grin.

She glanced at the buffet line. No oranges. "Where—" She stopped herself. He wanted to impress her. She didn't want to give him the satisfaction. The pleased look on his face told her he knew anyway.

"I can conjure more than just pennies." He spread his arms wide.

What a show-off. "Thank you. But an orange doesn't forgive you for ruining last night's session."

85

"So that's why you're being aloof this morning. You're miffed. But I didn't ruin it. I added drama."

"I established contact with Felix, for your information. And something else that could be behind this disturbance. You interrupted. I might've figured out what he wanted if not for you dragging in that stray kitten. We could've been done last night."

He dropped his head backward and pretended to fall asleep. "Snooze. That's too easy. Your viewers want to see you struggle. Fight for it. The audience is going to love it." He crammed a piece of bacon in his mouth and licked his fingers. "Just watch me conjure ratings."

"That kitten is not Felix."

"I know. There is no Felix. I was only stirring things up a bit. It'll pay off. You'll see."

She scowled a little harder. But she picked up the orange and peeled it.

"So what will we do today?" he asked as he cut a bite of soggy biscuit.

"Review footage from last night mainly." She yawned. "Reassure the family. Nothing too exciting. Then another session tonight, of course."

He put his fork down and scrubbed his mouth with a napkin. "Listen, I wanted to ask you—" His phone rang. He glanced at the number, smiled, and took the call. "Hi, Amber. Great to hear from you. How are you this morning, sweetie?"

Unable to stomach his glib gloating, she refilled her coffee again. His countenance changed in the short time she was away.

"Well, I . . . I don't know. I can look into it, I suppose." When he paused, she could hear Amber's brittle voice chirping on the other end but couldn't make out any words. "Yes, but . . . I'm pretty busy this week with *Wantland Files*—" He fell silent as Amber's voice interrupted again. He offered a smile, then turned away, speaking barely above a whisper. "Listen, I can't really talk right now. We'll have to discuss this later—" More shrill chattering. "Of course I want you to be happy. Yes . . . I know . . . okay, I have to go. Talk to you later. Bye." He hung up quickly as though afraid to let Amber speak again.

"How's Amber?" She tried to hide her delight in knowing something wasn't so perfect in the relationship he insisted on rubbing in her face.

"Can I ask you something? About Amber?" He stared at the table, voice soft.

Unexpected. She took another gulp of coffee, wondering if this was merely another ruse to make her look foolish again. "Okay."

"You mentioned . . . you said she's just a gold digger, and I should break it off. Why do you think that?"

"She's more than a gold digger. And I know because . . . I read her spectrum and I could just tell. It's what I do."

"What does that mean? Her spectrum?"

"Her chakras. You know what chakras are?"

"I've heard of them. And heard you talk about them. More silliness."

"It's not silliness. We all have them. Colorful, spinning energy sources that align along the spine."

"What?"

"Here." She scooted her chair closer to his and held her hand over his lap. "Here at the base of your spine, behind the groin, is the red chakra. It's the seat of your basic survival instinct as well as greed and lust." She moved her hand slightly higher. "Above that is the orange chakra, which allows us to feel intimacy and connection with others. Creativity flows from the orange chakra. Above that is the yellow chakra, where we gain our confidence and self-control. And humor." She paused to gauge his reaction.

His eyes danced.

She moved her hand up to his chest. "Next is the green, or heart chakra, which governs love, forgiveness, and compassion. Here at the throat is the blue chakra, which is the seat of communication. The indigo chakra sits between the eyes, thus it's often referred to as the third eye, and offers intuition and our sixth sense. Often ignored." She glanced at him again, waiting for him to comment on her barb. But he didn't. He must be waiting to pounce at the end of her lesson. "And then the violet chakra, here at the top of the head, connects us to the divine, to a state of bliss."

He lifted his hand to catch hers from where it hovered in front of him. His dark eyes bore into her.

Unnerved by his silence, she offered another opening to joke at her expense. "You didn't know you were a walking rainbow, did you?" She attempted to smile even though her heart pounded against her chest.

"No, I didn't," he murmured, his voice rough with a husky rasp she hadn't heard before.

She retracted her hand and scooted back to her place at the table, hoping her face wasn't turning pink.

She downed the remainder of her coffee. "Anyway, Amber's red chakra completely dominates her actions. She's controlled by greed, desire, lust. Everything she does is to ensure her survival, no matter the cost to anyone else. I detected virtually no influence by the other chakras. No warmth or compassion, no humor or sympathy. No love. And there's something else. Difficult to describe. A dank, ancient residue about her."

Sterling cleared his throat and shifted in his seat. "I don't believe that stuff. But you're right that she asks for a lot of things. Designer purses, crazy-expensive new shoes, shopping sprees for entire new wardrobes every week. New gadgets. If it catches her eye, she wants it. And wants me to buy it for her. Now she wants me to take her on vacation to a private island in the Bahamas. I'm trying to watch my expenses. If my show isn't renewed, I'll be unemployed. I'm not broke, but . . ."

"A vacation to a private island for someone you've only been dating a few weeks? Doesn't that sound unrealistically demanding? This proves my point. She's—" She stopped, unwilling to open herself up to his criticism.

"Go ahead and say it. Only after my money. And maybe the attention of dating someone on television. She loves when the paparazzi start snapping pictures. Sometimes I think she calls to tell them where we are." He pushed his plate away and propped his chin on his fists. "Why would anyone date me if I didn't have my own show?"

His tone tugged at her heart. She knew, knew for sure, she was asking for ridicule. He wouldn't believe her and would probably laugh at her. But she preferred his laugh to the gloom. "It isn't your fault. You're a victim here. Amber is . . . a succubus."

A glimmer sparked in his eyes. "A what?"

"A succubus."

"You mean, like a witch?"

"More like a demon, really. They prey on men, sucking them dry. She won't stop until you have nothing left. Or until you break it off, which is extremely difficult if not impossible if you've slept with her. A succubus uses sex as a means of control. The fact that you're even discussing this leads me to think you haven't slept with her yet."

He squirmed. "I don't . . . that isn't . . . look, that's just nonsense. A succubus?" He forced a laugh.

"Believe me or don't. Just don't go to bed with her. The sex will be unbelievable, but afterward you will find her irresistible—every request, every whim—until she bleeds you dry. And then, when she abandons you, you'll be ruined. Not just financially but emotionally and mentally. You'll spend the rest of your life unsatisfied, feeling like something is missing. No sex is worth that."

"Sorry. I don't believe in mythical creatures. Show me one tangible shred of proof that witches, demons, spells, any portion of any myth is at all true. You can't. I've looked and never found a thing."

"You can't see ultraviolet radiation, either, but it will burn you if you don't wear sunscreen."

"How can you say that? You're comparing scientifically proven radiation to the existence of a succubus?"

"I'm suggesting you put on some sunscreen. Tell her no. To everything. No vacations, no gifts. And absolutely no sex. If she likes you, she won't need those things. She'll want to spend time with you, get to know you, do things for you. And if she doesn't, why would you want to be with her anyway?"

He sat motionless.

She stared into her empty mug.

"You're right," he finally said. "Not about the ridiculous succubus thing, but she is extremely demanding. Greedy, even. Better to break it off now than to wait for her to decide my bank account isn't big enough to buy her everything she wants and dump me. Better to dump than be dumped."

"Not exactly what I was getting at, but if that helps you feel better about it, then okay." Her stomach growled, and she decided to look for oatmeal or whole wheat toast or something somewhat healthy.

His phone buzzed again, a single ping this time. He picked it up and grinned. "Yes! Our video is trending. And I've gained about a thousand Twitter followers already. Fantastic."

"What are you—" The video he'd made. He must have uploaded it. "Are you talking about the video from yesterday? With me in it?"

"Yep! Did you see it? I tagged you." He turned his phone to her, beaming, seemingly quite pleased with himself. "Exactly what I'd hoped for."

"No, I didn't see it. And I don't want to. I thought you planned to have someone upload that anonymously."

"I did. But then I realized if we get good publicity out of this, Hoffmeier and company will want to know who did it. And I want to be able to take the credit. Decided it was worth the risk of getting in trouble for posting without permission."

She stood and left him glowing in his own brilliance to peruse breakfast options.

He followed her. "But I'll share the credit with you. Seriously, you should retweet it. You can't buy this kind of publicity. We can both say it was our idea. Together."

"I don't want that kind of publicity. Whatever you may think to the contrary, my show is not a circus." She flipped through the instant oatmeal packets. "Don't they have anything that isn't loaded with sugar?" She flipped through the container a second time, slapping the envelopes against one another.

Sterling raised a hand in front of her face, a packet of plain oatmeal between two fingers like a playing card, smile stretched across his face.

"How . . . where . . . ?" She clenched her jaw. Once again, she'd played right into his hands before she caught herself.

"A good magician never reveals his secrets." He was brimming with delight.

91

She snatched the packet from his hand. She wanted the oatmeal more than she wanted to refuse him the victory. She grabbed a bowl, ripped open the envelope, dumped the oatmeal in, and depressed the lever on the hot water dispenser.

"You just can't stand to think someone has the upper hand, can you?" He leaned closer as she fished a spoon from the cutlery tray and stirred her oatmeal. "We're partners now. We watch out for each other, right? You watch out for crazy gold diggers, and I watch out for your bizarre dietary demands."

She clutched the bowl and turned to face him. "We're not partners. You're a guest on my show. I've built this show from nothing, on my own, and without any inflammatory, desperate, blatant attention-mongering like you're attempting."

She stalked back to her seat, Sterling close on her heels.

"This week is my chance to win over my network. To convince them to renew for another season. Please? Look, it works for you, too. My show gets renewed, I go away. Won't bug you anymore. No more challenges, no more comments on your show. I promise. Let's blow up the Internet. Get everyone talking about our awesome episode. And us. Money follows attention. We both win from an alliance."

She stared at her bowl, stirring the oatmeal. Those eyes of his really were too much. She found it difficult to think clearly when he looked at her like that.

Sterling had been antagonizing her online with his claims of fraud and challenges to let him debunk her show for more than a year. Here was a chance to get him off her back. All she had to do was help him this one week, then life could go back to normal. Better, since he would no longer harass her.

"Fine. I'll help you this week. Just stop trying to trip me up. You may enjoy drama and conflict, but I don't. And I know what you did. You took the only plain oatmeal and hid it so you could conjure it for me."

He held his hands out and shrugged. "Did I? Or was it magic?" He winked at her and turned to leave.

"Happen to have any honey or cinnamon on you?"

He spun around and reached into a pocket.

She sat forward. *No way.* If he gave her cinnamon and honey for her oatmeal right now, she'd forgive all his transgressions.

He whipped his hand from his pocket with a flourish. They both stared at it.

Empty.

"Sorry," he said. "Magic only works for true partners, not temporary allies."

He bowed and left.

14

Kimberly watched her crew clustered around laptops and cameras, headphones pressed to their ears, blank stares indicating deep concentration, sheer exhaustion, or both. Analyzing last night's footage would take most of the day, but it would be worth it. Anything they could glean would help guide tonight's session.

Rosie rushed to Kimberly's side. "Girl, you are all over the Internet. I didn't want you to find out from anyone else."

"Sterling told me at breakfast. That reminds me." She thrust a hand into her quilted burgundy Michael Kors bag and pulled out her phone. She tapped on the Twitter app and scrolled through—*Good grief, how many notifications?*—to find Sterling's video.

Rosie peeked over her shoulder. "You did not just retweet that!"

She pursed her lips and said nothing.

"Well, at least do it right. Hashtag it *wantlandfilesdrama* and include at *sterlingspookbuster* so it shows up with the others."

"The others what?"

"You're a thing. Look." Her stylist pointed to the side of the phone, where "#wantlandfilesdrama" headed the trending topics.

She gave Rosie the phone. "Here. You do it. I don't know how."

Rosie's thumbs flew across the screen in a blur. "Done. Now, did you eat anything?"

"Yes, some plain oatmeal from the hotel breakfast."

"The hotel didn't have any plain. I checked. I figured you'd refuse to eat anything on their buffet and show up here exhausted and starving."

"Maybe they brought some out after you left."

"Nope. I checked. I even made the busboy look in the kitchen. They don't keep plain. No one eats it. I have some yogurt and berries in your trailer."

"I . . . well . . . I . . ."

Sterling breezed into the living room, chipper and smiling. "Morning, everyone. Someone found that kitten a home yet?"

Rosie watched him breeze past. "He must roll out of bed looking like that every day."

"Please. He hasn't spent the last several years sleepless." Kimberly watched him chat with Elise, who perked up and giggled at whatever he said. "Make sure I look at least that good before we tape tonight. Allow extra time for makeup."

Michael pulled his headphones off and broke away from the equipment at the table. "How are you this morning, doll?"

"Been better, been worse. How's the footage? Please tell me we got something."

"Nothing earth-shattering yet. But we just got started."

His phone rang. He glanced at the screen. "It's RandMeier. Give me a minute." He took a deep breath. "Good morning, Mr. Hoffmeier. I'm . . . yes, things are going very well. They're working great together." He frowned. "What video?"

She froze. RandMeier already saw the video? And called midmorning to discuss it? She should've gone with her original plan to distance herself and let Sterling take the heat. Maybe even get fired.

"No . . . no, I didn't . . . okay. Oh, I'll get to the bottom of it. Of course. Yes, I'll talk to you later. Bye."

He tucked his phone into his pocket.

She attempted to soothe her facial features into innocence. "What was that about? Just checking on us? Did I hear you say 'video'?"

"You're a terrible liar, Kimmy. Always have been. Spill."

She slumped. "It was Mr. Wakefield. He asked TJ to record us and had Rosie mike him and then he acted weird and started an argument about calling me Kimmy. It's all a publicity stunt."

Sterling appeared and propped his chin on her shoulder. "Hey, partner. Mr. Wakefield is my dad. Call me Sterling. You guys discussing our video?"

She shrugged him off. "Your video. I had nothing to do with it."

"You must've had something to do with it," Michael said. "You've apparently retweeted it."

"Well, yeah . . . just now. But Mr. Wakefield made me. At breakfast this morning he told me I had to retweet it or . . . or he'd . . ." The cogs in her brain spun, but she couldn't think of a plausible threat.

"Yep." Sterling rolled his eyes. "Absolutely what happened. I held a refined white bagel to her side and told her to retweet my video or I'd force-feed her bacon. I'm a monster!" He covered his face in mock shame.

She whirled on him. "That's not funny—"

"Just stop." Michael held up a hand. "You both clearly knew about it, and you've put me in a terrible position. I knew nothing about this. I sounded like a fool to RandMeier."

Rosie joined the bickering group, her phone in hand. "Look how many views since you retweeted, Kimberly."

Sterling snatched the phone. "We've hit a hundred and fifty thousand! Yes." He pumped his fist. "You retweeted it, too?"

Rosie seemed to melt in the heat from his smile. "Of course."

"Apparently everyone is retweeting it," Michael interrupted, "and RandMeier wants to know who approved the leak. He's quite concerned you two are 'spending time alone' in your trailer. What is that about?"

Rosie choked on her coffee. Sterling shuffled his feet.

Kimberly's cheeks flushed. "We weren't alone, Michael. He only said that to pique interest. The whole video is nonsense—"

Michael held up a hand. "All I know is, RandMeier wanted drama—"

"Most of that video is us arguing," Sterling said.

"And you two are talking about being alone in your trailer. Which sounds like you're getting cozy."

"That was all her." Sterling pointed at her.

"What? That's ludicrous."

"I set up the arguing bit, but she started talking about us in the trailer."

"You twisted what I said. Michael, I never suggested we were alone—"

"*And* you have a girlfriend." Michael raised his eyebrows at Sterling. "A very well-known fact."

"Not anymore. Kimberly convinced me to dump her."

Michael's and Rosie's heads both swiveled toward her, eyes wide, jaws slack.

"Not like that. Not because I . . . you don't understand the whole story. Sterling, tell them it's not like that."

97

Sterling's phone rang. "Oops. It's Amber. She must've listened to my message."

"Your message? You broke up with her via voice mail?" Kimberly shook her head. *What an ass.*

Rosie stepped closer. "You're really unattached again?"

Kimberly whirled on her stylist. "Rosie, please focus." Why, why, why did she agree to cooperate with his scheme? And why didn't she wait until later to post that damned video? Then she could've honestly feigned ignorance, and no one could have proved otherwise.

Sterling stared at his phone. "I can't talk to her. She'll be upset, won't she?"

"Probably. So what did you do? Call her in the fifteen minutes it took to get here from the hotel?"

"You said it was important. That she's dangerous." He pocketed the phone. "Well, I missed the call. Just as well."

"You call her back right now." She tugged at his arm. "Man up and do the right thing. If you're not going to tell her to her face, at least call back."

Michael turned toward the front door, then grabbed both their arms. "Sorry, this will have to wait. The family just arrived. Put on your biggest smiles." He took a deep breath, followed his own directions, and moved to greet Danielle and her kids. "Good morning! How did everyone sleep?"

"Rosie—"

"Black tea." Her assistant started toward the trailer, then spun on her heel and placed a hand on each side of Kimberly's face. After twisting her head side to side and peering into her eyes, Rosie continued. "With mint. And lavender spray. And your hematite crystal."

Sterling watched her scurry out the door, raising a hand to wave good-bye. "Don't worry about me. I'm fine. Don't need

98

anything. Probably just triggered the rage of a gold-digging psychopath. But I'm good. Really."

"Oh, stop it, you big baby. Amber's at work. You're at work. No chance you'll see each other until this weekend." *When you won't be my problem anymore.* "Relax."

"Ms. Wantland?" Danielle hurried to her side. "What happened last night?"

"We are still reviewing footage. But we made good progress."

"But Felix is still here?"

"Clearing an entity takes time. And finding the root cause of the manifestation is necessary before we can clear it. I made a connection last night. That's the place to start."

"We'll know more in a few hours," Michael said. "You can go back to the hotel or take the boys to the park—"

"Drew needs his toys. And Josh needs his crib. He barely slept last night. Which means none of us slept last night. Poor Stephen. I dropped him off at work late. He looked terrible. I really hope you get rid of Felix soon. We need our house back." The young mother bounced the infant in her arms. The toddler stood beside her, two fingers stuffed in his mouth. He rubbed at his eyes with his other hand.

Sterling stepped forward. "Nothing to worry about. I'm positive I found the source of your disturbance."

Danielle narrowed her eyes. "*You* did?"

Michael draped an arm around her shoulders. "Why don't you settle the boys and let us complete our review. Then we can discuss it."

"Maybe all three of you can nap," she suggested. The last thing she needed was two wailing kids while she and the crew listened to sensitive recordings.

"Would that be okay?" Danielle asked, relief in her voice.

"Absolutely." Michael steered her to the bedroom.

"Come with Mommy, Drew." The exhausted mother took the little boy's hand and allowed Michael to lead her away.

"Hey, TJ." Sterling beckoned to the young cameraman. They huddled on the other side of the room, voices low.

Great. Plotting again. Just what I don't need.

She joined her crew at the dining table. "Anything yet?" *Please.*

Elise spoke first. "I haven't found anything to indicate previous paranormal activity. No significant pet tragedies reported in local newspapers, but that's not surprising since—"

"Danielle recognizes Felix from her past."

"Right. Previous occupants were an older couple. The wife died peacefully in her sleep. The husband fell into depression after losing her. Best I can tell, a younger brother moved him out of state and placed him in an excellent facility near his home. So he could be close. But he didn't last long without his wife."

"Did their kids sell the house? Maybe we can ask them about prior disturbances. See if their parents ever talked about strange things happening on the property."

"I'll work on that and let you know what I learn."

Rosie returned from the trailer with a mug of hot tea.

Kimberly held it to her face and inhaled the mint vapor. "Perfect. Thank you." She sipped the soothing liquid, relishing the radiating warmth. "Better already."

"Here. Let me put your hematite on. It'll help calm and ground you."

She lifted her hair and allowed Rosie to drape the necklace around her and clasp the chain.

"There," Rosie said. "Breathe deep."

"Okay, Kimmy, they're settled in the bedroom." Michael motioned her to the table to continue footage review. "Let's see what we can see, shall we?" He took his seat and snapped headphones over his ears.

15

Kimberly stood behind Michael, watching the footage from the main camera.

TJ returned to his laptop, placing his camera nearby. *Odd.* He wouldn't need to record anything until later tonight.

She eyed Sterling. He merely smiled. *Definitely up to something.*

"Here, Kimmy. This is during the EVP yarn session."

She bent low for a better look.

"Here's where the yarn moves." He handed her the headphones. "Do you hear that?"

She pressed her hands to the headphones and closed her eyes. She heard her own voice, then in the silent interim, a soft susurrus.

She leaned forward. "Was that . . . ?"

"I'll run it back and isolate it. Watch the screen this time."

She kept her gaze on the gray-scale images. Just as the yarn twitched, she heard it again.

Michael rewound and played it several times. "What do you think?"

"It's faint, but without question it sounds like a cat's meow."

He nodded. "My thoughts exactly."

She couldn't help but smile. Finally they were getting somewhere. The crew returned to their own tasks looking reinvigorated. She allowed a glance at Sterling—his chin was propped on his fist, boredom etched in his features.

"Don't give me that triumphant look. One fuzzy sound distortion doesn't offer a shred of proof," he said.

"All the little pieces create the larger image. I've done this for years. We've seen it over and over."

Michael took his headphones back. "I've only listened up to this point. We left the camera and recorder running all night. So I may find more."

She patted his back. Sterling rolled his eyes.

"Ms. Wantland." TJ waved her over. "I think you should look at this."

She maneuvered around the dining table to join the young man at his screen. "You know how I thought we saw an image of a cat, like, rising up on the little guy's bed? Watch this. I found more images like it throughout the night."

He clicked from one still-frame image to the next, each time capturing a similar red haze in the bedrooms.

She watched, fascinated, then beckoned to Michael. "Look at this. It almost looks like the cat is patrolling. Maybe searching. Look how it keeps going from one bedroom to the other and stretching up on the beds. Peering over the sides. Like it's looking for the family. And it keeps returning to the crib."

"It, like, gets in the crib at one point." TJ pulled up the image for her.

Michael's brow furrowed. "I see it. I think you're right. The cat seems to be looking for the family. That image in the crib makes my skin crawl. Can you imagine if the baby was in there?"

She remembered her vision and shuddered. How could she determine what the cat wanted? And if she couldn't, how could she get it to leave?

Sterling snorted. "More hazy blobs? That doesn't look anything like a cat to me."

TJ glanced at the kitchen and picked up his camera.

"I'm telling you," Sterling continued, "those red images could be anything. Or nothing. And may I remind you that I found Felix in the backyard last night?"

"What?" Danielle stood in the kitchen doorway. "What do you mean you found Felix?"

"Why don't you go ahead and show her, Michael?"

Michael moved back to his computer and fast-forwarded to the end of the footage. Danielle watched Sterling walk in the back door with the kitten in his hands, proclaiming to have found Felix.

The young woman whirled on him, eyes blazing. "How dare you? Did you not even look at Drew's picture? That kitten looks nothing like Felix. I knew you would ruin this for me."

All at once, Danielle collapsed onto Kimberly's shoulder, tears soaking her blouse. She raised a hand and hesitantly patted the distraught woman on the back. "It's okay. I know that isn't Felix. He hasn't ruined anything."

Danielle raised her watery, bloodshot eyes. "Really?"

"Of course. I told you I connected with Felix last night. Felt his presence. I know he's here. Sterling just found a kitten. And I think, deep down, he knows that." She locked gazes with Sterling. *He'd better cooperate.* "I think he's just trying to be very . . . thorough. To make sure we explore every possibility. So when doubters watch the show, they'll see he did his best to disprove supernatural activity." The words came out of her mouth slowly, pieced together. Anything to soothe the woman.

Rosie tucked a tissue into her hand, which she passed on to Danielle. "There you go. No need to worry. Right, Sterling?" Sterling started. "Right. I'm just being thorough. After all, that's why I'm here. To rule things out. And to keep Kimberly honest." He smiled.

Danielle blotted her tears. "I'm sorry. I'm so tired." Her voice quivered. "We haven't slept well since the apparitions began. And Josh didn't sleep at the hotel last night. I hoped we wouldn't have to go back there anymore."

Michael stepped forward and guided the woman gently from the kitchen. "Why don't you rest now while the baby is asleep? Let us handle this."

"I'm sure Josh will wake up and need to nurse soon. Maybe later I can lie down. If I can rest at all, wondering what you guys might find. And if Kimberly can get rid of it."

She heard Michael's reassuring murmur as he led her down the hall. After they left, the crew exchanged glances.

"This is why we do what we do, guys," she said. "Let's see if we can wrap this up tonight. This family needs us."

"Oh, please," Sterling crossed his arms over his chest. "Why do you persist in offering people false hope?"

She felt her irritation surge. "What are you talking about?"

"Encouraging this, letting them believe there's a 'ghost' in their house, and that you can somehow make it all better. It's disgusting, really."

"I can't wait to see your face the first time you encounter an entity. Come talk to me then, Mr. Wakefield."

Sterling signaled TJ, who lowered his camera.

"Seriously? Again? Your first idiotic video got us in all kinds of trouble."

"No, it attracted lots of attention. Now we keep hitting them with more. Keep stirring the pot. This time I'll tell Michael first and let him go to Hoffmeier with it. And would you please call me Sterling? Mr. Wakefield sounds like a stuffed shirt."

Stan motioned for her. "I think you need to see this, Kimberly."

She knew him well enough to recognize his serious voice. She bent over his computer screen for a better look.

"I noticed this a couple of times and didn't think anything of it. It's easy to dismiss, just a dark spot. But it's always the same. So I took a closer look." He flipped through several images he isolated from the footage. Like the cat, the image drifted from room to room throughout the night.

She pulled an empty chair beside Stan's and dropped into it. He'd captured the dark image she'd seen in the toddler's room. The form was not as clear as the cat's. "I saw this last night. Felt it. But couldn't establish a connection. It avoided me. Didn't seem to want me near it and felt very unsettled."

"What is it?" Michael leaned across the table for a look at Stan's screen. Sterling came around the table for a look, too.

Stan flipped back to the images. The entity hovered primarily between the toddler's room and the master bedroom.

"It's a dark spot. Nothing," Sterling said.

"If I saw the image only once, I'd dismiss it, too," Stan said. "But not when it appears throughout the night and in different rooms."

Sterling leaned closer as Stan looped through all the images again.

"And watch this. Here's where Kimberly connected with the cat and tried to engage the other entity. Watch how it reacts."

She thought back to the night before, the cat perched on the toddler bed, hissing. The dark, unknown entity pulling away from her. The footage supported her perception—the hazy figure drifting near to the bed, then pulling away.

"It wouldn't connect with me. I had the feeling it doesn't want me here."

"Did you get anything from it?" Michael asked.

"I reached out to it. And all I felt was cold and empty. Then it retracted. It doesn't dissipate though, until Sterling interrupts."

"Are these two manifestations related to each other?" Michael asked. "And why does Danielle see only the cat? She didn't say anything about this other entity."

"Because there's nothing there," Sterling said. "I have to hand it to you guys. You have the most incredible imaginations I've ever seen. You take blobs and shadows that could've come straight from a Rorschach test and make up some fantastic stories."

"As I've said before—"

"Kimmy, let's just focus on the footage. Sterling, save it for your Confidential Corners. The quicker we complete this review, the sooner we get to break. Break early enough, maybe we can all grab a quick nap before tonight."

She bit her tongue and shot Sterling a look, hoping her irritation was conveyed. He smirked and shrugged.

Michael put his headphones on, joining TJ and Stan in their search for evidence of supernatural activity.

She periodically circled the table and watched over shoulders but mostly remained in her seat. Her function was to encourage the entities to manifest, to engage and connect. Whatever evidence the footage provided would guide her tonight.

Elise made a few phone calls and hunched over her laptop, looking at property records and searching for news articles about the house or its previous owners.

The minutes ticked by. She yawned. She felt rather useless.

Footsteps shuffling through the kitchen caught her attention. The little toddler walked over to the table and peered at the computers, two fingers in his mouth. He leaned against Kimberly.

"Hi there, little guy. Maybe we should find your mommy." She looked at Michael, but before he moved to help, the boy pulled his fingers from his mouth and clambered into her lap. "Oh. Oh, okay. We're doing this now?"

He situated himself, leaned back against her, and lifted a piece of paper clutched in his fist. He stared at her. "Tat."

"Michael, what do I do?"

"Elise, why don't you see if Danielle is awake?"

Her research assistant nodded and hurried from the room.

Michael reached for the paper. "Whatcha got there, buddy? Did you draw another picture? You're a great little artist."

"Yes," Kimberly agreed, because it seemed like the right thing to do.

Elise returned from the bedroom. "She is out like a light. Snoring. And the baby is curled up next to her sound asleep, too."

Michael handed the drawing back to Drew. "We'll just hang on to him out here then. I think six adults can handle one toddler." He tousled the boy's hair.

Drew pushed himself backward, pressing closer against Kimberly. He held his drawing up to her face, slurping his fingers.

"That's . . . so nice. What a great picture."

The boy smiled and pushed the paper into her hands.

"This must be . . ." She turned the paper upside down and then flipped it again. Neither angle helped. "Umm, is this an elephant?"

Drew laughed a deep belly-giggle around his fingers. "No! Tat!"

"Hey." Stan took the paper. "This looks like . . ." He looked back and forth between the computer and the paper. "Did you draw your room, Drew?"

"Wait, what?" She leaned over for another look. *Seriously?* Stan saw something in the mess of scribbles?

"Look." Stan pointed. "That's his toys there. This is his closet. There's his bed. Right, little man?"

Drew poked the paper with a soggy finger. "Tat."

"That's the cat?" Stan asked. "There on the bed? Sitting next to you?"

Drew shoved two fingers back into his mouth, smiled around them, and nodded.

She stared at the picture and with great effort saw what Stan suggested. The rudimentary crayon lines shifted into a closet door, a jumble of toys, a bed with a stick figure child and a cat. And something else.

"What's this, Drew?" she asked, pointing at black scribbles beside the bed.

Drew whimpered and turned his head, pressing it into her chest, muffling his response. She wasn't fluent in toddler to begin with and couldn't catch anything he said.

"What is it?"

He raised his head and repeated himself. "The dark." He pressed his head back into her chest.

Even she understood that. "Is this a picture of you at night? Does the cat come see you at night?"

The boy wiggled closer and shook his head.

She felt fear as the little boy shook. Danielle believed he was afraid of the dark, but perhaps that wasn't exactly right. Perhaps there was more to his nighttime fears than they realized.

109

"Are you afraid of the nighttime, Drew?" She reached out to read his emotional reaction.

He shook his head, still buried in her chest.

"Can you tell me about the dark?"

He lifted his head and spun around. "Tat. Dark." He jabbed a finger at the two figures.

"And you don't like the dark?" She felt his red chakra flair.

The boy whimpered again.

Michael held his hands out to Drew. "That's enough about the dark. Come here, little guy. Let's go play until Mommy wakes up." He took the toddler to the train track in the living room.

She held the drawing beside the still frame of Drew's bedroom. "Okay, so it's just a bunch of scribbles, but does anyone else think this looks a lot like what we saw last night? I don't think he's saying the room is dark. I think he's calling this other entity 'The Dark.' And he's scared of it. I could feel his fear when he talked about it."

Stan took the drawing from her. "Oh, my God. I think you're right. Look, it has the same shape, minus a few stray lines."

"Danielle said he's had nightmares and cried about the dark since they moved into the house. What if he's not crying about dark*ness* but about this entity he's calling The Dark?"

Michael returned to the table. "Okay, let's see how long he can keep himself busy." He stopped short. "What? You all look like you've just seen a ghost." He laughed at his own joke, but no one else did.

"There's definitely another entity in the house. We need to figure out what it is. Tonight. Because I'm worried the kids might be the target."

16

Kimberly yawned so widely she thought her jaw might dislocate. She glanced at her watch. Already nearly four. She rubbed her weary eyes for the umpteenth time. They continued watering.

She pushed away from the table. "I'm done."

Michael removed his headphones. "What did you say?"

"I'm done. I can't do anymore right now."

"I think we've found everything we're going to find." He leaned back, stretching his arms behind him. "Everyone take a break. In fact, crew go ahead and break for dinner."

Everyone at the table glanced at watches and stood, stretching and yawning before shuffling out the door like zombies.

Sterling's head snapped up so quickly she wondered if he hadn't dozed off. "Wondered when we'd get some food again. Worked right through lunch."

She shot him a look. "You're fine. I saw the enormous breakfast you ate. And we ate quite late."

Danielle emerged from the back of the house, Josh propped on her shoulder. "Did I hear you guys are leaving?"

"Yes," Michael said. "We'll take a dinner break and come back for the night."

"I'll pick up Stephen from work soon. And then I guess we have to go back to the hotel tonight?"

"I know you don't like being away from home, but I don't think you'd get much sleep here with us shooting."

"I can't believe I slept all afternoon. And that Josh slept that long, too. And Drew didn't disturb you."

You and me both, she thought, but also noted the woman's eyes were far less red and puffy. *Poor thing.* She needed rest.

Michael brushed aside her concerns. "He did fine. Played. Watched us. Took quite a liking to Kimmy."

Danielle beamed. "Really?"

"Kept climbing in her lap."

"Thank you so much. On top of everything else, you babysat so I could sleep." The woman's voice rose in pitch, her eyes tearing again.

"It was nothing. We're glad to help any way we can. And I want to talk to you about Drew."

"What's wrong?"

"Nothing's wrong. He may have helped with the investigation."

"Seriously?"

"He drew another picture. Let me show you."

Michael signaled Stan, who picked up his camera and moved closer.

"He pointed to this and said, 'Cat.'" She watched the woman carefully for her reaction.

Danielle shifted Josh and took the paper. "It's another picture of Felix. Sitting beside him on the bed?"

"That's how we interpreted it. He also pointed at this and said, 'Dark.'"

"He's been scared of the dark ever since we moved here. He slept with Stephen and me before. Our apartment had only one bedroom."

"So his fear of the dark definitely coincided with moving into the house?"

"That's right. Why?"

"I discovered something in his room last night. We captured it on the recording. It manifests as a dark patch on camera. No strong form, simply a dark patch."

Danielle looked as if she might cry again. "Are you saying he isn't scared of the dark, but that he's been trying to tell me there's a ghost in his room?"

Sterling interrupted. "That's a huge leap. It's more likely your son is adjusting to sleeping on his own, and he's afraid of the dark. Which isn't at all unusual for a child his age. He did not say *ghost*. He said *dark*. I say he simply drew a picture of himself in bed at night."

"Does Drew have any knowledge of ghosts?" Kimberly asked Danielle, though her gaze remained fixed on Sterling. "Why would he use the word *ghost*? He's saying he sees a dark figure in his room. Otherwise, why didn't he color the entire room black? Why does his drawing resemble our footage?"

"He's three! You're looking at this from an adult perspective."

"And what about the cat? He keeps drawing Felix."

"I've already addressed this. He's a three-year-old boy. He drew a cat. Maybe he wishes he had a pet cat. Maybe he overheard you guys talking about a cat. There are so many rational explanations—I don't know why you keep going to ghosts. You're skewing the observations to make them support your desired outcome. You want to see ghosts, so you do."

"Except you leave out the part where I saw the dark figure myself. And I've seen the cat. And so has Danielle, for that matter."

"That poor boy." Danielle sniffed, her voice thick with choked-back tears. "He's been trying to tell me all this time. He kept saying, 'The Dark.' And I didn't understand. I told him to be brave, that he's a big boy now. Like Sterling, I didn't want to be bothered, so I didn't listen."

"What? I always listen to what people say." Sterling sounded offended. "I may not agree with the conclusions they draw, but I listen."

"No, you dismiss people as soon as their ideas don't align with yours." Danielle wiped her nose on her sleeve.

Sterling rubbed the back of his neck and took a deep breath.

Kimberly cut him off before he could speak. "You're doing the best anyone could—"

"I didn't listen to Drew. I assumed it was nothing. I've been so busy with the baby, and sleep deprived, and worried about the cat. All this time I've been sending him back to his bed, where something terrifies him."

Kimberly rested a hand on the woman's shoulder. "You knew you needed help and you called us. Even drove to our office to insist we help. It's our job to fix it. So don't worry. You did great."

"I feel like I'm failing the entire family. And everyone thinks I'm crazy."

"I don't. I know we're dealing with something here. I'm glad you invited me to come help you."

"Really?"

Kimberly patted Danielle's arm. "You're doing great."

Josh leaned forward, eyes huge, drool trailing from his open mouth to his bib. "Gah!" The infant's entire body jerked as he expelled the sound.

Danielle sniffed and smiled through her remaining tears. "Kids just seem to be drawn to you. Want to hold him?"

"Oh. I don't know if that's a good idea—"

The baby dived forward, and before she knew what was happening, he was in her arms. She adjusted the wobbly thing until he sat on her hip, peering up at her. "Hi there." She giggled at the baby's unstable head, huge blue eyes, and O-shaped mouth.

He was so unsteady, so innocent. And so trusting, the way he leaned right into her arms knowing she wouldn't let him fall. The image of the cat standing over this little guy's lifeless body flashed through her mind. She instinctively clutched him to her, holding his bobblehead to her chest. "I won't let anything happen to you," she murmured before passing him back to Danielle.

"We'll figure this out," she promised the young mother.

Danielle nodded, took a deep breath, and gathered up Drew. "Nearly time to go get Daddy, Drew. Let's pack up a few things for tonight."

"Don't tell me you don't play for the camera," Sterling said after Danielle retreated to the bedroom.

She saw Stan's camera focused on her. "Actually, I forgot Stan was recording. And none of that is likely to make it into the episode. That was all genuine."

"Sure."

"Please don't antagonize the family anymore. She needs hope and reassurance. Whatever is happening here—or whatever you believe is happening—it isn't her fault. Stop trying to snatch her hope away. Say whatever you want about me, but leave her alone."

"Hey, I'm not heartless. Tell her whatever you want. But the way I see it, you're offering false hope, which is worse than no hope at all. She needs real help, not fantasies." He cocked an eyebrow at her, then reached for his ringing phone.

As much as she wanted to be annoyed with him, that cocked eyebrow set her pulse racing. *He really is too cute for his own good.*

"Oh no! It's Amber again." He looked to her as though expecting directions.

"What do you want me to do? You have to talk to her."

"I can't. I can't do it."

"Come on, Mr. Black and White—do the right thing."

"Not right now. Later. I need to talk to Michael before he leaves for dinner."

"You could have dinner with him and talk to him then. He'd love the invite."

"Nah. I need to grab something quick and take a nap. I'll never make it tonight otherwise."

"Wow. One night and you're done. I knew you couldn't handle it."

"I've pulled plenty of all-nighters on my show. But someone needs to be well rested around here. I'm starting to wonder if all of you simply experience sleep-deprivation-induced hallucinations."

"You're consistent if nothing else. Every time I start thinking you're okay and maybe we can get along after all, you remind me I don't like you one bit."

Rather than the ruffled feathers she expected, he lit up. "You're starting to like me? Hey, Mikey, she likes me!"

She clenched her jaw. "Case in point."

Michael joined them. "Glad to hear it, Sterling, but could you stick to Michael, please? I don't care for Mikey."

Sterling stared at her and spoke deliberately, as though reading from a script. "I'm so sorry. I'll never call you Mikey again. I didn't realize. I'm glad you told me."

She closed her eyes and clutched her hematite stone. *Breathe in. Breathe out. Just a few more days.* Fewer if she unraveled the source of the haunting and cleared the house.

"Sterling, didn't you want to talk to Michael about something?"

"I have another video. Call Mr. Hoffmeier back and tell him it's for publicity. And tell him we have"—he glanced at his phone—"over two hundred fifty thousand views! This is fantastic! We're trending. And we have another video to leak."

Michael nodded. "I like that approach. I'll talk to him over break. Kimmy, get some rest. You look terrible."

"Thanks. I so appreciate the brutal honesty."

"Honey, if I don't tell you, no one will."

Sterling raised a hand. "I will. You look awful."

The twinkle in his teasing eyes didn't keep her from smoothing her hair. Somehow it sounded worse coming from Sterling. "One wise guy is more than enough. Rosie! Let's get some food. Girls only."

17

Kimberly squeezed her eyes shut while Rosie brushed finishing powder over her face.

"There. Gorgeous!"

She checked her reflection. An hour of sleep had done wonders, and Rosie had covered up the last of her dark circles and managed to brighten her eyes. "You're a miracle worker. I don't know what I'd do without you."

Rosie glowed. "Makeup can't make an ugly person pretty. It just highlights the pretty that's already there."

"We both know I'd be a mess if you weren't here."

"So." Rosie's tone told her she wouldn't like what her makeup artist was about to say. "Sterling is back on the market again. And you somehow convinced him to get rid of his drop-dead gorgeous supermodel girlfriend?"

She blushed. "You mean his succubus. It's not like that. He already had some serious doubts. He talked to me about it over breakfast. Against my better judgment I let him know she's a succubus, and, as expected, he said that was ludicrous and didn't believe me." She left out the part about teaching him where his chakras live in his body and the smoldering look in his gaze when he'd taken her hand. "She keeps asking him for expensive gifts. He called her a gold digger. He didn't take much convincing."

Rosie flashed a huge smile. "And here you are poised to comfort him."

"They've only been dating a couple of weeks. He doesn't need comforting. He's the one that ended it."

"All the better. He doesn't need to recover. He can move along to better and smarter. And lucky for him that woman happens to be right here."

"You know I'm not going to do that."

"Oh, come on. What would it hurt? I know you don't want anything serious. So just have a little fun. I know you remember how."

The door opened, and Sterling walked in, looking refreshed and carrying a drink tray like the night before. Tonight, however, he balanced three cups instead of two.

"Hello, ladies! Coffee anyone?"

"Absolutely," Rosie replied, reaching for her beverage.

"I got you mocha again. I hope you like it. If you don't, speak up. Otherwise I'll just keep getting it." His brilliant smile lit up the room.

She noticed Rosie's flush and decided to exit. "I'm finished here. The chair is all yours." She forced a smile as she stood to leave.

"No need to race off. Here. I brought you coffee. I don't know if you got that nap or not but I figured a shot of caffeine would do us all good either way. Dark roast, no sugar, skim milk." His dark eyes crinkled, radiating warmth.

She accepted the cup, brushing his fingers with hers. "Thank you. That was very thoughtful. I appreciate it." She couldn't break his gaze. *This will never do.*

She looked to Rosie for help but found only an irritating grin plastered across the woman's face. "I'll leave you two alone and get started on the house."

"Stay and visit with us. I won't need much makeup. Just a smidge of powder. Then we can go inside together. Like partners."

The butterflies in her stomach danced. *Stop that. Remember how annoying he is.* Still, no need to be rude. "Okay." She sat in a chair and took a big drink of coffee.

"Okay, ladies. Tell me about the times you've been dumped. Best and worst."

Rosie picked up the powder brush. "I have so many breakup stories. Hmm, best—"

"Wait a minute," Kimberly interrupted. "Is this about Amber?"

"Yep. I'm trying to figure out what to do about that."

"I told you, you need to call her. You still haven't?" How could this guy be so charming and such a jerk at the same time? *Oh, wait.* Wasn't that always the case? What guy wasn't a jerk deep down? On the plus side, at least the butterflies were gone.

"I don't want to call her back until I know what I'm going to say. So I don't get caught off guard. She's going to be upset. Will she yell? Cry? Tell me off? I need to be prepared for every possible contingency."

"Maybe she'll say she was about to dump you and is glad you saved her the trouble. Have you considered that?"

Rosie shot her a look and dusted powder over Sterling's face. "Nobody likes to get dumped. She could respond any of those ways. Although, probably not the way Kimberly suggested. She'll get over it. Just call her back and let her vent. Then it'll be over."

"I don't want to hurt her feelings. I just don't want to be with her anymore. We're not a good match."

Kimberly scoffed. "Just yesterday you were raving about how great you two are together. How you were both so willing to work for the relationship."

"You saw right through that. That's what I wanted to believe. Sure, she came and met me for dinner, but she asked me for money while she was here and suggested I book an island getaway for us. When you told me she's a gold digger, I knew my concerns were valid."

"I never said—"

"Look," Rosie interrupted, "just be honest with her. That's what every woman wants. You can be nice about it, but be honest. Don't make up a story. Don't tell her you've realized you want to be a Catholic priest. Or that your mom is dying and you needed the money from her checking account to get back home and you promise to pay her back. Or that you're leaving for a yearlong cruise and won't be able to write and then not have any excuse ready when she sees you two months later at the bar where you met her. Or—"

"We get it." She knew Rosie's examples of horrible breakup stories could go on for days. "Rosie makes a good point. You don't need to prepare because all you need to do is tell her the truth. You don't want to be with her. Honesty is better than BS every time."

Rosie nodded. "Exactly."

"Okay. I hear you. I get it. I'll call her first thing in the morning."

"Call her now!" What was with this guy?

"My makeup is done. Time for us to figure out why Danielle thinks she has a ghost in her house."

She stood. "News flash. The show doesn't start without us. Take a couple of minutes to check in with Amber. You'll feel much better afterward. We can leave you alone, right, Rosie?"

Rosie linked an arm through hers. "Of course. Get this over and done so you can move on to better things."

She stomped Rosie's foot.

Sterling seemed not to notice as he pondered the idea. "Nah. I don't want to be rushed. Or stressed or distracted. I'll call her in the morning before we have breakfast. Meet you in the dining room?"

Rosie dug an elbow into her side. Never one for tact or grace. She took another drink of coffee. "I'll probably be there the same time. Sure. We can eat together."

He stood and offered a gorgeous smile. "Okay. Let's do this."

18

Michael raced to her side the moment she entered the house and gripped her forearm with both hands. "RandMeier called me before I had the chance to call him."

"And?" She couldn't tell if his enormous eyes and crushing grip were excitement, terror, or disappointment. With Michael, it could be anything.

"He is thrilled! The video is trending, everyone is talking about *Wantland*. He says he isn't too pleased I didn't consult him first, but this is exactly what he wanted. The publicity is fantastic. I told him we have another clip ready to release, and he gave me the thumbs-up. Says to keep building the hype."

Sterling slapped him on the back. "I knew this would work." He pumped a fist in the air and smiled at her. "Didn't I tell you? Okay, I got another clip this morning—"

"Actually, I'm going to use the one from last night, where Kimmy comforted you," Michael said. "I think it's perfect. We come back from the one where she loses her cool and show her softer side."

Sterling blinked. "I thought we should stick with what worked before. The two of us disagreeing, arguing our different viewpoints."

"No. RandMeier wants to focus on the relationship developing between you two now. Build on what's attracting the attention. Everyone is gossiping about the two of you alone in the trailer."

"We were never—"

"Doesn't matter, Kimmy. The suspicion is fueling attention. And he said the next clip needs to leak something about the haunting. So I'm hoping we get something good tonight."

Sterling put his hands on his hips. "But—I kind of have this worked out. I mean, this was my idea."

"And you're lucky he decided he liked it. And that I was able to play it off that I was in on it. RandMeier doesn't like being out of the loop."

Kimberly couldn't help but smirk. "I don't think you get it. RandMeier gets what RandMeier wants. That's the only reason you're on my show this week."

"Sorry you still feel that way," he muttered.

She opened her mouth to reply, but Michael spoke before she could say anything.

"No one says no to RandMeier. We will have to release clips the way he wants now."

"Don't worry, Michael," she said. "The entity will be my main focus tonight. Something tells me it's the key to this haunting." She watched Sterling, waiting for the usual snarky reply. But he said nothing and wouldn't look at her.

Michael clapped his hands once. "Okay, let's get the cameras rolling, record the recap, and go dark. We have a house to clear. Elise, you have a research update?"

She could tell he felt much better than this morning, unlike Sterling, who remained quiet and distant. Michael had a little bounce in his step as he set up with the crew.

She sat at the table with Elise. "Have you been able to find out about Danielle's grandmother? Anything about witchcraft in the family?"

"Not that I can tell. Not an easy question to ask, but I see no evidence of it."

"I'm less convinced the cat is the real problem here. I'm not sure how it all ties together but I have a feeling—"

Sterling dropped into the seat beside her. "Didn't you forget someone, partner?"

That tone again. "Nothing personal. Just used to working alone." She offered a smile, but he didn't return it.

"You ready, Kimmy? Can we start recording?"

She thanked Elise for her help, moved to the camera, and waited for Stan to bring them into focus. Michael counted her in.

"Last night we discovered the Williamses' home is host to not just Felix the cat but also another unknown entity. Is it a previous occupant? Are the cat and the dark shadow related? Though I interacted with both entities last night, I don't yet have answers to those questions. Elise, did you find out anything more?"

"I talked to the previous owner's brother, Frank. Frank said his brother, Dale, and his wife, Edna, lived here for forty years. They never had children, so Frank oversaw the sale of the home for Dale since he was the sole surviving relative. He says he remained pretty close to Dale and Edna, but neither of them ever mentioned any strange occurrences. I don't think the house itself is the source of the haunting."

"Were you able to learn if any deaths have been reported in the house?"

"Edna passed away here, of course. Prior to that, I'm not sure. I'll keep digging."

"You said she died peacefully in her sleep. Nothing traumatic?"

"That's right. And Frank confirmed it. Said it was 'just her time.'"

"Okay. Thanks." She tried to hide her disappointment. She'd hoped the black figure might be explained by the history of the home. But she still had no idea what it was or what it wanted. Hopefully it would show up again, and perhaps this time she would successfully connect with it.

"What was that about?" Sterling asked.

"Sometimes we can glean information about a haunting from the home's history. A sudden, traumatic death can wrench a spirit from the body and leave it wandering the earth, unaware it's dead and needs to move on. If that was the case here, I might be able to intervene and explain to the spirit it needs to leave this world behind and translocate to the next plane of existence. But Elise found no evidence that's the case here."

"Sure."

"The important thing tonight will be connecting with the unknown entity. I have to discern why it's here and what it wants. And if it's somehow connected to Felix. Then I can determine how to get them out of here. For good. We don't want repeat hauntings."

"Good luck. Hard to imagine you connecting with anything."

What did that mean? Aware of the camera still rolling, she shook the confusion off her face. She could talk to him later, offscreen.

"And cut," Michael said. "Okay, Sterling, let's get your Confidential Corner recorded and move on from there."

"Sure." He moved to the corner of the living room. Stan raised his camera and cued Sterling to start.

She couldn't help but overhear.

"After the first night spent watching this 'investigation,' I can say they all truly believe they see signs of activity. This is not a joke or a scam. Sadly, Kimberly believes she possesses the ability to speak with spirits and to influence them. And the people she surrounds herself with believe in her so-called abilities. So they all see what they want to see. They want to see ghosts and make their observations fit the conclusions they desire."

Whoa. She stepped to Michael's side. "You're going to let him say these things? I thought he was starting to like me. He even brought me coffee." She lifted the cup and downed the last swallow. "Now he's running me down again."

"Relax. It's just for show." Michael watched him for a moment. "I think."

Sterling continued. "I'm also not convinced the camera operators don't manipulate the equipment to produce shadows and smudges on the recordings."

She jumped as TJ spoke over her shoulder. "That's crazy. I just record. I don't mess with the footage."

"I know you don't. He's grasping for anything negative to say."

Sterling raised his hand, revealing a camera. "Tonight I'll be carrying my own camera. Digital. No tampering. We'll see if I can produce the same results they record. Or if the 'images' they claim to see are absent on my recordings."

Where did that camera come from? He didn't have it earlier.

"Our cameras are digital," TJ said. "We don't tamper. He won't get anything different. To think I helped that tool record his stupid video."

Her young cameraman's tone brought a smile to her face. "Hoffmeier is happy. People are paying attention to us. Come on. Let's move to the bedrooms."

She went to the master bedroom first, hoping the crib would offer new clues. Nothing jumped out at her immediately.

"Let's try an EVP in here."

TJ passed a recorder to her and continued to capture footage. "What about Michael?"

"It's just an EVP. Nothing to direct really. Let him hang around Sterling while he records out there."

She depressed the "Record" button. "Second night of the investigation, Williams house, master bedroom EVP session."

She remained silent to allow a baseline of the room's ambient noise level. They would later compare any deviations with the baseline to verify a change. She hoped something would register.

"I'd like to talk to whoever is in the house with us. I saw you last night. Not the cat. We played with yarn yesterday. Who else is here?" She listened. If anything answered, it wasn't audible to her. "Can you tell me why you're here? Did you live here before? Does it bother you that someone else lives here now?" Another silent pause. "What about the cat? Is Felix your pet?"

That was something she hadn't considered before. Perhaps the spirit of the cat followed the spirit of Danielle's grandmother. She didn't have an answer to why the grandmother would be haunting Danielle's family, but it was possible. But why did Danielle see only the cat? She needed answers, not more questions.

"Will you talk to me? Do you like the family that lives here? Do you like the children? Are you—"

A noise behind her interrupted.

"What was that?" she asked. "It sounded like it came from the crib."

She crossed the room and peered into the infant bed.

Michael arrived. "Kimmy, you started without me?" Sterling and Stan trailed after him with a few other crew members.

"Just an impromptu EVP. But I heard something. It sounded like a clatter or a jingling." TJ moved to her side, aiming his camera in the crib as she shifted items.

She bumped the overhead mobile, which plinked a few sad notes before falling silent. "That definitely wasn't it."

She reached into the crib. A blanket. *No.* An assortment of stuffed animals. *No.* Her hand brushed something hard and plastic. *A rattle.* She lifted and shook it.

"That was it! That was the sound," TJ said.

"Yes." She shook the rattle, reproducing the sound again to confirm when they reviewed footage. But she felt certain the rattle was the source.

Michael and Sterling joined her at the bed.

"We have activity?" Michael asked.

"Yes. Right in the middle of the EVP. I wanted to see if I could prompt the unknown entity to answer me. We heard this"—she shook the rattle—"just as I asked if it likes the children."

"I wish we'd had the FLIR on the crib. We might've noticed if the cat was in the bed when you heard the sound."

"Funny," Sterling said, "how you never have the camera in the right place to catch proof of paranormal activity."

"I'm sure the recorder caught the sound. It was very audible," she countered. "And we can bring the FLIR in now and leave it on the crib all night. We might still record something. But I'm not sure it was the cat this time."

Sterling raised his camera to record her. "What does that mean? You think there's another ghost?"

She turned away from him. "You know I do. You saw the images yourself." Sterling's on-screen personality got on her nerves. She liked the guy at breakfast and the one who brought her coffee. What had set him off later?

"Want to continue the EVP?" Michael asked.

"Sure." She laid the rattle back in the crib and moved to the center of the room. The crew shifted out of the way. Stan entered the room with the FLIR. "Was that you?" She continued her attempts to engage the entity. "Did you shake the rattle to let me know you're here? Do you want to tell me something?" Silence. "Can you shake the rattle again? Or talk to me? If you want to talk, this device can record you."

Michael held up the K-II device that monitored the electromagnetic fields. "EMF readings are spiking, Kimmy. Keep engaging."

"Can you let me know why you're here? What is it you want? You're scaring the family that lives here. The mother wants her children to be safe—"

The rattle shook again.

The crew gathered around the crib.

"EMF is through the roof, Kimmy. You've definitely poked this bear."

"My camera is acting up," Stan said. "Batteries are draining, and the image is grainy. Gonna have to swap battery packs." He left the room.

"Did someone kick the bed?" Sterling asked, pressing forward with his camera.

"No one was anywhere near the crib, Sterling. You saw that yourself if you were paying attention."

"Then maybe—"

"Save it for later. Please. I don't want to disrupt the connection."

"EMF is falling."

"Ms. Wantland," TJ said, "my battery pack drained, too. I need to swap out."

"Go ahead. Too much commotion in here now."

"We definitely had some activity," Michael said. "Good job!"

"I'm afraid we may have scared it off for the time being. Or shaking the baby rattle may have used all the strength it could muster."

"My batteries are fine, by the way," Sterling said, still recording. "I know you're going to say the drained batteries are a sign a ghost attempted to appear, but mine haven't been affected."

"We experienced several signs of supernatural manifestation," Michael said. "I'll be interested to see what we recorded."

"Your batteries are drained now, by the way." Kimberly turned the camera back to face Sterling. "Hope you have some extras up your sleeve."

"What?" He spun the screen around. "No way. I just put brand-new batteries in it."

"I'm sure we have extras if you didn't get any. Go see TJ."

She started down the hall but stopped in Drew's room. She'd had luck in there the previous night. Probably too much to hope for a repeat scenario, but she sat on the bed, closed her eyes, and took deep breaths.

She tuned her senses to other frequencies, like turning the dial of a radio, moving past the static to find the one broadcasting.

No one wanted to talk.

She gripped her crystal and sank further into herself, receptive to anything out of the ordinary. Blocking out the noise of the world around her, she listened. Nothing.

She thought she should feel something residual from last night's manifestation. She placed her hands against the toddler bed. *Come on. Talk to me. While everyone else is busy and distracted. Just us.*

Who had shaken the rattle? If Danielle was correct, her grandmother's cat began appearing during her second pregnancy. The crib was a hot spot. Kimberly had experienced a vision there the first night. And now the rattle tonight. The cat had also been in the toddler's room. Maybe it wasn't just the baby. Maybe both children were the target? But why?

She recalled Drew's crayon-scribble drawing. The boy drew his room, with the cat beside him on the bed and the dark figure to the side. He'd seen both entities, she was sure. *Tat. The Dark.*

As she sat cross-legged on the miniature bed, dread, hopelessness, and vulnerability overwhelmed her. She found herself in the child's place, experiencing what he lived through at night. She clutched something—a teddy bear?—to her chest. Her heart pounded. She squeezed her eyes tight and dared not open them even to peek just the tiniest bit because she knew—somehow she knew—the dark figure lurked in a shadowless corner, hiding, waiting for her to fall asleep.

Her frantic mouth worked feverishly in a single repetition, "Mommymommymommy . . ." Yet no matter how desperately her burning lungs gulped breath after breath, she produced no sound.

A soft meow broke through her paralyzing terror. She opened her eyes.

The entity stood before her.

This time the form, though still hazy, appeared more human. She even saw faint facial features, twisted into a grimace.

The entity held out a hand. Did it want to communicate? Could she communicate in her current state? Pushing down the fear, she attempted to gain control, to open herself, and to accept a connection.

The figure drifted closer. Coldness gripped her. Her entire body shook as though the temperature had dropped below freezing.

The figure's mouth appeared to move. Words? She couldn't tell and couldn't break the grip it held on her.

The outstretched hand reached for her. Unable to move, she watched the hand creep closer, closer until the fingers— tendrils—closed about her neck. Her skin burned where the entity touched her. No, *froze*. No, the tendrils were so cold they burned. She didn't know and lost the ability to care as she choked and gasped for air.

She heard her name, distant, distorted as if someone called her while she sat underwater. Was that why she couldn't breathe? Was she drowning?

"Kimberly?"

She heard the voice more clearly, followed by a frantic, "Kimberly!"

The entity turned toward the doorway, then dissipated. Drained, she pitched forward. Strong arms caught her before she hit the ground and encircled her as she lost consciousness.

19

Kimberly opened her eyes, a strong scent of lemon surrounding her. She turned her head, trying to get her bearings. Rosie hovered over her, brow furrowed and anxious. Michael and Sterling stood behind Rosie. Stan trained his camera on her from the foot of the couch. The rest of the crew was scattered about the living room.

Something slid off her forehead. Rosie caught it and repositioned it. "Be still. You were really wiped out this time. Give yourself a few more minutes to recover. The lemon oil on your feet and arms should help rejuvenate your energy."

She listened to her and remained still, careful not to disturb the chakra crystal on her forehead. She took a deep breath, noting the weight of a crystal on her chest, as well. Breathing felt so good after choking. "How long was I out?"

"Just a few minutes," Rosie said. "Sterling carried you to the couch."

"Sterling did?" She sought out his eyes, but he wouldn't meet her gaze.

Michael knelt beside her. Rosie shifted to make room for him. "Tell me what happened. Sterling is convinced you have an undiagnosed medical condition."

"That's ridiculous. I connected with the other entity—the shadow. I fell into a spiritual coexistence, morphing into the toddler's awareness and experiencing The Dark through Drew. That little guy is incredible. I'm not sure how he braves it. It turned hostile. Choked me. I couldn't breathe. What did we get on tape?"

"We haven't had time to review," Michael said. "We were too worried about you."

"Can I sit up now?"

"Not yet," Rosie said. "I have some tea almost ready. Just lie still and breathe lemon for a bit longer." She scurried away.

Sterling stepped forward. "You okay?"

"I'll be fine. Not the first time this has happened."

"Right. I saw an episode where you passed out. Thought you must be faking. Guess it's not an act."

"That's really offensive." She didn't like lying helplessly on the couch. Especially with him here.

"People don't pass out for no reason, Kimberly. You must have some underlying cause. Even if it's sheer exhaustion. That was really alarming."

"I'm not faking. The underlying cause was being choked by a spiritual manifestation."

"Sure. Have you been to the doctor for a checkup recently? Maybe you have low blood sugar. Or something more serious."

"I appreciate your concern, but I know exactly what happened. And it isn't medical. You'll see it on the recordings. Probably." She really hoped somebody had caught *something* on tape.

"I was standing right there. I had my own camera going. I didn't see a thing except you having a seizure and not breathing. I've never been so scared. I wanted to call nine-one-

one, but Michael forbade me. Not sure what kind of friend he is if he isn't concerned about your safety."

"Michael knew I wasn't in danger. And we certainly didn't need an ambulance disrupting the investigation. Rosie is trained to help me recover when my spiritual energy has been depleted. Think of it like your batteries being drained in your camera. When I open myself to an entity, I invite them to tap my energy for themselves, hoping they can connect with me. I'm certain that's what happened tonight. I even saw some facial features and had the distinct feeling we're dealing with a female presence. She didn't want me interfering. But she was more than happy to drain my energy and show what she thinks of me."

"That's nonsense," Sterling growled. "You should be at the hospital having tests run."

"No. I need to be here taking advantage of a charged spirit that seemed ready to communicate."

"If you consider choking a form of communication."

She sat up, spilling crystals on the couch and floor. Sterling caught one and held it in front of her. "What is this?"

"Jade."

"I recognize the stone. Why is it sitting on your chest? With all these other crystals?"

"I'm recharging my depleted spiritual energy. Anytime I need to recharge or focus on a specific chakra, I wear the corresponding crystal." She held up her clear quartz on her necklace. "I always wear my quartz because it helps hone and harness the sixth sense. I add more if I feel lacking in a particular area. Rosie used all the crystals at once and placed them directly on the chakra zones to recharge fast."

"You can't possibly believe you draw strength from rocks. Like Popeye eating spinach?"

She laughed softly. "Rocks are of the earth. So are we. We draw all our power from the earth. Where else would we get it? Well, the earth's energy comes from the sun, but we'll keep it local for now. All the chemicals and elements that formed us come from the earth. The earth supports us. Of course we draw strength from the earth."

"I . . . I don't even . . . ," he sputtered and shook his head. "You're trusting your health to rocks and voodoo. You're too smart for this nonsense."

He thought she was smart? "It's not nonsense. Look." She placed a hand on each side of his face and forced eye contact. "Are my eyes dilated? Bloodshot? Yellowish? In any way unusual?"

He leaned closer and stared into her eyes. "I'm not a doctor, but they seem normal."

"What about my skin tone? Pale? Flushed? Clammy? Anything wrong? Go ahead. Examine." She lifted his hand to her cheek.

He swallowed hard. "I'm not really qualified to say, but I don't see anything wrong."

She saw his pulse quicken in his neck. So she wasn't the only one who felt an inexplicable spark between them. *Not good.*

Michael cleared his throat. Sterling dropped his hand and jumped to his feet.

"You good, Kimmy?" His gaze bounced between her and Sterling under a furrowed brow.

She stretched. "I think so."

Rosie bustled in through the front door, tea clutched between her hands. "I haven't cleared her. Tea first."

She accepted the decoction, wrapping her hands around the hot mug. She held it to her face and inhaled deeply.

"Ugh. Rosie! Not the Super Perk. You know I hate this one."

Rosie crossed her arms. "Every drop." She whirled on the crew. "And I better not catch any of you pouring it down the drain. She needs to drink it, so don't listen to her sob stories."

Rosie collected the crystals and left for the trailer.

Aware of every eye in the room on her, most filled with pity, she scowled. "Okay, find that ghost. Tape, run EVPs, thermal scan, see what you get. The ghost is hot—go!"

"Yes, everyone, let's do what we do." Michael clapped, and the room cleared.

Sterling sat beside her. "The ghost is hot?"

"Charged. Potentially more visible and more active. You can record, too, if you'd like."

"So what's in the tea?"

"Blah. It's Rosie's special recipe to treat all the chakras at once. She throws pretty much everything in her cache into a pot and boils it. Ginger, lemon and orange, honey, garlic, peppercorns, mushrooms, roots. Who knows what else? Meant to cleanse and energize. I know sometimes she adds sage to ward off spirits. I'll need to wear something protective since this entity threatened me."

Sterling leaned over the mug, sniffed, and wrinkled his nose. "Price of celebrity? Or just the price of your bizarre health practice?"

She narrowed her eyes at him and sipped—and couldn't disguise the gag it prompted. She pressed her fingers to her forehead and rubbed.

"Headache?" Sterling asked.

She nodded. "A headache always follows an episode. It's associated with contacting another spiritual plane."

"Headaches are also associated with seizures, strokes, any number of other serious problems. Maybe you're prone to migraines. Modern medicine can treat those. May be as simple as taking a pill."

She shook her head. "Not migraines. Thank you for your concern, though." She forced down a gulp of tea and shuddered. "Jeez, it's worse than beer."

"Don't like beer, huh? Interesting. Here." He took the mug and set it on the coffee table. Placing his fingers on her temples and his thumbs on her forehead, he rubbed gently.

Immediately the throbbing pain lessened. The rhythmic, circular pattern soothed. His touch dissipated the stress. "That's fantastic. Thank you."

Rosie came through the front door and gasped. "Did you finish the tea?" She marched to the abandoned mug. "As I suspected. Drink the tea first, then massage." She shook a finger at Sterling.

"Rosie, come on. It makes my stomach hurt."

"You've never once puked it back up. Drink."

Michael leaned around the corner. "Kimmy, Sterling, I think we've found something." He jerked a thumb over his shoulder.

She shrugged at Rosie and helped gather her chakra stones. "I'll have to drink the tea later." She placed her hands on the cushions and eased herself off the couch.

Sterling jumped to his feet and rested a hand on her shoulder. "Sure you're okay? No dizziness?"

She stood still and took stock. "No dizziness. Let's see what Michael found."

She crossed the living room slowly, Sterling at her elbow.

The moment she rounded the corner into the hall, she felt it—an icy wall slammed into her with the force of an arctic front. She gasped and stopped abruptly, pointing toward the door to the master bedroom.

Sterling curled an arm around her waist. "You got up too soon." He attempted to guide her back to the living room, but she held her feet in place.

139

Teeth chattering, she jabbed her finger toward the entity drifting in the hallway. Which she knew he wouldn't be able to see. "Camera . . . there . . . record." She removed his arm from her waist and turned him to face the master bedroom.

"What's wrong with you?" Sterling asked, lifting his camera.

"C-cold."

Michael held out his thermometer. "Kimmy, I've found it. Cold spot, right here. TJ, get the FLIR. Stan, stay on Kimmy. Sterling, you recording?"

"Yes." He fiddled with the "Record" button. "Why is Kimberly cold? She said the ghost was hot."

"Figure of speech. Means it's active. Charged. This is not a warm-blooded creature we're dealing with. Elise, what's the EMF look like?"

"Nearly one hundred. And climbing."

"Unbelievable. Everyone stay on this. It's building toward something big."

Kimberly saw eyes boring into her from the entity's face. It drifted closer, beckoning her. She shook her head. "No way. I'm not coming closer. One draining is enough for today. Tell me what you want."

Without hearing a voice or even actual words, she knew the spirit wanted her gone.

"I won't leave. Not until I know the family is safe."

"Who are you talking to?" Sterling said. "No one told you to leave."

"She did. The ghost. She doesn't like us here."

"EMF at one hundred and ten," Elise murmured.

"Cold spot moving. It's drifting down the hall. This is unreal. Kimmy, you good?"

"I'm fine. I'm prepared this time."

"Sterling, don't flip out," Michael said.

"Why would I? There's nothing there."

"What do you want?" Kimberly asked the entity. "Tell us why you're here. We can help you."

She saw the figure stop, hover. She worried it would deplete its energy and dissipate before she learned anything more.

It rose higher, then swooped down at her, passing over Sterling.

"What the—is a window or door open? I felt a breeze."

"No, Sterling, that was her. She's directly between us now."

He turned, aiming his camera at the space. "Still nothing." He yanked the camera from his face. "I thought I saw—"

"Tell me what you want." She wrapped a hand around the quartz crystal hanging from her neck and focused all her energy at the entity. She saw images of Drew and Josh sleeping in their beds. Her stomach churned.

The entity turned, raced past Sterling, and dived through the ceiling, leaving behind a trail of wispy residue.

Sterling smoothed his ruffled hair. "I felt that breeze again."

"Not a breeze." She gulped deep breaths, trying to compose herself before speaking directly into Stan's camera. "She communicated with me. She wants the children."

20

Kimberly slid her plastic keycard into the slot and swung the hotel door open. Bed had never looked so good. Physically exhausted and spiritually drained, she went to the bathroom and peeled the contacts from her eyes.

She turned the shower on as hot as she could stand, filling the room with steam. She lost track of time, savoring the heat against her skin, soothing her aching muscles.

Sleep tugged at her. She turned the water off and patted herself dry with a thick, white towel. She slid into her Victoria's Secret nightgown.

The clock read 4:15 a.m. when she finally crawled between the clean, soft sheets. The bed wasn't hers. No telling how many heads had rested on the pillow. But she was too worn-out to care. She closed her eyes, eager for sleep.

Someone knocked on her door.

She groaned. *Go away.* Surely it was a mistake. Everyone who knew she was here worked on the show. And not only did they know better than to disturb her but they also wanted to sleep while they could.

Another knock. Louder, more insistent.

142

Could it be a fan? She hadn't noticed anyone trailing her. She'd been relatively fortunate as far as stalkers went—nothing serious.

Another knock. Rapid raps this time.

She groaned, pushed the blankets away, and forced her head off the pillow.

She peered through the peephole.

Sterling. What in the world?

She unlatched and unbolted the door, then cracked it open. "What are you doing here?"

He threw his weight against the door and pushed past her into the room, slamming the door behind him. He bolted and latched the locks.

She blinked, mouth agape, and clutched at the neckline of her nightgown. "What are you . . . you can't . . . please get out of my room."

He pressed his back to the door, shaking his head. "I can't." He spun around and peered through the peephole.

"What are you doing?"

"She's here."

"Who's here?"

"Amber. And she's upset."

"Here at the hotel?"

"Yes! She flew back, and she's been waiting for me. In my room. She's. In. My. Room. I came back ready to sleep, opened my door, and there she was."

"You never called her, did you? This is what happens when you don't deal with problems. They get worse."

"I was going to call her in the morning. I didn't know she'd show up. How the heck did she get into my hotel room anyway?"

"I suspect she bewitched some poor hotel employee. Male, of course. Would've been easy for her."

"What do I do?"

"Go back and talk to her."

"I can't go back. I'm lucky I got out in the first place."

"What do you mean? What happened?"

"She was all over me the second I walked through the door. Tried to get me in bed. You don't understand what it does to a man when a gorgeous woman demands sex and won't take no for an answer." He finally turned from the peephole, leaning against the door. His gaze took her in. "Nice nightie."

She attempted to draw the silky gown closer, as if that would make it less revealing. She wished she'd grabbed her robe before he'd barged into her room. "It looks like you need to tell her no and send her on her way." She reached for the handle to open the door.

He caught her hand in his, expression pleading. "I can't. Something happens to me when she's around. I can't think clearly."

He continued to hold her hand. She didn't resist. "That makes sense. A succubus knows how to prey on a man's weakness. She's trying to reassert control over you."

"I need your help. I don't know how to deal with an obsessed woman."

He stood so close. Those dark eyes seemed to cast their own spell on her. Could he resist a succubus? And seek her out instead? "I don't have experience with situations like this. But you managed to break the spell and escape." She paused. "How *did* you get out of the room?"

He blushed. "I kissed her a few times and then told her I wanted to go get her a present. I told you—I couldn't think straight. I wanted out of there."

Kissed her a few times? And now he was in her room? She removed her hand from his and crossed her arms. "You could've dealt with this over the phone. Now you have to deal with her in person when you're strongly influenced by her feminine allure. All the more difficult because she's a succubus. Mr. Wakefield, you have to leave—"

"I'm not going back in that room. And call me Sterling." He offered his most charming smile.

"You have to handle this."

"I will. But not at four thirty in the morning. I'm tired and need sleep." He looked around the room. "Hey, you got a king-size bed. This is a nice room."

"I need sleep, too. You go deal with the mess you made and tell me about it over breakfast."

"Maybe I can just sleep here."

Her heart skipped a beat. "You cannot sleep here. That is out of the question. Completely inappropriate."

"Do you have a second room? I'll take the extra bed."

"I only have the one room. One bed. And I need to get in it and sleep."

"But it's a huge bed. I promise I'll stay on my half—"

"Are you insane? We are not sharing a bed."

"I'll sleep on the couch, then. It's sort of in its own room."

"You're not listening to me. You cannot sleep here. You do not understand the kind of gossip that would provoke if word got out. And it would."

"How?"

"Amber is sitting in your room, waiting for you to return with a gift. She expects you'll then take her to bed for incredible sex. If you don't, she'll be more spiteful and ready for revenge. She will talk to anyone who will listen."

"She won't know I was here."

Her heart beat against her chest at the idea of this man sleeping in her room. He hadn't reacted in any way to her

145

reference to sex with Amber. He wanted to stay with her. But that was a bad idea. "You're being ridiculous. You can't sleep in my room."

"You said she's dangerous. That she'll steal my soul. How can you send me back?"

"Call the front desk and report an intruder in your room. They can send security to escort her out. You can use my phone." She crossed to the bedside table and lifted the handset.

He joined her by the bed and returned the phone to its cradle. "Until she convinces another unsuspecting employee to let her back in. While I'm asleep."

She could smell his cologne, musky and masculine. Why did she lead him farther into the room? "They can't open the door from the outside if you latch it. My idea makes much more sense than your sleeping here."

"And then she comes back tomorrow even angrier. What will she do to me? What if she tries to kill me? Is this a *Fatal Attraction* situation?"

"You've said repeatedly you don't believe she's a succubus. Are you telling me you aren't man enough to show her the door?"

"I *don't* believe she's a succubus. But I do believe this woman is mentally unstable. She was crazy tonight. Absolutely unhinged. She crawled all over me, clawed my back. Her eyes were wild. She kept saying I'd never get away from her. She'd never let me go, and no one else could have me. I'm scared. There. Are you happy? You made a grown man admit he's scared."

Had he heard nothing she'd said about a succubus? "She won't kill you. She wants you alive."

"Oh, I feel much better now."

"I'm sorry. I'm exhausted and need to sleep."

"Me, too. So can I kick it on your couch tonight? Please?"

"And then what tomorrow?"

"I'll deal with Amber tomorrow. When I'm not completely exhausted. I need some time to figure this out. Develop a game plan."

"Avoidance is not a game plan."

"Lesson learned. I should've listened to you. Now can I sleep on your couch?"

He looked so pathetic. And genuinely scared. Her resolve wavered.

But she couldn't let him. The risk of scandal was too great.

She took a deep breath. "If you truly don't want to go back to your own room, let's see if you can stay with Michael or one of the crew. We can't risk the gossip by having you stay here, even for a few hours."

"Will you come with me to ask them? I'm scared I'll run into her somewhere."

"I don't feel up to running around the hotel in my pajamas."

"What if Michael is already asleep? What if no one answers when I knock? If you toss me out and no one else lets me in, then what?"

She took another deep breath and rubbed her temples. This was deteriorating into one of the most difficult weeks ever. RandMeier had never foreseen this when he invited the guy to come cohost.

Just a couple more days. She could get through this. But she needed to sleep. Her head hurt, her eyes hurt, everything hurt.

She walked to the closet, opened it, and yanked out the extra pillow and bedding from inside. She pushed them into his chest. "Couch. Do not tell anyone. You will sneak out in the morning. No one can know you slept here."

He dropped the bedding to the floor and threw his arms around her, crushing her in a hug. "Thank you so much."

Startled by the unexpected physical contact, she gasped. Every muscle in her body tensed. She hadn't allowed anyone to hold her in a long time and had forgotten how nice it felt. Her pulse quickened.

He smelled good. She relaxed, melting into the warmth of his embrace and breathing deeply.

He apparently noticed the shift. He pulled her closer, lowering one arm to curl around her waist. And his orange chakra pulsed.

What was she doing? This guy challenged her online. Called her a fraud. Distracted her when she needed to focus. He hoped to make a fool of her on her own show. Allowing herself to become entangled with anyone—especially him— would be a huge mistake.

She pushed him away. "None of that."

"Right." He cleared his throat and smoothed his hair. "I really appreciate this. You won't know I'm here."

"*No one* better know you were here."

He spread the sheet over the couch. She wished there were a door or divider between the two spaces. Something. She wasn't worried about her safety or about Sterling trying anything. Despite their differences, she could see he was a mostly decent guy. Just a major pain in the butt.

She crawled back into bed and pulled the blankets to her chin. She heard the sound of him removing clothing. Heard the clothes drop to the floor. And realized he was now in her room undressed. Her heart thumped as she listened to him settle onto the couch. She tried to forget that an extremely attractive and undressed man was sprawled across the couch a few feet away. And how good he smelled. And how nice his arms felt around her. And the way his orange chakra resonated for her. When her mind wandered to imagining him in the bed snuggled against her, she chided herself. The orange chakra indicated nothing but lust. It wasn't proof he had any serious feelings for her.

He would be gone soon, and she couldn't risk developing feelings for someone who wouldn't be around long. Better to keep her distance than deal with the heartache of abandonment. Someone like Sterling wasn't a good match for her. *No way. No how. No.* She fell asleep to the soft sound of Sterling breathing, trying to convince herself she didn't care.

21

Kimberly woke to the sound of the shower. Her head popped off the pillow, and her pulse raced as she remembered Sterling was in her hotel room. She stretched and blinked, her eyelids like sandpaper: 7:58 a.m. Only a few hours of sleep. She felt as if she'd been hit by a truck. Her head throbbed, her body ached, and her brain screamed for sleep.

She knew she should get up. They needed to review hours of footage from last night and gear up for tonight's investigation. Plus the hotel would stop serving breakfast at nine. Did she care? Her sleep-deprived state left her stomach sour and uninterested in food. She lay back down, preferring a couple more hours of sleep to breakfast. She could arrive at the Williams house later. She was getting too old for these sleepless nights.

She heard the shower turn off and then the sounds of rustling as Sterling pushed aside the shower curtain and grabbed a towel. She blushed as she pictured him naked. She hoped he was on his way out. Staying the night in her hotel room had not been a good idea. Why had he come to her for help? He ridiculed her incessantly. Maybe he simply didn't know where else to turn.

The bathroom door opened, spilling light into the room. She gritted her teeth. No matter how exhausted, she couldn't sleep with light glaring in her face.

She opened her eyes. Sterling stood in front of her, a towel wrapped around his waist, wearing nothing else. His skin glistened with droplets of water. He scrubbed at his hair with a second towel. She bolted upright, turning her face away and shielding her eyes. "What are you doing?"

"Nothing like a hot shower to wake you up. Can I make you some coffee?"

"You can put some clothes on."

"I'm covered. At least in the critical areas. This doesn't bother you—does it?"

"Covered, sort of. Get dressed." She hadn't looked away fast enough to avoid seeing his broad chest, thick biceps, and rippled abs. Her imagination hadn't done him justice. Yes, it bothered her to have a half-naked man standing in her room. Particularly this man. The way she reacted to the sight of him would not lead anywhere she wanted to go. "You should go deal with Amber."

"I'm going, I'm going. Still meeting me for breakfast?"

"I think I'll skip. Thought I'd try to sleep a few more hours."

"You promised me breakfast. I'll be waiting in the dining hall. I'm pretty pumped about the footage review today. Very interested to see how my footage compares to your cameramen's."

She turned to face him. "Yes, I'm looking forward to that, too. Quite eager to see your reaction." No way would he see anything different on his own footage. She wasn't sure anything would wipe the smug grin off his face, but the thought that he might actually see something he couldn't explain was absolutely delicious. He'd see. Nothing fake about

151

her show. Her eyes drifted lower. Nothing fake about those abs, either.

He turned to go into the bathroom, the towel drawn tight around his waist, outlining his backside. Her gaze lingered a moment before she looked away, her heart skipping a beat. Yes, she was ready for this week to be over. Ready for life to return to normal. Ready for this distraction to be gone.

She lay back down and squeezed her eyes shut. She heard him pulling on his jeans and T-shirt. Heard him lift his jacket from the couch. As he headed out the door, he called, "Breakfast! Don't stand me up."

She lay still, hoping to drift back off. But she couldn't relax or calm her mind enough to fall asleep. And, although she didn't want to admit it, the image of Sterling in a towel kept her worked up.

She gave up, pushed the blankets off, and left the warm cocoon of the bed. She turned the water up almost unbearably hot and allowed it to pound against her back. By the time she finished, she admitted Sterling was right—nothing like a hot shower to rejuvenate a weary body and mind. Her headache didn't go away completely, but it was much more tolerable. She pulled on an outfit but didn't bother with makeup since Rosie would apply some later.

In the dining room, Sterling sat at the same table they'd shared the previous morning. A single daisy in a bud vase rested in the center of the table.

She stopped in her tracks and nearly fled. Perhaps he'd misunderstood. Allowing him to sleep in her room last night had been a decision made by an exhausted mind that wanted rest. And no matter how good he looked without a shirt, she wouldn't be someone's rebound. Even if she was interested in a relationship. Which she wasn't. Especially not with Sterling Wakefield.

Her concern must have shown on her face. He stood. "Relax. Just a thank-you for last night."

She took a deep breath and started for the table.

A voice behind her halted her steps. "A thank-you for last night?"

She recognized the voice. *Not good.*

"A-Amber," Sterling stammered. "I thought you went home. You were gone when I got back to my room."

"I was there until eight this morning. I know you spent the night elsewhere." The pale woman narrowed her eyes, the vapid, bovine emptiness gone. Fury burned in its place. "And now I know where."

Kimberly stiffened her spine and crossed her arms, clutching her quartz necklace. Had she realized she'd be involved in a confrontation this morning, she would've prepared by wearing her ruby necklace.

No matter. She could handle a succubus, although only Sterling could sever the connection. "He doesn't want you, succubus. Leave him alone."

Amber grimaced and bared her teeth. "He is mine." She stepped closer.

Kimberly held her ground. "I don't want him. But he doesn't want you. So go."

"You don't want him? Then what is all this?" The girl held out her phone, which displayed Sterling's leaked video, as well as the video RandMeier had requested they post. "The two of you alone in your trailer? You comforting him on set? You look pretty cozy to me. And everyone else in the world."

"Those are publicity videos. Nothing more. And I never said we were alone in my trailer. Or my hotel room." Okay, so they had been alone in the hotel room, but if that got out, no one would believe nothing had happened.

Amber attempted to step around her, but Kimberly countered and continued blocking her way.

The young woman tried another approach. "Sterling, let's go back to your room and discuss this alone."

He cleared his throat. "You know I'd love to, but I need to eat breakfast and get to work."

The man would never learn. She raised her voice. "Be honest with her, Sterling. Don't extend false hope. Lying will only drag this out."

"You surprised me, Amber. You should've given me some warning—told me you were coming."

The young woman spoke through clenched teeth. "How could I tell you when you wouldn't take my calls and wouldn't call me back?"

"Oh. Ha. Well, yes, that is rather a good point," Sterling mumbled.

Kimberly wished she'd opted to stay in bed. "You already know I agree. You could have handled this much better. Man up and do the right thing. Tell her the truth."

"I—I . . . think maybe we should get drinks later. Maybe grab dinner before the show tapes tonight? We can talk about this then. I think maybe it would be better for us both if we took a break."

Amber once again attempted to step around her. "I know you don't mean that. Let me take you back to your room and you'll remember how badly you want me. Want this." She pressed her hands to her breasts and squeezed.

Sterling whimpered.

Kimberly nearly threw up a little bit in her mouth. "I'm finished running interference, Sterling. Either say the words or I'm leaving—leaving you to fend for yourself."

The threat worked. "I don't want you, Amber." His voice wavered. "I'm breaking it off. I want you to go."

Amber recoiled as if punched in the gut. She heaved several deep breaths before she spoke. "I'll go. But you can't make me leave. I'm getting my own room. And charging it to your credit card." Revenge burned in her eyes and wrath rolled off her in palpable waves as she whirled on her heel to go.

Kimberly didn't normally lash out. At least not at the still living. Perhaps Amber's emotional state fueled her own. Or maybe she was truly concerned for Sterling's safety. Whatever the reason, she couldn't stop herself. *"Et abiit, maleficus!"* She hurled the words as the threat she meant them to be.

Amber turned, her gaze on her perceived rival. "You cannot stop me. I will—"

"Just try it. I know your weakness." Kimberly's lips twitched into a smile.

Fear passed over Amber's face. Then she smiled at Sterling. "I won't be far when you change your mind. Call me." The young woman sauntered from the dining hall.

Kimberly crossed to the table with the daisy.

Sterling opened his mouth. "I—"

"Don't call her."

"I won't."

"You gave her a credit card?"

He rubbed his temples. "Sometimes guys—"

"I suggest you call immediately, report it stolen, and cancel it. Amber is probably at the front desk by now."

"Shit!" He yanked his phone out of one pocket and his wallet from another. "This isn't how I expected our breakfast to play out."

"No doubt. You call. I'll get coffee."

She left him at the table, filled a mug from the coffee urn, and added a little milk. His frantic voice told her he got through to someone. She flipped through the oatmeal packets.

No plain. She glanced over her shoulder to find him watching her, apparently on hold. He smiled.

Stale pastries, dried-out bread, soggy pancakes, and the burned, greasy remnants of a pan of bacon constituted this morning's options. Not a single piece of fruit in sight. *Ah, well. Who needs food anyway?*

"Sorry about that." Sterling stood directly behind her.

She jumped. "Don't sneak up on me."

"Sorry. Wasn't intentional." He shook his head.

"That's okay. They don't have anything I want to eat anyway."

The mischievous gleam returned to his eye. "Why don't you come sit with me while I eat?"

She gripped her coffee cup and accompanied him to the table, where he pulled a seat out for her. Her place was set with bowl and spoon. A plain packet of oatmeal leaned against the bowl. A carton of berries sat to the side. "How did you—"

He held up a hand and indicated she sit, then settled into his own seat beside her. "That's not all." He reached inside his jacket pocket and with a flourish produced a packet of honey. Before she could say a word, he reached behind her ear and withdrew a little bottle of cinnamon.

She gasped and accepted it. "This is . . . when . . . where did you . . . thank you so much."

His eyes crinkled into a smile. Not his usual self-satisfied smirk but a warm, genuine smile. "Just want you to know how much I appreciate you letting me be on your show this week. I have a good feeling about it. I know they'll renew my show now."

"I hope so." She meant it. Not just to get him out of her hair. She knew how stressful waiting for renewals could be.

"Plus I need to thank you for helping with Amber. She's really shown her true colors. What a psycho. She's right,

156

though, that our videos are trending." He held his phone out to her. "Look. We're generating so much buzz. The new one posted on *The Wantland Files* site has even more hits than the one I leaked. We are a viral sensation. I owe you so much more than a decent breakfast. You're awesome."

Her cheeks grew hot. She was accustomed to people asking for her autograph and telling her how much they loved her show. But Sterling's compliment made her squirm in her seat. "I'm glad you're having fun. I'm going to make my oatmeal."

She scurried to the hot water dispenser, attempting to calm her breathing while the steaming water filled her bowl. She had to get a grip. If Rosie saw her like this, she would immediately know something was up. Kimberly could trust the woman to keep her confidences. But she also knew Rosie would flip out. Especially if she admitted Sterling had slept on her couch last night. Even though she was bursting to talk to someone, she needed to keep this to herself. Bad enough Amber had overheard and misinterpreted what Sterling had said. Still, she laughed to herself as she pictured the look on Rosie's face if her friend ever found out.

She returned to the table and found Sterling yawning widely. "What did we get last night? Three hours of sleep? I have a newfound respect for you. Takes real grit to keep at this season after season."

She added the honey and cinnamon to her oatmeal, incredulous she was enjoying her favorite breakfast away from home. She knew he wouldn't be able to handle the rigorous demands of the schedule, but his admission surprised her.

"I'm also impressed I haven't figured out your secrets yet. Or at least not all of them. There's not an illusionist alive that can fool me for long. I see through everything. I figure you're just acting your bits. Quite good, I must admit. Did I get the capsicum thing right? Is that how you make yourself sweat?"

She swirled her oatmeal and said nothing.

"Do your cameramen doctor the footage prior to the review? That would make sense. But what about the little guy? Drew? He keeps drawing pictures that seem to support your claims and even match the footage. Did you tell the mom to have him draw those?"

As much as she wanted to enjoy the oatmeal, her appetite faded. "There's no trick. Nothing to figure out."

"Come on. I thought we were sort of friends now. Can't you let me in on it?"

She swallowed and lowered her spoon. How did he manage to irritate her so badly just as she was starting to like him? Or at least, not actively dislike him. "There is no trick. No one is in on anything. We just investigate and capture what happens."

"Uh-huh. Okay." He dug his fork into a stack of pancakes. "I thought maybe we could collaborate. You let me in on what you plan to 'find,' and I'll have my explanation worked out in advance, too. No surprises that way."

"I don't know what I'm going to find until I see it on our recordings. You saw how we work. I'm unclear why you think you're missing out on something. We investigate, and I use my abilities to resolve any hauntings we encounter. And I'm good. People invite me to come because they know I won't fail. And because they're tired of the skepticism of people like you. Do you know how many people I have to turn down? Thousands. Every day. How can you continue to deny the existence of anything supernatural when so many people report experiences they can't explain?"

"I have never once seen actual proof of anything supernatural."

"What about last night? You saw how the spirit affected me, even if you couldn't see it yourself."

"I saw you suffer some sort of seizure and convince yourself of an encounter with a ghost rather than admit to needing medical help."

"I can't believe you won't acknowledge it. You even felt her. You said so. You felt her brush past you."

"I felt a gust of wind. Open window? Open door? Wind blowing through a house isn't proof of supernatural activity."

"But it is. No wind blew through the house. No windows were open. It was nearly freezing last night. The gust of air was room temperature. Surely you noticed that. And can acknowledge wind would've been cold."

"So maybe someone on your crew turned on a fan."

"Wow. Okay. And here I thought we were starting to work together. I see that's not the case. Thank you for the oatmeal, Mr. Wakefield. I truly appreciate it. I will see you at the Williams house for the footage review." She picked up her bowl, intending to finish it alone in her room.

He grabbed her arm. "Mr. Wakefield again? Don't go. Are you so insecure that you can't have a discussion with someone who disagrees with you?"

"This isn't a discussion. This is you continuing to tell me I'm a fraud. And you'll believe anything, no matter how much of a stretch, rather than accept what truly happened."

"I could say exactly the same thing. You're telling me I'm wrong. And as far as I'm concerned, you'll believe anything, no matter how preposterous, rather than the simplest explanation. I believe in applying Occam's razor. Your conclusions rely on so many untestable variables, they simply cannot be sustained."

"Danielle saw the ghost of her grandmother's deceased cat. Repeatedly. I feel a presence in the house. We've caught disturbances on camera and will probably see more evidence in the footage from last night. Even a three-year-old presented us with his version of evidence. And helped us determine a second entity in the house. For the life of me, I can't understand why you refuse to acknowledge this *is* the simplest explanation. To me, it's as easy as one plus one equals two."

"Except the evidence you cite isn't real. Those things are all circumstantial at best and imaginary at worst. That's not objective evidence. Your equation is null."

"Why did you want to be on my show if you think I'm such an idiot?"

"Whoa. I didn't say you're an idiot. Sit back down. Please. Finish your oatmeal. We can agree to disagree."

She sat but continued to seethe.

Sterling cut another bite of pancake. "I didn't mean to offend you. I think you're a brilliant woman."

"You have a funny way of showing it." She spooned another bite of oatmeal.

"Brilliant minds clash sometimes. I wouldn't bother trying to talk to you if I didn't think you were smart." He grinned, sending her stomach fluttering again. "Now eat. You need your strength today."

22

K imberly slumped in her chair at the Williamses' dining table. Her crew sat at the dining table, as well, wearing headphones, engrossed in footage analysis. She wanted to skip to the two exciting scenes at the end of the night, but that could leave evidence undiscovered. They needed to watch and listen to every moment. They'd encountered a couple of potentials—shadows and sounds and blips on the recordings—but ultimately ruled out supernatural causes.

Rosie still hadn't shown, much to her irritation. Her stylist wasn't required until a couple of hours before the investigation. But normally Rosie came during the day anyway. She knew her friend enjoyed keeping up with the investigation but also liked to think she came to spend time with her.

Of all the days not to show, why today? All the way to the Williamses' home, she'd pictured Rosie reading her emotional state on her face and dragging her off to the trailer to talk. And once there, the woman wouldn't relent until she'd pulled all the juicy details out of her.

Where was she? And for that matter, where was Sterling? When she'd left him sitting in the dining room, he'd nearly finished eating. So why wasn't he here? All that talk about looking forward to analyzing footage must have been a lie.

Or did he run into Amber after Kimberly left? Did the woman manage to lure him back to the bedroom? That would be so typical. She shouldn't have left him alone. She understood the power of a succubus. Sterling didn't even acknowledge their existence. What if Amber got to him? Or what if he resisted, and she turned violent? The woman had seethed when Sterling had rejected her. Kimberly stood up and paced, no longer bored.

Where was Rosie? She needed to talk, needed calming tea, needed—

"Kimmy." Michael gestured her over. "We've got something."

She turned to the computer, glad for something to distract her thoughts.

The front door opened. She turned on her heel, hoping Sterling would walk through. So she could relax that he was safe. Not because she felt a small pang of jealousy whenever she thought of him with Amber. She couldn't afford the distraction of jealousy.

Danielle bustled into the house, lugging a wailing Josh in a baby seat in one hand and clutching Drew with the other. The baby seat banged into her leg every few steps. Drew nearly tripped her in his haste to bolt to his train track. The young mom looked even more exhausted than she had the previous day.

"Good morning," Kimberly greeted the worn-out woman with as much smile as she could muster while the baby shrieked.

"How did it go last night?" Danielle asked, dropping the baby seat onto the couch. "Please tell me Felix is gone and we can sleep here tonight."

"Well . . ." Not sure how to answer and distracted by the baby's cries, she looked to Michael for help.

Michael took the baby seat and passed it to Elise, who lifted the crying baby and rocked him until he quieted.

Finally, she could think. At least a bit. Lack of sleep and a raging headache still clouded her thoughts. She led Danielle to the dining table. "I made some great progress last night. We haven't finished reviewing the footage yet, but Michael was about to show me something."

"So Felix isn't gone?"

"Not yet. I'm convinced, however, that another entity may be the real root of the disturbance here."

"Two ghosts to get rid of? Great."

"I know it sounds like a setback rather than progress. But this is good. We have to determine the root cause to know how to clear it." She rested a hand on Danielle's shoulder and smiled.

The woman burst into tears, talking through snot and heaving sobs.

Kimberly couldn't understand a word of it. Michael shrugged at the look she threw him. Okay, she'd talked Michael down from inconsolable crying jags. Usually when a boyfriend had dumped him. She could do this.

She patted the woman's back. "I'm sure it's not that bad."

Danielle sucked in a breath. For a moment, Kimberly thought her words had worked. The young mom seemed to be collecting herself. Just as she smiled, the woman melted down completely, sobs racking her body.

"Oh, God. I made it worse. Michael, do something."

Her director threw his hands up in the air. "I don't know a thing about women."

Baby Josh joined in the wailing. "Guys, I think her crying scared him. Can you get her to stop?" Elise asked.

She glared at her research assistant. "I tried. You saw what happened."

Rosie stepped through the front door, carrying a bag from what appeared to be a boutique. Her stylist had gone shopping? Was that where she'd been? Before she could ask why, Rosie took one look at the situation and raced to Danielle's side. "Divorce? What?"

Apparently Rosie understood incoherent blubbering fluently. She nodded as Danielle started all over, occasionally interjecting words of encouragement like, "He wouldn't really divorce you over this," and "He didn't mean it. You're both exhausted and stressed," and "All men are pigs."

Josh continued to wail. Danielle wiped her eyes, breathing in ragged gasps. "I . . . think . . . he's hungry."

Rosie took Josh. "Here's what we're going to do. You're going to come to the trailer and feed your baby. I'll make some relaxing tea and light some candles. You need to relax. Put that husband of yours out of your mind for a while. Drew can stay here and play for a bit."

Danielle allowed herself to be led from the room.

Rosie looked back at her. "We need to talk, Kimberly. Soon."

She recognized that look. Her stylist's eyes brimmed with gossip. No telling what she'd heard. This was the most drama Kimberly had experienced during her entire three-year run.

Her ears rang in the silence that engulfed the house after Danielle and Josh's departure. She shook her head to clear it. Her crew stared back, shell-shocked.

"Okay." She smoothed her hair and clutched her crystal. "Michael, you were about to show me something?"

"Right. Yes. Stan? TJ? Did one of you get some of that?"

Both men flashed thumbs-ups.

"Good. Let's show her what we found." He steered Kimberly in front of TJ's monitor, where she stood in front of the crib.

"The rattle! Did you get something from that?"

"We've determined you definitely heard the rattle, both times you noticed noise. We isolated those segments of the recording and compared the sounds to the rattling you produced with the toy. Same thing."

TJ played the clips for her, then pulled up the sound recordings. They were, as Michael said, identical in frequency and fluctuation.

"Did we catch anything visual? Anything around the crib when we heard the sounds?"

TJ shook his head. "No, unfortunately not."

"And the FLIR didn't catch anything, either," Stan said before she could ask.

"No manifestations after we left the room? That makes me think the entity truly wanted to communicate with me. But what was it trying to tell us?"

TJ played the footage of her during the EVP. The rattle seemed to be a response to her question, "Do you like the children?"

A shiver ran down her spine. "I'm more convinced than ever this entity has some interest in the children. I just can't see how the cat figures into it."

"You'll sort it out. You always do," Michael said. "We only caught the end of your encounter in the toddler's room. Because you didn't wait for us." He gave her his angry look.

"But someone recorded part of it?"

TJ nodded. "I looked for you after getting fresh batteries. Found you and started recording. You kind of looked like you were in a trance, so I didn't want to disturb you. At first nothing happened. You just sat on the bed. But I kept panning the room. Watch this."

The eager look on his face told her how excited he was to share his finding with her. When he hit "Play," the image

165

swung from where she sat cross-legged on the toddler bed to the closet door. Back and forth. Back and forth. The grainy images still struck her as creepy, even after years of working with them. The camera moved to sweep across the room again, then jerked back to focus on the closet. The door crept open several inches.

"The closet," she said. "Of course. I felt the presence originate from the closet."

TJ beamed. "There's proof. I can't wait to show this to Sterling. He can't write this off as tampering with footage. He'll have to admit this is proof."

She crossed her arms. "He won't. He'll say it was wind, or someone behind the door, or a wire we can't see on the recording. He ruined what would have been a lovely breakfast by badgering me to tell him how we fake things."

TJ's face fell. "But I've been here a year now. I'm not a moron. I'd know if it was fake. This stuff is legit. Surely he'll see—"

"There's more, Kimmy. Go ahead, TJ. Show her the rest."

"Right. After the door swung open, I saw a shadow in front of the closet." He returned his attention to the monitor, forwarded the footage, and paused to isolate the image of a human-shaped shadow. "After that, an elongated orb moves toward you on the bed."

He played the footage for her. Sure enough, something drifted across the room toward her on the bed. "If I'd seen this last night, I'm sure I would've yelled and ruined everything."

"You have no idea what moves around us while we go about our lives," she said. "Probably best most people can't see it. Too overwhelming and frightening."

"This next bit really got me," TJ said. "You just sit there with your eyes closed. Almost looks like you can't move. When the orb reaches the bed, something leaps from the floor. Took me a while to isolate this. I don't see anything on the floor beforehand. And nothing is on the bed with you after. But watch this."

He hit "Play." The figure remained beside the bed. A shadow streaked from the floor toward where she sat. TJ replayed it several times before he spoke. "That's Felix, isn't it? The cat. And it looks like the other entity lifts a hand right before the cat leaps. See? The shadow lifts its hand, the cat leaps, and then you open your eyes and respond."

Michael pressed forward, leaning close to the screen for a better look, finger and thumb curled around his chin and his brow furrowed. "Play that again?"

TJ obliged, playing and replaying the footage. She watched the dark, grainy, cat-size shadow appear to jump from the floor toward her. Almost as if aiming for her lap. Or maybe . . .

"I see it," Michael said. "The entity does appear to be directing the cat to attack right before it leaps at you. Did you see the cat or feel threatened? You talked about seeing a dark shadow, but you didn't mention Felix."

"I didn't see the cat but thought I heard a meow. TJ, can you play it again, but slow it down?"

He rewound yet again and played the same few seconds of footage, this time in slow motion.

"Watch carefully," she said. "Looks to me like Felix is jumping not toward me but in between the other entity and me. Do you see that?"

Michael nodded. "I think you're right. It appears to be attempting to get between you. What do you think? What happened from your perspective?"

She thought back to that moment when she was unable to move. "I felt paralyzed. And then I thought I heard a cat meow. I felt like I was jolted from a dream. After I heard it, I could move again. Can you turn the sound on? So we can listen?"

TJ pulled the headphones from the jack, adjusted the sound on the laptop, and pressed "Play." She didn't hear a meow. Michael and TJ glanced at her, questioning looks in their eyes. She shook her head. TJ turned up the volume, rewound, and tried again. Still nothing audible on the footage.

"I'll analyze the sound more closely later. If there's anything there at all, I'll be able to find it."

"Yes, move on," Michael said. "You look like you can't breathe in the next part."

She heard the concern in her director's voice as TJ adjusted the footage and continued playing. The dark entity raised an arm, reaching for her, before the fingers seemed to elongate and drift closer. The tendrils wrapped around her neck, choking her. Just as she'd experienced the night before.

The sound remained on, and she heard Sterling call her name in the background before he dashed into the room. He dropped his camera on the floor and caught her as she pitched forward off the bed. She felt slightly ill watching her limp body carried from the room. She'd never seen herself look so helpless. The entity had hurt her. No wonder Sterling looked so shaken.

In the recording, TJ continued to follow Sterling as he carried her to the living room and settled her onto the couch, where Rosie took over. No mistaking the genuine concern on Sterling's face as he hovered nearby, wringing his hands. TJ stopped the footage as the camera came to rest on her pale, still face. She looked dead.

She shuddered. She couldn't let the entity get its hands on her again. It was more powerful than any she'd dealt with before. She had to get it out of this house.

23

The front door opened and Sterling entered. Right away Kimberly noticed the change in his disposition. His shoulders slumped, his brow was creased, and he refused eye contact. She felt the shift in his chakras, as well. Where he'd been predominantly governed by yellow and green before, now his red and orange dominated.

Something worried him. *Amber?* She couldn't tell.

Best not to ask in front of the entire crew. Distracting him with work would hopefully help him focus elsewhere. Maybe when Rosie finished dealing with Danielle's crisis, her stylist could make some calming tea for him. With sage to ward off spirits. Amber wasn't a spirit, but sage would interfere with her powers regardless.

"Mr. Wakefield," she called, "come join us. We just reached the part where you carried me to the couch."

He shook his head. "You just won't call me Sterling, will you? Ready to admit you had a seizure yet?"

Sharing personal information with this man went against her best judgment as well as her desire to guard her personal life. On the other hand, he'd shared his incredible abs. She wasn't sure which made her more uncomfortable.

"I've had these episodes before. They're not seizures. Do you honestly think I don't see a doctor regularly? I'm probably evaluated more often than you. I don't suffer from any chronic condition."

He shrugged.

"I was depleted by a charged spiritual entity. And you raced to help. Thank you." She placed a hand over his and squeezed.

He met her eyes, then quickly looked away. "Of course. That's what partners do. Right?"

She flushed at his use of the word *partner*. And for a moment she thought she might actually miss him in the future.

"So did you find your ghosts?" He gestured to the table of equipment.

TJ jumped to his feet. "Indisputable evidence."

Sterling cocked an eyebrow. "Indisputable, huh?"

She rushed to TJ's side. "Instead of going back, let's move on. Sterling can see the footage later." Pleased to see her cohost smirking again, she didn't want TJ to jeopardize the improvement by antagonizing him.

"You recorded in the hallway, Mr. Wakefield," she said. "Let's compare your footage to Stan's and TJ's. Sound good?"

"Very. I'll get my camera." He started for the door but stopped. Holding up a fist with his little finger extended, he said, "Promise you'll include my footage?"

"What?"

"I want your promise you'll include my footage, even when you don't find anything."

She hesitated, partly because his serious tone caught her off guard and partly because his dark eyes mesmerized her. "Yes, okay. Even *if* we don't find anything. But we will."

He crooked his finger at her. "Promise."

"I just did." Did the guy want it written in blood?

"Pinkie promise." He lifted her hand, capturing her little finger by curling his around hers and squeezing. "Do you pinkie promise?"

The twinkle in his eyes prompted a giggle. "Yes, fine. I pinkie promise. You goof."

"That's binding in a court of law." He squeezed again before releasing her captive finger. His hand lingered on hers a moment. "I'll get the camera."

Rosie returned with Danielle and Josh. The baby was now sound asleep. Danielle knelt beside Drew, who played with his train track. "You okay, little man?"

The boy had been so quiet while he played, Kimberly had forgotten he was there.

Drew, slurping on his two middle fingers, nodded and thrust a train engine in her direction. "Play train," he said around his fingers.

Kimberly went to Danielle. "Glad to see you got him settled down," she said, because the wailing didn't help anyone but also because she didn't know what else to say.

"I am so sorry," Danielle answered. "I keep having one meltdown after another. I promise I'm normally much more stable."

"We all have rough patches. I'm glad to be here to help you through yours."

"Play train," Drew said again, pressing a bright-green engine into the palm of Kimberly's hand.

She stared at it. Then she lined up the wheels with the grooves in the track and pushed the engine back and forth.

Drew popped his fingers from his mouth and clapped his hands, giggling.

"You're very good with kids," Danielle said.

She laughed. Hard. "Not really. I have no experience. If that wasn't completely obvious."

171

"You fooled me. You're very relaxed. And you take Drew seriously. He responds to that. He told me you see The Dark, too. It's important that someone believes us. Doesn't think we're crazy. Even a three-year-old can tell the difference."

"Believe me—I understand that. Completely."

"Could we stay here tonight?" Danielle asked. "The kids don't do well at the hotel. They need to be home. In their familiar surroundings. We're so tired and out of sorts. Steven told me this morning that he's thinking about divorce." The woman's voice wavered. "Rosie says he can't possibly mean it, and that it's just stress and fatigue talking. I hope so. But he said he's starting to think I really am crazy. And he said he must've been crazy to think you could actually do anything to help. Two nights in our house and nothing."

She bristled. "He sounds like Mr. Wakefield. I have made progress. I established contact with the cat. I've determined a second entity in the house." She stopped, not wanting to alarm the woman with the other piece of information she'd discovered—that most likely the children were the target of the haunting. One or both of the kids, she couldn't tell.

That was another reason she wasn't eager to allow the family in the house while they investigated. The children were safe at the hotel. In the house, they could be in danger. Still, maybe the woman's idea wasn't all bad. They might have more luck with the entity if the children were there.

"I'll think about that. I know it's tough having your life disrupted."

"Come on, Drew. Let's go to the park. And then we'll get some lunch at BurgerLand."

Drew dropped his trains and jumped to his feet. "I tan swing?"

"Yes, you can swing. Say bye-bye to Miss Wantland."

Drew threw his arms around her neck and squeezed hard. "Bye-bye. Make The Dark go away."

She clutched the little boy in return. "I will, buddy. I promise."

Danielle packed Josh in his baby carrier and ushered Drew from the house.

Rosie stood beside her, arms crossed. "Keep playing with those kids, and pretty soon you'll want one of your own."

She stood. "Not a chance. This show takes every bit of energy I have. Nothing left over. Besides, I think there's supposed to be another person involved in the process. A guy, I've heard. Don't have one."

Rosie smiled. "We should work on that. As I've said before."

She ignored the comment. "Where were you this morning? I missed you."

"I went shopping for a new outfit. That's part of what I wanted to talk to you about. Have you seen the posts about you and Sterling today? Amber is pissed off. Posting about you stealing her man. Let me show you."

Rosie lifted her phone from her purse and tapped on the Twitter icon. "Whoa, girl. The hashtag *wantlandfilesdrama* is still at the top of the trending list."

"What does that mean?"

"Everyone is talking about you and Sterling. Have you checked your newsfeed this morning?"

She shook her head. "You know I don't pay attention to that."

"You're the only one on the planet who doesn't. Soooo, Amber hasn't stopped tweeting since about eight o'clock this morning. Something happen at breakfast?"

Kimberly squirmed and shifted from one foot to another. Shaking her head, she opted not to delve into the story. Not with Sterling about to return with his camera. "Nope. We had breakfast together but—"

"Oh, stop. You couldn't lie convincingly to save your life. Look." Rosie navigated to Amber's profile. "Look what she just tweeted."

Just heard my bf spent last night with another woman @sterlingspookbuster CHEATER #you'remine and @KWantland BITCH #you'llpay

Her jaw dropped. *Bitch?* Her heart pounded. *That damned succubus.* She took the phone from Rosie and stared at the tweet. Amber had scores of comments, all of them supporting her, along the lines of "men aren't worth it!" and "wow, just call her Kimberly Bitchland." Tons of retweets, too. Everyone assumed Amber told the truth.

Rosie's eyes bored into her. "Nothing happened, huh?"

"It's not . . . we didn't . . . she misunderstood."

Rosie held up a hand, eyes wide. "Amber misunderstood you two spending the night together?"

"It's not like that! Nothing happened. We didn't—"

"Oh. My. God. He did, didn't he? Sterling Wakefield spent the night in your room."

The crew members at the table went silent.

174

24

There it was—the stunned look Kimberly knew would grace Rosie's face if she heard. "Shhhhh!"

Rosie laughed. "Oh, honey. Do you honestly believe any of them doesn't know yet? What happened? Tell me everything!"

"There's nothing to tell. He showed up at my door terrified because Amber was in his room. He asked to sleep on my couch. I told him people would gossip. He never listens. He's an arrogant ass. But I was exhausted, and I let him crash on my couch. And no good deed goes unpunished, so I'm the laughingstock of the Twitterverse."

"And Facebook. She's really ranting there. Much longer posts."

She glared at her stylist. "Thanks."

"But you're not a laughingstock. People are lapping this up. Every woman wants to be you. Every man wants to be him. Hoffmeier wanted a ratings boost. He's gonna get it."

"Not like this. Not at the expense of me and my show."

"It's not at your expense. It's just publicity."

"Sordid publicity."

"Who cares? You're three seasons in. You've had great success. But the viewers are starting to change the channel.

They want something new. In a drama the writers would kill someone off at this point. Or introduce a new love interest. But you can't do that. I think this is rather brilliant."

"You're saying the show is stale? Are you tired of it?"

"Girl, no. Never. I'm with you until the end. But I'd rather the end come another eight or ten years from now. Not next season."

She realized Rosie was right. True, she wasn't in danger of being canceled yet. But ratings were slumping. She hadn't wanted to admit it. She'd been upset with Sterling for using her show to boost his chances for renewal, but her boss was using him to boost her ratings, too.

"How are you going to answer Amber?"

"I'm not. I will not participate in mudslinging."

"You have to say something. Silence is an admission of guilt."

"Silence means I won't stoop to her level. What does she think this will accomplish?"

Sterling hovered in the entryway, camera in one hand, phone in the other, and a scowl on his face. His thumb tapped rapidly on his phone. He looked up and offered her a smile.

Rosie laughed. "Sterling just responded. Look."

OMG tantrum much? Some girls can't handle being dumped #getoverit #notacheater @amberbaby @KWantland

Rosie took the phone back. "That's what you need to do. Let people know you didn't steal anyone's man."

"Why did he include me in that? I don't want to be tagged on that."

Sterling joined them. "So it shows up on your profile and in your newsfeed, obviously. I see Rosie caught you up on this mess."

"I told you this would happen."

"Knew I wouldn't escape without an 'I told you so.'"

"I did warn you. And now you're answering her? You'll only make it worse."

"Worse? Look at the comments on my profile. 'Shame on you, Sterling.' 'Keep it in your pants.' 'Ur a manwhore.' I'm not going to let this psycho lie about me without at least telling the truth. I did not cheat. I broke up with her. I can see someone else if I want."

"Though nothing happened between the two of us that could be considered cheating, technically, you didn't break up with her until this morning over breakfast. It looked and sounded suspicious."

"I broke up with her yesterday. And the lunatic broke into my hotel room to ambush me. This is a *Fatal Attraction* thing going on here. I won't be portrayed as the bad guy or accused of things I didn't do."

"I don't think a voice mail breakup counts."

"I do. You should say something in our defense. She's attacking you, too."

"I won't participate in this ugliness."

He looked at his phone when it buzzed. "Here's a new one. 'Sterling Slutfield.' That may be my favorite yet. Took some real thought, that one."

"You should take the high road and ignore the comments. What do you think you'll gain by allowing her to drag you into this?"

"I intend to set the record straight. She's lying. People should know the truth."

"You honestly believe all these people saying nasty things about you will suddenly realize the error of their ways?"

"I think they'll realize there's more to this story than Amber is telling them."

"They don't care. They're just trying to be part of the latest scandal. Makes them feel important. If we participate, we only fan the flames."

"So you're going to sit there and let her lie about you and trash you all over the Internet?"

"Not much different than your continual posts about me being a fraud. Also a false allegation. Did I ever respond to your goading and harassing online? Would you have stopped if I had?"

"This is different."

"Not really. The best thing we can do is ignore her and let it blow over. The less attention paid to it, the sooner people will lose interest and move on to the next scandal."

Sterling leaned close. "Except it didn't work with me, did it? Because here I am on your show."

She had never in her life punched someone. But her right hand fisted while images of slamming it into his gut tantalized her. Even if she'd probably break her hand on those rock-solid abs of his.

Before she could reply, his phone rang.

She transferred her fist to her crystal, shut her eyes, and breathed deeply.

"She won't stop calling me. This is insane. Does she think I'll take her back after this?"

"Probably not. She's just trying to hurt you. And as agitated as you are, I'd say it's working."

His phone rang again. "Oh my God, crazy—" He glanced at the screen and did a double take. "It's my agent. I need to take this." He stepped away to take the call.

For the second time that morning, she became painfully aware of silence. Deafening silence.

Her head swiveled to meet the gaze of every crew member. Mouths hung agape, eyes wide as saucers. She turned to Rosie. "I thought you said they all knew."

Rosie pulled the corners of her mouth down into an overexaggerated grimace. "I assumed as much. Maybe I miscalculated."

Michael cleared his throat. "Footage review?"

"Yes. Yes, of course." She hurried to the table, where Elise offered raised eyebrows, a sly grin, and a thumbs-up.

"Sterling is . . . ?" Michael asked.

"He stepped out to take a call. From his agent," she added, to clarify he wasn't talking to Amber.

The silence continued, broken only by TJ clicking images on his screen. Until he spoke. "I can't believe you would . . . with Sterling." The cameraman spoke the name as though choking down vomit.

Elise spoke up. "She said nothing happened."

"Yeah, right."

"Really, TJ? After you asked for his autograph and sneakily recorded us and planned to upload the video?"

"That was before I realized he's a complete douche."

"TJ!"

"What? That's the way I feel."

Elise cleared her throat and tipped her head toward the living room, where Sterling stood. How long had he been there?

Michael spoke first. "TJ, you should—"

"If you're going to say apologize, Michael, don't bother," Sterling interrupted. "TJ is merely voicing the popular sentiment of the moment." He carried the camcorder to the table, set it down with a thump, and switched it on. When he depressed "Play," TJ spoke again.

179

"If you plug it into a laptop, we can all see the footage on a nineteen-inch screen instead of that two-inch postage stamp."

"Not a chance," Sterling answered. "No way will I let you mess with my recording."

TJ jumped to his feet. "I don't 'mess with' any recording. Nobody can see that screen. Especially not you. You have no idea what you're looking for."

"There's nothing to see. This is my only shot at objective evidence. I'm not giving you the opportunity to plant something."

TJ stepped toward him. "How dare you—"

"Okay, boys. Calm down." She stepped between them, placing a hand on TJ's arm. When he took his seat, she turned to Sterling. "I have to agree with TJ on this one—"

"There's a surprise."

"Since you've made me promise to use the footage. It's only fair we review it with you. You'll be standing right here, your camcorder will never leave your sight. We simply view it on the larger screen."

He shook his head. "I still don't like it."

"Why?" she asked. "Afraid we'll find something you won't be able to explain away?"

His brows met above his eyes. He picked up the camcorder and thrust it at TJ, then dropped into a chair beside the junior cameraman. "I'll be watching you."

"Bring it." TJ clicked the USB cord into place and brought up the footage.

She shook her head. In addition to finding and clearing a ghost, it looked as though she would also get to referee a pissing contest. *Terrific.*

25

Sterling's footage disappointed Kimberly. She'd hoped it would prove their evidence wasn't doctored. But the grainy, shaky recordings only proved that he'd never operated a camcorder before in his life. And induced queasiness.

TJ's periodic scoffs and interjections of "Amateur," and "Basic Camera Operation 101," ratcheted up the tension in the room.

When they reached the part where Sterling dropped the camcorder and raced to catch her as she fell from the toddler bed, she suggested a break.

"Yes," Michael agreed, one hand on his stomach. "And someone run to any place that sells Dramamine." He squeezed his temples. "And to Starbucks for double shots."

Elise gestured to several of the support crew and scrambled to fulfill his requests.

Sterling stretched. "You can criticize my technique all you want, but my footage proves me right so far." He walked to the kitchen for a glass of water.

She joined him, leaning against the counter. "Nothing yet, true. Though that's not terribly surprising. And you did see that no one shook or kicked the crib to set off the baby rattle as you thought."

"I'm one hundred percent certain the rest of the footage will be equally boring."

Rosie turned the corner into the kitchen, carrying two mugs of steaming tea. "Here we go. A decoction of lemon, ginger root, peppermint, and a touch of honey. One infused with sage." She handed a mug to Sterling. "One without."

Kimberly accepted the tea and smiled. "You read my mind." The ginger and peppermint would soothe the motion sickness wrought by Sterling's footage. And while she didn't want any sage in her system when she'd be inviting spirits to connect tonight, Sterling needed the help.

"Um, Kimberly?"

She turned and found TJ ashen. *Odd.* She sipped her tea and joined him at the table. "What's up?"

"You guys need to see this." His hand shook as he reached for the mouse.

"Hey!" Sterling strode to the table. "Did you go on without us? That wasn't the deal."

She rested a hand on his arm and felt his red chakra flair. "Calm down. I'm sure it's—"

Guilt settled on TJ's face. "I only wanted to get past the boring stuff."

She stared at TJ. "You did continue on?"

"This recording is now inadmissible!" Sterling reached for the camcorder.

"No!" TJ grabbed his arm.

"Whoa. Come on now. This isn't a court of law, Mr. Wakefield. TJ, I'm shocked you'd do this."

"You guys were standing right there. And I didn't expect to find anything. I only meant to fast-forward past where the camcorder fell on the floor and get to the hallway manifestation." He held up his hands in surrender. "I had no time to add anything. I didn't copy it. Check my drives. No downloads. Ms. Wantland, you have to see this. And if Wakefield is truly a man of science, he'll want to see it, too."

She looked at her cohost, who still seethed. "Please?"

He clenched his jaw and glared at TJ. His face softened when he turned his attention back to her. "Like anyone could say no to that face. Fine. Go ahead."

Her insides quivered at his compliment. Did he really find her irresistible? Rosie nudged her in the back.

"But as far as I'm concerned, this footage"—he jabbed a finger at the screen—"has lost all credibility."

TJ jumped from his seat. "As far as I'm concerned, you lost all respect when you jeopardized Ms. Wantland's reputation. Pompous prick."

"Fine! I'm an asshole. Everyone hates me. No one wants me here, least of all Kimberly. So I'll go." He turned and headed for the front door.

"Good!" TJ called after him.

"What the heck happened while I went to the toilet?" Michael intercepted Sterling.

"I'm leaving. No one wants me here. My presence doesn't add anything to the show. Because of Kimberly, I now have a psycho stalker—"

"That wasn't Ms. Wantland's fault!" TJ yelled.

Sterling rubbed his temples. "Because of my actions involving Kimberly, I now have a psycho stalker trying to convince everyone on the planet I'm a jerk. And everyone believes her. This week has been a disaster. I'm going to go."

"I'm sorry, but you're not going anywhere," Michael said. "You signed a contract to appear on this episode of our show. And it's all over the Internet now, with everyone excited to see it."

"Because you leaked it," TJ reminded everyone.

She held up a hand. "Okay, TJ. We know."

Rosie held up her phone. "Hashtag wantlandsavethedate already has over a half-million follows."

Michael nodded. "Believe me, I know. RandMeier calls me every few hours to crow about all the publicity we're getting from this and to gloat about what a smart idea he had to bring you on the show. You're stuck with us until we close this investigation."

Sterling muttered, "Coming on the show was technically my idea. Not his."

"Sure. But as far as RandMeier is concerned, it was his. And there is no way I'm calling to tell him you left."

Two days ago, she would've thrown streamers and confetti at Sterling's decision to leave. Now the idea of disappointing her producer and all the fans excited about the show made her blood run cold. "Sounds like you managed to record something no one else caught. Don't you want to see? Aren't you at all curious? Don't give up now."

Sterling turned his dark eyes on her. Something troubled him. She saw turbulence and fear, something that hadn't been there until now. Even last night when he'd worried what Amber would do to him, she hadn't seen this level of concern.

Finally, he spoke. "I suppose I have nothing to lose. Let's see what TJ imagined on the footage. Someone needs to be the voice of reason around here."

She heard a collective sigh of relief as Sterling returned to the table.

"Just for the record," Michael told Sterling, "I'm the only one allowed to pitch diva-style fits on set. Not even Kimmy has diva privileges."

Sterling glanced at her. "I suspect she manages to get what she wants without pitching fits."

Elise and the crew members returned with Dramamine and coffee shots, passing them around the table. Michael popped open the cap and chewed several tablets, washing them down with a gulp of espresso.

"Stan, if we have potentially exciting footage coming up, let's have you on camera to capture responses. Kimmy and Sterling, I want one of you on each side of TJ so we can get all three of you in the reaction shots."

Stan scooped up his camera and stood across the table from the trio. She and Sterling scooted chairs near TJ's and leaned in close. Michael counted them in.

"Okay," TJ said. "Sterling dropped the camera. You can see it's sideways, just laying there. When I had the headphones on, I heard all of us moving away, worried about Ms. Wantland. No one thought about the camera. But watch this."

He played the footage. The camera lens angled to include the edge of the bed. On the rough footage, a shadow appeared, as though creeping out from under the bed.

She saw it before TJ pointed to it and leaned closer. "What—"

"Wait," TJ said. "The form becomes clearer."

Sure enough, moments later, the shadowy blob looked distinctly like the silhouette of a cat.

Sterling shook his head. "Is that stray kitten I found still in the house?"

Stan swung the camera when Elise spoke up. "No. I can confirm the kitten is no longer anywhere near the house. I personally took it to the Humane Society shelter. And someone adopted it yesterday."

"But you admit you see the silhouette of a cat?" TJ asked.

Sterling hesitated. "I'm not sure what we're seeing. I'm admitting to seeing a dark silhouette I cannot identify at this time."

185

"You'll love the next bit then. This is where I called you over."

The image crept nearer to the camera, appearing to approach with caution. The closer it drew to the camera, the clearer the image became until the frame was filled with what very much resembled a rounded head with two pointed ears. As they watched, the head seemed to press against the camera, as though rubbing it. A coarse, reedy sound accompanied the movement.

"What is that?" she asked.

TJ adjusted the volume. "Let me see if I can clean up the sound a bit."

"No," Sterling said. "No adjustments or changes. I insist."

"Dude, it's only to clarify the sound. So we can figure out what that is."

"Leave the footage as is. That was the deal."

TJ blew out a deep breath and cranked up the volume even more.

Michael cocked his head. "Is that . . . purring?"

Elise nodded. "I wasn't going to say anything, but I thought purring, too."

"This is exactly why I wanted you to see this, Ms. Wantland. It's the cat, right? And it's rubbing against the camera and purring. It doesn't look angry or aggressive at all."

She stared at the screen. In three seasons, they'd never captured anything that so clearly seemed to be the entity they were tracking. *But Sterling shows up, drops a camera, and inadvertently records what could potentially be the strongest proof of a spiritual entity ever captured?* That just couldn't be. "Can you replay it, TJ?"

"Really? You're not convinced yet?" Sterling sneered at her. "Your crew seems ready to accept it, and for once you're balking?"

"I didn't say that. But I always want to be sure."

"Well, I'm sure that's not the ghost of a cat, but go right ahead and watch it to your heart's content."

"What do you think it is?" she asked as TJ began the segment again, and she saw the silhouette creep from under the bed. "Look at that. Something came out from under the bed. What is it?" At that moment, she hoped he had a good answer. She didn't want him to be the one who provided proof on her show.

"That could be anything—a smudge, something on the lens. Why do you always jump to spectral entity?"

"You just asked if the stray cat was still around here," TJ said. "You must've thought the same thing we did. You just won't admit it."

"No, I thought perhaps an actual cat crawled out from under the bed. Not a ghost."

"But there is no cat in the house. So where does that leave you? You saw a cat. There is no cat. What conclusion do you draw?"

"Honestly? I draw the conclusion that you tampered with my recording."

"Come on!" TJ's voice rose. "I would never do that. But even if I wanted to, I didn't have time."

While they bickered, the footage continued. The purring sound ended abruptly, and the silhouette disappeared.

"It's gone," she said. "It just disappeared."

TJ and Sterling turned their heads back to the screen. TJ reached for the mouse, but before he clicked it, a mist clouded the frame.

"What . . . is that?" TJ asked, adjusting his glasses and leaning closer.

"You mean you didn't see this part?" she asked him.

"No, I stopped and called you over when I heard the purring."

187

She and Sterling leaned closer, as well. A shadow fell across the frame. Darkness shrouded the room. The camera shifted forty-five degrees, so that the lens centered on the closet. The mist and darkness lifted, leaving a clear image of the closet door as it swung closed and latched shut.

26

Kimberly blinked at the screen. "I can't believe this happened while I was unconscious. If you weren't here, Mr. Wakefield, we would've missed it completely."

"Someone turning the camera? I'm afraid I'm not terribly impressed."

"No one turned it," TJ said. "We were all out in the living room with Ms. Wantland. And we're all recorded out there."

"Every single crew member is on-screen every second? Someone could've slipped away undetected and turned the camera."

TJ affected a pompous voice. "'Someone could've slipped away undetected.' What is this? The movie *Clue*? Was it Mrs. White? Or Colonel Mustard?"

"That's a completely possible scenario."

"And shrouded the camera in darkness and some kind of hazy mist? And closed the closet door without being visible on the footage?"

"I haven't figured out how you manage those illusions. But I will."

"They aren't illusions," she repeated for what felt like the thousandth time. "When will you believe me? This is your own footage. You recorded this. No one else handled the camera. And still you won't accept what you're seeing."

"Because it makes no sense!"

The screen went black. When the footage resumed, they were in the hallway. She heard her voice instructing him where to record. His camera caught the crew with their equipment, similar to what TJ and Stan had already seen on their own footage. She heard their voices and then her own, demanding to know what the spirit wanted. Sterling commented on feeling a breeze. He swung the camera around to face her.

Something flashed across the screen, a barely perceptible blip, just before Sterling commented that he saw something.

TJ paused the footage.

"Did you see that?" she asked. "I thought maybe I imagined it."

TJ shook his head. "You did not imagine it. Definitely something there. I need to flag this portion of the recording so I can come back and analyze it further."

"I said I don't want anyone tampering with my footage," Sterling said, a scowl on his face.

"They won't tamper with it," Michael said. "TJ and Stan isolate and enhance images from footage all the time. They'll take a still image from the recording. The process doesn't add anything to the recording at all."

"Then do it right here, right now, in front of me," Sterling said.

"It takes some time," TJ warned him.

"Do you have somewhere else to be? Because I thought analyzing footage was the goal for today. I don't have anywhere else to go."

Something in his voice caught her attention again. Something bothered Sterling. She thought about suggesting they speak privately in her trailer but hesitated given the

190

current rumors swirling around them. Probably best not to encourage any more speculation by disappearing into the trailer alone. She made a mental note to talk to him later.

Stan put down his camera and went to TJ's side. They viewed the recording frame by frame until the blur began to take shape. Once satisfied they had isolated the best frame of the image, they would magnify it as much as possible without distorting it.

Rosie motioned to her from the living room. She gladly left the boring technical portion of the footage review behind and went to see what her stylist wanted. She preferred results to the time-consuming analysis. Interesting Sterling had caught this image when neither Stan nor TJ had. Particularly since his comment indicated he must have seen something while recording.

Rosie stared at her phone, mesmerized by her Twitter app. "This is still blowing up. I don't know if you should keep ignoring it. At some point, negative publicity ceases to be good publicity. You need to consider your reputation."

"And a catfight between Amber and me is somehow anything but negative publicity and detrimental to my reputation? No. We should ignore it and let it blow over. It will. Something else will grab attention in a day or two."

"At least tweet hashtag justfriends. Or something. Anything to indicate you have no interest in Sterling."

"I don't have any interest in Sterling. And I don't think we are friends, frankly. What if I wish Amber all the best? I guess I could do that."

"What? No. Absolutely not. She'll spin that into passive-aggressive gloating. Like you're rubbing her face in it."

"Except I don't care about her or him in the slightest. I am indifferent. As a colleague I tried to keep him from being hurt. That's it."

"Apparently you convinced him to dump her. Even Sterling says so."

"What are you talking about?"

Her stylist turned her phone so she could read Sterling's latest post.

@amberbaby @KWantland was so right about you. U r a psycho #betteroffwithoutyou

The tweet had been posted five minutes prior.

She stormed back to the table. "Mr. Wakefield, if you insist on taking part in this disgusting, juvenile display, I insist you leave me out of it. Including me in your tweets implies I am complicit and I am in no way—"

TJ held up a hand. "Shhh."

She whirled on her junior cameraman. "Did you just shush me?"

"I have an image. It's a face."

"Kimmy, let's focus on the footage. You and Sterling can talk about personal issues during break."

Blood rushed to her face. Mortified, she slunk to her chair. Michael had never once reprimanded her. Especially not in front of the crew. Face burning, hands shaking, she sunk into a chair beside TJ and blinked away tears, aware of Stan lifting his camera to resume recording.

She noticed Sterling sneak his phone back into his jacket pocket.

Damn that man! He stirred up nothing but trouble and left mayhem in his wake. This was the last straw. She would insist the family sleep in the house tonight and expunge any spiritual entity that dared cross her path. The episode would end, and she could send Sterling packing. She squeezed her eyes shut and fisted her hands while rage burned through her.

Damn Michael and Hoffmeier for going behind her back and bringing Sterling on the show. She could shake things up all on her own without adding a man to the equation. To hell with them, too. She'd buy the rights back and fire anyone who tried to tell her how to run her show. Or she'd refuse to come back next season. She'd started this show from nothing, and she could start a new one. She'd—

"I know that face," Elise whispered.

She opened her eyes. Elise pressed her fingers against her mouth, eyes wide, unable to look away from the image on the screen. Kimberly swung her head to see what TJ had discovered on Sterling's footage.

A woman's face stared back at her. To be sure, the edges blurred into the surrounding air, translucent and undefined. But the black-and-white ethereal image included eye sockets, cold and empty. Gaunt cheekbones. The dark line of a mouth slashed below a delicate nose.

Michael rested a hand on the table and leaned closer to the screen. "My God. That is a face. Undoubtedly, unequivocally, undeniably . . . a face. This is what you saw?"

Sterling crooked a finger and thumb around his chin. "I didn't see anything in particular."

TJ replayed the footage immediately following the blurred streak that had caught their attention. Sterling's voice crackled from the speakers.

"I thought I saw—"

"You saw this while recording?" Michael asked.

"No. Not a face. Something startled me. Maybe a moth flew in front of me. Maybe that's the blurred image of Kimberly from a few frames earlier."

TJ shook his head. "Dude, do you have any idea how desperate you sound right now?"

Kimberly turned to Sterling. "I can't believe you captured this. We could submit this to journals as substantive proof of afterlife. And the fact that you saw it in real time—" She

193

stopped herself. The fact that he'd seen the entity in real time while recording meant he harbored some ability to connect with spirits, despite his adamant denials that they even existed. Was he aware? Had he seen spirits before but simply refused to acknowledge it?

This wasn't the time to discuss it. This was something he wouldn't want to hear or talk about on a good day. And he wasn't having a good day. His emotions were already raw from the Amber debacle.

"I said I didn't see it," Sterling insisted. "That could be anything. A blurry image is far from substantive proof. I don't think you even know what that is."

"That argument might carry some weight except Elise just said she knows who this is. Elise?"

Her researcher, still transfixed by the image, nodded and shook herself a bit. "Yes." She pulled a copy of a newspaper article from a stack of papers. "Here. Look."

Kimberly took the paper, noting the haunted look in Elise's eyes, and glanced over the article while the rest of the crew pressed close. "It's dated May 2014. 'Local Schoolteacher Retires After Sixty Years in the Classroom. Edna Miller presided over her final class of third graders today before her coworkers surprised her with a retirement party.'" She looked at Elise. "This is the woman who lived here before the Williamses?"

Elise nodded vigorously. "Yes. As always, I researched the previous occupants. But she was a teacher. She loved kids. There's nothing to indicate malice or resentment. When you said The Dark is angry and perhaps even hostile toward the children, I set this aside. But look at the picture."

The article included a photo of Mrs. Miller with her class of children. Kimberly stared at the pixilated likeness.

Sterling took the image from her and held it beside the image on the screen. "Sure. These images are exactly the same in that both appear to have eyes, noses, and mouths. We don't even know the image on the screen is a face. Look at it. It's a blurry, shadowy smudge at best. We could snap a picture of Kimberly from twenty feet away, print it in a newspaper, photocopy it, and I bet it would look exactly like this."

Michael took the page and stared at it a long time before he spoke. "I don't know, Sterling. I can see some uncanny similarities. I never want to rush to judgment, but this is giving me goose bumps." He passed the article back to Kimberly. "Your thoughts?"

"This would confirm my earlier impressions of the entity. We do seem to be dealing with a female spirit."

"This confirms nothing," Sterling said.

"I said *would* confirm. If true. Elise, did you learn anything else? Maybe something we dismissed before?"

"I actually had a long talk with Dale's brother, Frank Miller."

"Dale was Edna's husband, right?"

"That's right. Frank is a friendly guy, glad to chat with me. He said Edna didn't care for retirement at all. She went back to teaching the very next school year as a substitute. She and Dale had planned to travel once retired, but their finances didn't allow for much. Plus they were in their late seventies at that point and 'not as sturdy as they once were,' as Frank put it."

"You said she died in the house?"

"Right. Frank said Edna started getting forgetful. She called Dale several times to get her when she couldn't find her way home after school. She couldn't go to the grocery store alone. Would wheel her cart right out the door without paying or come back home with nothing. Really sad. She couldn't teach anymore. Then she had a severe stroke. Dale couldn't bear to put her in a facility, so he brought her home for as much time as she had left and hospice cared for her the last few weeks. She passed away in her sleep after a few days not recognizing even Dale. They'd been married over sixty years. Frank said it broke Dale's heart. He didn't know what to do with himself when Edna went before him. Frank moved him out to California, but Dale didn't want to go on without his soul mate and declined quickly."

She mulled this over. "So after she passed away, Dale's brother moved him to California, and the house sat empty until it sold?"

"Right. Frank said the Realtor had a handyman come through and take care of a few issues. No major renovations or remodeling but some minor updating and repairs. The roof needed to be replaced. They repainted. Things like that. Frank wasn't worried about making money from the house, so he made the minimum modifications and let it go cheap."

"Which allowed Danielle and Stephen to afford the move from apartment to home." She nodded, looking around the cozy older home.

"What are you thinking, Kimmy?"

"Normally, spirits remain behind only when jarred from the earthly body through a traumatic experience. That didn't happen here. She passed away peacefully. But her mind was confused. If she didn't know what happened and somehow didn't cross over, and then her husband moved, leaving her alone and even more confused, and then another family moved in . . ."

Michael cocked his head. "You think that could explain it? She's the dark entity scaring the family?"

Elise shook her head. "Everything I read and heard indicates she loved children. She wanted children of her own so badly and never had any. So she put all her efforts into teaching. Frank said her students took the place of having her own children. Since she couldn't have her own, she decided all children were hers."

She looked at Michael. "All children were hers. What if she feels that way about Danielle and Stephen's children? What if she's trying to take one of them with her permanently? The baby she never had?"

Michael rubbed his arms and shivered. "That's terrifying."

Rosie spoke up. "So anytime someone with memory issues dies, they stay stuck here, lost and confused forever? This is awful news."

Kimberly held up a hand. "Now wait. We've never seen anything to indicate that's the case. Remember when we investigated the retirement community? We didn't encounter lots of lost souls. What if this time, this particular woman became lost and couldn't figure out what happened? And she's still here? We don't know what the spirit world is like, either. Maybe she became further confused after passing. She may not remember much about her previous life at this point. We just don't know."

"That is the most factual statement I've heard come out of your mouth," Sterling said. "You just don't know. Yet you're fabricating a spirit realm you have no evidence exists, and you're imagining a deceased woman stuck there, lost and confused."

TJ brought a palm down onto the table. "Dude, *you* just don't know. I have seen so much stuff on this show. You've only been here a couple of days."

"And you think seeing years of smudges and shadows will change my mind? Ghosts do not exist. Black-and-white. Open-and-shut."

"Save it for your corner, Mr. Wakefield. We do have evidence of a haunting. The most convincing piece of which you captured yourself. No worries about us using that footage. It will definitely figure prominently in our episode. The linchpin, as it were, that helped us determine the identity of The Dark."

"That's ludicrous. I didn't help with your investigation. And that's a huge leap. This smudged image proves nothing."

"It does support our conclusion. And like it or not, you did help with the investigation. You were invaluable." She gave him the widest smile she could muster.

"Don't put that on me. If you're going to claim that's a spirit, don't associate me with the footage at all. I don't want anyone to think I agree with you."

"It's right there in front of you. Why do you keep denying it? You wanted the truth, and you discovered it. The Williamses are experiencing a haunting."

"You know what I've learned this week while I've been here? People don't want the truth. Yes, I came here, excited, exuberant, ready to blow everyone out of the water with the truth. Guess what? No one wants it. They want to believe in gossip and lurid stories. And fairy tales and magic and ghosts and supernatural creatures. People want to believe they're special, that they can communicate with the dead, that they have special powers no one else has. The truth is we're all stuck on this planet hurtling through space and we're all the same. Fairy tales and wishes don't come true, just because you work hard doesn't mean you'll be rewarded for it, and sometimes crappy things happen to good people. I get it now. You're not a fraud at all. You're not out to fool anyone. You just want so badly to believe in ghosts that you see them even though they don't exist. And so do all your pathetic fans. Guess what? There are no ghosts. And you're not special. You're just a regular person who wishes she were extraordinary."

27

No one said anything. In the silence, Kimberly grasped her crystal and took deep breaths. If someone had told her a week ago that Sterling Wakefield could crush her feelings by calling her ordinary, she would've laughed. He'd been calling her a fraud online for months. Never once had she felt threatened or hurt.

But after spending the last couple of days with him, thinking they'd developed something of a friendship—even almost allowing herself to imagine them as something more than friends—his words stung. More than she wanted to admit.

Still no one moved or said anything. They all seemed to be waiting for her response. Somehow her mouth wouldn't form words. She watched Sterling seethe until he met her eyes, and his scowl softened. He stormed to the couch in the living room and flopped down.

Michael cleared his throat. "Maybe it's time for a break." He looked to her for affirmation.

She couldn't find any words to say. What had caused him to lash out like that? She felt hot energy flowing off him but couldn't ascertain the cause. Did she really infuriate him so? Had Amber's behavior set him off? Was it stress from the ugly comments about him online? "Sterling Slutfield" was pretty rude. But he didn't strike her as the type to take something like that to heart. She assumed he had much thicker skin than that. Maybe she could encourage him to rise above it.

"Okay, since no one else will say it, I will," TJ announced, his voice forceful. "We should finish this footage review. Look at all the amazing evidence we've seen on his recording already. Who knows what else we might find? I don't think we should bail on this just because he had a tantrum."

Michael looked to her, and she nodded.

"You're right," Michael said. "We have a job to do here, first and foremost. You and Stan keep going. Push through and see if you find anything else." He pinched the bridge of his nose and shook his head. "I don't think this week is going at all the way RandMeier expected."

Rosie rushed to her side. "That was harsh and uncalled for. I'll go make some more tea."

TJ popped his headphones in place, muttering, "Told you that guy's a douche."

She saw sympathy in everyone's eyes and stood up straighter. She didn't need coddling, or "spoiling," as Sterling put it. She was a grown woman. This wasn't her first brush with scandal. "TJ, that's very vulgar language," she told her young cameraman. "And, Rosie, I'm fine. Mr. Wakefield's opinions are his own, he is entitled to them, and they don't affect me in any way." She projected her voice so that Sterling would hear from the living room.

Rosie crooked an arm through hers and spoke softly. "How many times do I have to tell you—you couldn't lie to save your life?"

She forced her lips to curl into a smile. "I'm fine. Really. But I will take some hot tea since you offered. Maybe with some peppermint for my stomach?" Sterling's words left her insides churning worse than the terrible quality of his footage.

TJ jumped and yanked the headphones off his ears. "Holy shi—" He glanced at her and continued. "I mean, holy cow! Okay, Wakefield. Come check this out. This is raw footage. No one has looked at it or tampered with it. I want you to be present when we review it as a group and record it for the show. We will definitely want to record this, Stan."

Sterling slouched back into the dining room. "Now what are you blathering about?"

"Here." TJ thrust the headphones at him. "Wait, though. Watch before you listen. Here's the footage from Stan's camera."

Stan turned his screen so everyone could see. With a click of the mouse, the night-vision footage played, their eyes glowing neon green as they stood in the hallway. Stan pointed to Sterling's hair. "See there? Your hair ruffled. And then here you reach up to smooth it back down. Clearly you felt whatever ruffled it."

"I've already said I felt something. Presumably wind."

"Wind that affected no one else?" Stan rewound the footage. "See? You're standing near Kimberly. You honestly believe her long hair is impervious to a gust of wind that set your short hair on end?"

"I'm significantly taller than her. A wind gust above her head would be unnoticed by her but felt by me."

"Oh, come on!" TJ yelled.

Stan held up a hand. "Just show him the rest. We know he felt it. Move on."

Grumbling and shaking his head, TJ continued. "Here's the FLIR footage from the camera I carried. Watch." He switched to the rainbow-hued images from the heat camera. He slowed the footage, allowing them to see a burst of red color as it swooped from Kimberly to Sterling, racing over his head and disappearing through the ceiling.

She leaned forward. "That's at the end of the session. Right after the entity let me know she's after the children. She flew through the ceiling."

"Yes," TJ said. "But she had a message for Wakefield on her way out. Aside from messing up his hair." He turned his attention to Sterling as Stan stepped closer with his camera. "Mr. Wakefield, your camera remained with you, in your possession from the time our session ended last night until you handed it to me a few minutes ago. Correct?"

Sterling shifted and crossed his arms. "What does that have to do with anything?"

"No one could have tampered with this footage except you, since it remained in your possession. Correct?"

"I didn't tamper with the footage. I didn't touch the camera. You can ask Kimberly. I was with her all night."

Her jaw fell open. "It wasn't—"

TJ rested a hand on her arm and murmured, "Don't worry. I'll edit that part out." He turned back to Sterling and raised his voice. "Do you swear you neither tampered with nor allowed someone else to tamper with this footage that you recorded last night?"

"Why would I? That's ludicrous."

"Answer the question, Wakefield."

"I said I didn't tamper with it."

TJ held up his hands in victory. "*Post hoc, ergo propter hoc.*"

"What is this? Kid thinks he's Perry Mason or something."

"Perry Mason? Who the heck is that?" TJ asked.

Sterling shook his head. "You've never heard of *Perry Mason*? The courtroom drama?"

"No. Worked as a paralegal for a few years, though. Guess it shows." The younger cameraman sat up straighter.

Sterling rolled his eyes. "Yeah. Especially since you just labeled your own argument fallacious."

TJ uncrossed his arms and sat forward. "What?"

"Nothing. Can we please get on with this?"

She turned to Stan's camera. "By Mr. Wakefield's own admission, this footage remained with his camera"—she gestured to the equipment—"in his possession since we ended last night's session." She gave the camera her gravest look. "TJ?"

TJ passed the headphones to Sterling and indicated he put them on. "Wakefield will now hear the audio on his personal footage at the precise moment his hair ruffles on Stan's footage and the entity flares red on the heat camera."

TJ turned and locked eyes with her, a smirk on his face, as his finger hovered above the mouse.

He depressed the button, and the footage continued.

Seconds later Sterling jumped up so fast, his chair clattered backward to the floor. He yanked the headphones off his head and stared at TJ, accusation burning in his eyes. "No, you . . . that's not . . . you . . ."

TJ stood, facing Sterling. "This is raw, unenhanced footage. We listened to it for the first time minutes ago. We didn't have the opportunity to add anything to the footage, which remained in your possession at all times. Unless you added this yourself, you recorded it last night."

Sterling's hands shook as he ran his fingers through his hair. "I didn't hear anything last night. That sounds like someone is standing right behind me, speaking into the camera microphone. But there was no one there."

"Spiritual entities leave us messages via EVP," TJ said. "Happens all the time."

"There is no way the camera recorded sound that wasn't there. If someone spoke, I should have heard it while it happened."

Kimberly watched the exchange until she couldn't stand it. Normally she sprang exciting tidbits on others. She'd had enough of Sterling stealing her thunder. Now TJ, too? *Enough.* This was her show. "We have audio?"

"We sure do," TJ confirmed.

"Can you analyze it a bit? Determine what's being said?"

"Don't need to." TJ's smirk resembled the one that normally graced the face of now-deflated Sterling, as if it had hopped from one to the other.

Her hands curled into fists. "TJ, you are rapidly becoming the most annoying person in the room. Let the rest of us hear."

"Sorry, Ms. Wantland. I just wanted to build suspense."

"You've built it. Let's hear if the payoff is worth it."

"Right." TJ unplugged the headphones from the sound jack and rewound the footage. "Here it is." He pressed "Play."

In the background, voices of her crew chattered. A female voice overpowered them all, clear and distinct, as though standing behind Sterling, but no one had stood behind him.

"Get out."

28

Kimberly sat once again at a table in the hotel restaurant with Rosie and Michael. She tried and failed to ignore a despondent Sterling at the bar. At four o'clock in the afternoon, the restaurant was between lunch and dinner crowds and mostly empty but for her crew, exhausted but intrigued by the footage.

After everyone had recovered from the shock of hearing the dark entity speak on Sterling's recording, TJ had played the isolated section over and over. *Get out, get out, get out.*

Her fanboy waiter drifted to the table for the fourth time since bringing their meals. "How is everything? We still doing okay? Ms. Wantland, do you need anything?" He seemed eager for an issue that he could fix. Anything to extend his contact with her.

She looked about the table. "I think we're still good."

"Okay. If you need something, just let me know." The young man lingered as if hoping she would suddenly think of something.

"We will." She smiled at him until he backed away.

Michael and Rosie didn't speak, both sipping their diet sodas with the nervous countenance everyone in the crew wore. This was huge, and they all knew it. She felt very strongly that Edna Miller had remained in the home after passing. And for some reason was now hostile. Whatever left the spiritual entity in this current bitter form, she needed to resolve the issue for the Williams family.

Could she help the woman move on? She had helped spirits before. Once she determined who they were in life, she could usually help them understand it was time to cross over. But Edna Miller demonstrated hostility toward her and wanted them to get out. Would the confused woman be able to remember who she had been in life? Would she listen? How could Kimberly entice the hostile spirit to leave the Williamses' home and translocate to the next plane of existence?

Michael swirled his straw through his soda, clinking the ice cubes against the cup, which dripped a puddle of condensation on the table. "What are you thinking, Kimmy?"

She sipped her hot tea while she pondered how best to answer. What she was going to suggest probably wouldn't thrill him. "I'm trying to decide how best to proceed. With what we saw and heard today, I feel pretty confident I know what we're dealing with." Out of the corner of her eye, she noticed Sterling signal for another drink.

Rosie rested her arms on the table and leaned forward. "I think you need to proceed with caution. This entity has already tried to strangle you. She's told us to get out. This is a dangerous disturbance you're dealing with."

She took a deep breath. "That's true. But that's why I'm thinking we might need to try something a little more unconventional. We need to get that thing out of there. I keep imagining her strangling that little toddler boy. I'm sure he's seen her." She shuddered.

Michael cocked an eyebrow at her. "Unconventional? In what way?"

"Something we don't normally like to do. But I think we should continue our investigation tonight with the Williamses in the house." She watched him carefully for his reaction.

He frowned. "Why in the world would we do that? You just said you're worried about the entity trying to hurt one or both of the children. Why do you want to put them in harm's way?"

"I want to resolve the disturbance. And I think the best way to do that is to lure the entity with the children. I believe she's been looking for them this week. And part of her hostility may come from believing we've taken them from her. If she's focused on the children and not me, I should be able to handle her better."

"It seems like too much of a risk. We send the families away for a reason."

"I know. And normally I'd agree. But not this time. Besides, we'll all be there. If I truly felt like this would endanger any of the family, I wouldn't suggest it."

Michael pursed his lips. "I don't know. I really don't like it."

"I knew you wouldn't."

He rubbed his hands together. "Maybe we need to take it slow another couple of nights. You know more about the entity we're dealing with. That should help you handle it."

"On the contrary, that's exactly why we need to wrap up this investigation. The Williamses need this entity purged. Sterling appears to be having a meltdown. Let's pull out all the stops tonight and go in aggressive."

"Would the family even agree to that?" Michael seemed to be grasping for a way to say no.

"Danielle asked me this morning if they could come back home. This has taken such a toll on them. I don't know how much more they can take."

207

Rosie nodded. "It's taken a toll on their marriage, too. Stephen is threatening to leave. I told her he didn't mean it, but I'm not so sure. He's exhausted and missing work. Danielle says he doesn't want to admit to his boss what's really happening at home, so he's blaming her, claiming she's suffering from postpartum depression so severe it's endangering their baby. I think he's said so many negative things about her, he's actually starting to believe it. Look at them."

The family occupied a table in the back corner of the restaurant. Drew sat in a high chair, dragging a spoon through his plate of food. Danielle and Stephen didn't speak. Baby Josh perched on Danielle's knee, gnawing a fist and oddly silent.

"That's absurd. Danielle would never hurt her children. But the tension is so thick, even the baby feels it," she said. "Stephen doesn't believe we can help and didn't want us here to begin with. We have to end this, Michael."

Michael nodded. "Okay. I'll call RandMeier and give him a heads-up. We'll need to go back early to reset cameras and wire for remote sound and images. We can change the dinner table from footage review to real-time footage tracking. It's doable."

A huge weight lifted off her shoulders. "Thank you, Michael. Trust me. I can do this. I won't let The Dark hurt those kids. Rosie, we need anything and everything in our arsenal tonight that can combat a hostile spirit. And can charge my energy. I have to do more than connect tonight. I have to get through to her and convince her to translocate. I'll talk to Elise about—"

"Oh no."

Rosie's tone of voice startled her more than the interruption. She followed her stylist's gaze. Amber had just walked in and was threading her way through the tables toward Sterling.

"Ugh," Kimberly said. "Doesn't she have clothes to be wearing somewhere? Sterling said her schedule kept her busy, but here she still is."

Rosie elbowed her. "Might be a good time to go check on your cohost. I'm not sure how much he's had to drink, but I am sure it's enough he's in no position to handle the situation that's about to unfold."

She fought the urge to jump and run to his side. "He doesn't need or want my help. He made his opinion of me and my show amply clear at this morning's footage review."

"You know better than that. Something is bothering him. I don't believe deep down he meant what he said. Just go over and say hi. Maybe invite him to come sit with us."

"If he wanted to sit with us, he wouldn't be at the bar. And if he wanted to share what's bothering him, he would. He doesn't want to share. At least not with me. You can go talk to him if you want to." She wouldn't admit how much it bothered her that he chose not to share with her. She stayed in her seat but strained to hear what the succubus said to him. And she couldn't help but watch out of the corner of her eye.

Amber shoved her way next to him, standing between two bar stools. "Hi, sweetie."

"Get lost, Amber. I'm not your sweetie. I don't know how you have the balls to come anywhere near me after the shit you've been saying online."

"How did you expect me to react when you tried to break up with me?"

"Like a normal human being. You overreacted like a crazy person. And I'm done. I didn't try to break up with you. I did break up with you. We're finished. Go home."

She felt the angry heat rolling off Amber at his words. Did Sterling have any idea how much danger he was courting? Amber didn't act like a normal person because she was a

209

succubus. He'd never get that through his thick skull. But Amber's next move surprised even her.

The young woman placed a hand on either side of Sterling's face and pulled him in for a lengthy kiss.

Kimberly jumped to her feet, expecting to see Sterling dazed and entranced again. But he still seemed very much in control of himself. *Impressive.* Or perhaps it meant he'd developed feelings for someone else.

"Okay, Amber. We can keep going out if you like. But the circumstances will be very different. No shopping sprees, no extravagant meals, no movie premieres, and definitely no private island in the Bahamas. You good with that?"

She sat back down. Was Sterling actually taking her advice? Severing Amber's connection with him by cutting off all gifts and trips? She couldn't stop the smile that bubbled to her lips. He'd listened to her. Her irritation dissipated, replaced by a warm-and-fuzzy feeling she hadn't experienced in quite some time.

Amber, smiling as if at a petulant child, rested her hand on his arm. "Stop trying to punish me, silly. I'll forgive you. We can go back to the way we were. Like none of this ugliness ever happened." The young woman gave him her wildest smile and batted her thickly lashed eyes.

"I'll never forgive you for what you said. But I'm not punishing you. I'm just being honest. I won't be able to take you out or buy you anything. Still interested in me?"

"Sweetie, stop this silliness." Amber looped her arms around his neck and thrust her breasts forward. "I'm not just with you for the money."

Kimberly squirmed in her seat and lifted her tea to distract herself. Amber could writhe all over Sterling if she wanted to. It was none of her business, and she didn't care.

Rosie gave her the look. "Girl, go deck that floozy, and get it over with. Your eyes are burning with hate right now. I can tell you want to throw her out the door."

Kimberly sipped her tea again. "It's not my place. He can do whatever he wants with his life."

Rosie clicked her tongue. "It's your place if you want it to be."

Sterling unhooked Amber's arms from his neck. "I'm glad to hear that. Considering I'm unemployed now. You'll need to make some pretty significant sacrifices. Might even have to pay for dinner occasionally."

Amber dropped her arms and jumped back as though burned. "What?"

"My agent called today. *SpookBusters* didn't get renewed. I've been canceled."

Amber gaped at him. "You're lying."

"I wish I was. It'll be announced tomorrow. Ought to be all over the Internet a second later."

The pale young woman narrowed her eyes. "I don't do canceled." She turned and strutted out of the restaurant, stilettos clacking angrily with each step.

"Oh, my God," Rosie said. "Did you hear that? No wonder he's a mess."

She nodded, not sure what to say.

"Well, what are you doing just sitting here? Get over there. He needs someone right now. And it needs to be you."

She didn't know what her stylist meant by that last sentence, but she couldn't let Sterling sit alone now that she knew what was eating him up. No one should cope with news like that all on his own. She tried to imagine how she'd feel if *The Wantland Files* was canceled. She shivered. The show was her life. She knew no show lasted forever, but she always thought of life after the show as the distant future. Three seasons. How many more did she have left before she would be faced with the same devastating call Sterling had received today?

She stood up and crossed to the stool beside him, sliding into it wordlessly.

The bartender sidled in front of her. "Get you something, Ms. Wantland?" His voice carried the intentionally casual cadence of someone trying not to geek out.

"Something nonalcoholic, please. Cranberry juice and soda water?"

"You got it." His nod and half smile indicated he understood her need to remain sober, and he had her back. And that he believed they'd shared a moment. His brush with fame he could share with friends and family for years to come. He grabbed a martini glass and picked up a bottle of juice.

"Come to gloat?" Sterling asked as the bartender added fizz to the juice. "Point out how much people love your show and hate mine?"

"Not at all." She accepted her mocktail and slid five dollars across the bar.

"On the house," the bartender said, holding up a hand to decline her payment.

"Your tip, then."

He accepted the money, folded it, and slid it into a pocket. "Classy lady," he said to Sterling as he moved down the bar to a man in a suit who looked as if he'd had a rough day.

"Oh yeah. Everyone loves Kimberly Wantland." Sterling tossed back the remainder of his beer and signaled for another.

"Don't you think you've had enough? We have another session tonight. You'll need to be lucid and alert."

"You don't need my help. And it doesn't matter anyway. I'm sure you heard my show's been canceled."

"I did. I'm sorry. I know you were hoping cohosting my show would help. It seems early to make that decision. You have plenty of fans, too. What reason did the network give?"

"Oh, the usual. My agent says they cited budget cuts as the deciding factor. Get this—my show and I have become so popular, they can no longer afford to keep me. Particularly in light of the growing interest surrounding the crossover on *Wantland Files*. And the drama with Amber."

"What? That makes no sense. They should be glad for the extra attention."

"I thought so. My agent said he thinks they'd already decided not to renew and are trying to spin this unexpected turn of events so they don't look bad. The network is losing money. They're going to try to lure in a younger crowd with some teen-based shows. So I got the ax. Wish I'd known before. Wouldn't have wasted your time." He lifted the beer the bartender placed in front of him and swallowed deeply.

"Are you kidding? What have you been saying the past few days? We're blowing up the Internet. People love us together. Rosie says there's a new hashtag trending. Wantlandsavethedate. For the season finale with Sterling Wakefield."

"It'll be my last show. Need to figure out what I'm going to do next. Would you excuse me? I need to be alone before we shoot tonight. I . . . I'm really sorry I blew up at you earlier."

"No worries."

"No. There's no excuse for it. I reacted poorly to upsetting news, and I'm sorry. I will be completely professional tonight."

"Don't be professional. Be yourself. You're fun. I think that's what people are responding to. You bring a new energy to the show. And I didn't want to admit it, but I needed that to

213

boost my own ratings. But maybe stop drinking now. I'd like you to at least be sober-ish."

He grinned at her—the grin that just a few days ago had irritated her to the point of distraction but now set her stomach quivering. "Don't worry. I'm a good Irish Catholic. I can handle my liquor."

"Catholic? Really? You don't accept what I tell you about spiritual entities in the world around us, but you believe in the Immaculate Conception and Jesus rising from the dead?"

He raised an eyebrow at her. "That's a conversation for another day. I feel like we've arrived at a truce. Let's not endanger the progress we've made." He lifted his beer bottle and clinked it against her martini glass. "Here's to us. Let's go out with a bang."

"That's the plan. Tonight we finish this investigation. Whatever it takes. Just, maybe, don't disrupt me anymore."

"No worries, m'lady. I am ever your humble servant. And tonight I do naught but your bidding."

She felt his orange chakra flare and saw something dance in his eyes that sent another quiver through her stomach. She pulled her gaze away, focusing on her martini glass. "I seriously doubt that. I need to talk to Michael. I promise everything will be okay." She rested her hand on his. "So don't worry anymore. And stop drinking."

She scurried away from him, not sure if the idea taking shape in her mind was a good one, but knowing she needed to try. And knowing she also needed to get away from the stomach quivering Sterling's smoldering gaze produced.

"Michael, have you called RandMeier yet?" she asked as she took her seat at the table again.

"Not yet. Thought I'd call when we head back to the Williamses'."

"Okay. I have something else I want to run past him."

Rosie lit up. "What is it?"

"I don't want to say yet. You'll find out soon enough, if it works. Right now, I need to talk to Danielle and Stephen and iron out everything for tonight."

29

Kimberly sat cross-legged on the floor of her makeup trailer, envisioning all her stress and distractions evaporating from her body. Eyes closed, she pictured herself in the middle of a field of flowers, temperate breezes playing across her brow. Incense burned around her. Sounds of babbling water and soft birdcalls filled the air.

She allowed her head to drop forward and slowly bent until her spine curved in an arc and her forehead rested on the floor. Breathing deeply, she hummed lightly.

"I guess I'm not surprised Danielle and Steven opted to come back tonight when you offered. But I'd be completely weirded out by a camera crew in my house at night," Rosie said.

She remained hunched over her lap. "They didn't hesitate a bit."

Danielle and Stephen had readily agreed when she'd approached and suggested her idea. Michael had also questioned whether or not the family would be able to sleep knowing a crew of people with cameras and microphones lurked throughout their house.

"I'm so tired," Danielle had countered, "and so eager to be back in my own bed, I think I could sleep through a tornado."

Even Stephen had perked up a bit at the idea of this ordeal coming to an end.

Rosie shook her head. "I guess different people make the world go round. I couldn't handle it. They're not worried about the spirit coming after the kids? Or does Danielle just trust you that much?"

She slowly uncurled her spine until she sat upright once again. "It didn't exactly come up."

"You didn't tell them your theory?"

Stretching to the side, she breathed deeply. "Danielle looked about to cry when I said they could come back and we'd complete the investigation with them here. She assumed we did it to accommodate them. I didn't want to further distress anyone. And Steven would have scoffed anyway. He doesn't believe in spirits or our ability to help."

"So you didn't tell them?"

"Don't judge me. Otherwise I might need to bring up Ramón, who tried to convince you to run away to Europe with him. Just four easy payments of a thousand dollars."

Rosie sighed. "That's not exactly what happened, and you know it. Still, good thing I was completely broke and didn't have anything to give him. Fine. The makeup trailer shall be designated a judge-free zone."

When Kimberly felt thoroughly relaxed and loose, she shifted to her massage table. Rosie placed chakra stones on all her chakras to recharge and align her energies, then rubbed essential oils into her skin as she massaged her shoulders and hands. She needed to be her strongest yet most relaxed self tonight.

"How are you feeling?" Rosie asked.

"Good. Very good. And confident we can wrap this up tonight."

"That's what I wanted to hear. I know you can do it. Now, how do you feel about Sterling?"

"You're supposed to be helping me relax and focus. Not distracting me with guy talk."

"You're running out of time, though. If you finish the investigation tonight, he'll be leaving soon. I think you need to ask yourself if you're okay with him disappearing from your life."

Did she dare admit to Rosie the very same thought had been on her mind since her conversation with him at the bar? Sure, he frustrated the heck out of her sometimes. And they operated from completely different beliefs and approaches. But she'd spoken the truth at the bar—even though part of her wanted to deny it and claim she'd wanted only to cheer him up.

"He needs a new job. I don't have much say in the situation."

"He may want a new job. But he doesn't really need one. Not immediately anyway." Rosie removed the chakra stones.

"What do you mean?" She sat up and accepted a cup of tea.

"He comes from money. His parents gave him a tidy sum when he turned twenty-one, and he invested it very well. He works because he enjoys it. But he's not hurting for money."

"That can't be right. He told Amber he wouldn't be able to take her out to pricey restaurants or on vacations or anything."

Rosie raised an eyebrow at her. "He took your advice. Don't you see? You suggested that was the only thing that would get rid of her, and he listened. Though apparently Amber 'doesn't do canceled.'"

That warm, fuzzy feeling tingled in her stomach again. She turned to Rosie and narrowed her eyes. "How did you know about his money when Amber didn't?"

"I'm a busybody. You ought to know that better than anyone. The point is, he doesn't need to race off and go pound the pavement for a new job. He may decide he wants to. Then again, maybe if someone gave him a reason to hang around, he would. And I get the feeling you wouldn't mind having him around a bit longer."

Her silence appeared to tell Rosie everything she needed to know. With a smile, her stylist picked up the boutique bag from the counter. "I never showed you what I found for you this morning in the most adorable little boutique. They had some fantastic outfits. I know you prefer your earth tones over everything else, but I think we need to brighten you up for this last part of the investigation. I know you absolutely won't wear red, but what about a jewel tone?"

Rosie reached into the shopping bag and brought out a deep-purple blouse. The neckline dipped low, the center gathered in the middle, clearly intended to accentuate the breasts. She did like the flutter sleeves, though they were not a good choice for the chilly evening temperatures.

Rosie held it up to her. "Your green eyes pop against this color. It looks fantastic on you."

She turned to the mirror. "You really think a different outfit will convince Sterling that he likes me? The differences are too fundamental. A new shirt isn't going to change his mind."

"Dress to impress. How do you think I caught Donovan? I lured him in with a sexy outfit."

"Donovan . . . wasn't he your first boyfriend after your divorce?"

"Excellent memory! He really was incredible."

"Until he cheated on you with your best friend."

"Ex–best friend. Enough about me. Judge-free zone, remember? The point is, you'll give off a more open vibe if you dress a certain way. Sterling likes you already. I can tell."

"I can't tell. I think you're imagining it. And if he doesn't like me as is, then too bad. If he wants someone who looks like Amber, he should look elsewhere. I'm not changing my wardrobe to impress a guy."

"Come on. At least try it on for me. You'll look phenomenal. End this season looking like a million bucks."

She pulled the shirt closer and noticed the tapered middle contoured nicely to her slender waist. "That is a good point. A lot of people could be watching this episode. Some maybe for the first time. Wouldn't hurt to look especially nice. Maybe I'll win over some new fans."

She slipped out of her blouse and wiggled into the new one. Just as she tugged the fabric into place around her middle, the trailer door opened and in barged Sterling, coffee tray in hand.

Flustered by the intrusion, she snapped at him. "How about knocking next time?"

"Except there won't be a—" Sterling caught sight of her. His eyes took her in head to foot. "Wow. Nice shirt. It looks very nice on you."

She tucked a lock of hair behind her ear and smoothed the shirt over her hips, not sure where to look. "Thank you."

He walked by Rosie as if she didn't exist. "Not that you didn't look nice before. I just . . . I mean, usually . . ." His gaze lingered on her cleavage before he shook his head slightly and blinked several times. "I, um, thank you for earlier. I don't like to admit when I need help, but I did, and you were most gracious." His eyes looked anywhere but at her breasts.

"No problem. Of course," she answered. After a moment's hesitation she added, "That's what partners do."

His eyebrows rose. "Partners?"

She nodded.

"Okay." He couldn't contain the smirk. It blossomed into a full-blown smile as he stepped closer and fumbled with the cups of coffee in his hands. "I brought coffee again. No sugar. Skim milk."

"Thank you." Her hand brushed his as she accepted the welcome beverage. "I really appreciate this. Did you get some? Are you okay to shoot tonight?" Asking if he was inebriated seemed a poor choice at the moment.

He ducked his head and grinned sheepishly. "Yeah, I'm fine. Like I said, good Irish Catholic. I won't screw up your show tonight. Scout's honor. Plus, I've had two double shots. Of espresso."

She giggled. Giggled. She didn't giggle. Ever. And yet Sterling Wakefield had just made her giggle. What was happening?

She dealt with fans routinely, the especially fanatic of which always gushed and breathed rapidly and didn't know how to act or what to say. She never gave it a second thought. Autograph something, smile, snap a picture, and off they went, happy. But Sterling's behavior caught her off guard. She hadn't attempted a relationship in years, and the feelings bubbling through her were scary. And yet they weren't entirely unpleasant.

Rosie tapped her foot. "Did you bring me mocha again? Like my beautiful skin?"

"What? Oh! Right. Yes. Coffee for you." He lifted a cup from the carrier and passed it to her.

Rosie accepted the cup and mouthed, "I told you so." No chance Sterling would notice. His eyes hadn't left Kimberly.

"So, Amber is gone?" she asked as the silence stretched to the point of awkwardness.

"Yeah, I think so. Thanks for the help with her, too, by the way. You've really been terrific this week. I'll miss you."

Her heart thumped, and she knew she should look away. But she couldn't break his intense gaze and didn't want the moment to end.

The trailer door opened, and Michael stepped in.

She and Sterling jumped apart like two children caught misbehaving.

Michael glanced at his watch. "What's the holdup? Are we shooting tonight or what? Ooooh, nice shirt, Kimmy. Good choice, Rosie. I know she'd never pick that herself."

Rosie came to the rescue. "Kimberly went over the plan for tonight, and Sterling needs a touch of powder. They'll be right in."

"Great. Let's do this." The trailer door slammed behind him.

Sterling ran a hand through his hair. "I'll, uh, go ahead. I think I'm good on powder. I'll see you inside, Kimberly."

"See you inside, Mr. Wakefield."

He shook his head. "Sterling. Partners, right?"

Her knees turned to jelly at the look he gave her. She nodded. She would've agreed to anything at that moment.

After he left, Rosie clapped and hopped up and down. "I knew it! I told you! This is awesome! If only Michael hadn't interrupted. If only I hadn't been here!"

Sure she was blushing, Kimberly sipped her coffee and attempted to compose herself. "I guess you were right. About the shirt." She turned to the mirror. Did she really look so different in this?

"Oh, I was right all along. It wasn't the shirt. Sterling Wakefield has liked you since day one. Never doubt Rosie's

222

intuition. It's almost as good as Kimberly Wantland's ability to clear a house of any disturbance."

"Speaking of, do I look okay? I have a ghost to transition."

"You look like a million bucks. Go get her! And then get him."

30

Kimberly pinched the bridge of her nose and entertained second thoughts about her brilliant idea to allow the Williams family back into their home before wrapping the investigation. Danielle had been so relieved. Seeing a smile on the poor woman's face had made her feel like a hero.

But as Drew tore through the dining and living room on his fifth lap, naked, hair soaking wet, and cackling maniacally, she realized she hadn't completely thought this through. Then again, how could she possibly know what a bedtime ritual consisted of when she'd never lived with a child?

Sterling raised his hands and wriggled his fingers at the streaking, laughing toddler. "Booga-booga-booga! I'm gonna get you!"

Drew screamed with laughter and employed a burst of speed, tearing down the hall for another lap. Stephen puffed after him. "Come get your pajamas, Drew-man. Come on. Daddy is too tired to chase you."

She scowled at Sterling. "I don't think you're helping."

"Sure, I am. Think how good he'll sleep after racing around like this. I'm helping wear him out."

"Maybe let his dad dress him first?"

"Fair enough." Sterling picked up a train engine from the track snaking around the living room. "Oh no, Drew! The trains need help!"

Drew stopped in his tracks and whirled to face Sterling. "They need help?"

"Yes," Sterling said, eyes huge with feigned concern. He looked to her. "What kind of problems do talking trains have?"

She shook her head and shrugged. "I have no idea. You're on your own with this one."

"A . . . cat is . . . sitting on the track. No one can get him to move."

"A tat?" Drew stopped running and joined Sterling at the track. His eyes followed the length of the winding railway system that would surely cause an engineer heart palpitations.

Stephen knelt beside him and used the moment of stillness to maneuver the toddler into his Pull-Up and pajamas.

"Stephen?" Danielle called from the back bedroom.

He rolled his eyes and stood. "Next crisis," he murmured and ruffled Drew's hair before he walked away.

"No tat!" Drew giggled and stared at Sterling as if waiting to hear it was a joke.

"Well, not a real cat." Sterling ducked his head and flushed. "I was playing pretend."

"Pretend tat?" Drew made a face.

"Sorry, buddy. Just pretend. I was only playing."

Drew shrugged. He picked up an engine and choo-choo'ed it along the track, crawling beside his circuitous railway until he bumped into Sterling. The boy blinked at the man. "Tat tan help."

"I'm sorry, I don't . . ." Sterling looked to her for rescue, as if she possessed some ability to interpret toddler-speak. "Kimberly?"

Drew turned his head in her direction and mimicked the adult. "Kimuhly?"

Danielle appeared from the hallway, Josh balanced on a hip. "That's Ms. Wantland to you, mister. Remember your manners."

Drew dropped his head. "I sorry, Miss Wan-land."

"No, he's fine," she said, heart breaking at the sign of his crestfallen face. "Drew, can you tell your mommy what you told Mr. Wakefield?"

The boy raised his head to his mother, nodding with each word and speaking distinctly. "Tat tan help."

"Cat can help? What does that—is he talking about Felix?" The young mom gasped, eyes wide.

Kimberly suspected the boy was, in fact, referring to Felix, but she downplayed the connection for Danielle. No sense alarming the woman at bedtime. "Who knows? He and Sterling were playing pretend." She smiled and left it at that.

Danielle seemed to accept her story. "Bedtime, Drew. Let's go read your night-night story and go to sleep. Say good night."

Drew stared intently at his train engine, pressing it against the track and devoting all his attention to rolling it.

"Drew, come on. No fussing tonight. Let's go."

The boy shook his head.

"Mind me, young man."

Drew whimpered. "No bed, Mommy. No Dark."

Her heart melted at the boy's words, as did Danielle's apparently. The woman softened her tone. "I know you're scared. But Ms. Wantland will be here tonight. She's going to make The Dark go away for us. Tonight."

Hearing the promise spoken aloud to the toddler caused her heart to skip a beat. What if something went wrong? What if she couldn't? The boy's reaction only intensified her anxiety.

"Miss Wan-land tan stay?" The boy looked at her as if he didn't believe the words.

"I'll be here with you all night. I won't let anything happen. Okay?"

Drew stood and placed a hand on Sterling's shoulder. "Good night."

"Good night, buddy."

He shuffled to the dining room table and crawled in her lap, laying his head on her shoulder and squeezing tightly with his chubby toddler arms. "Good night, Miss Wan-land."

"Good night, Drew. Sleep tight."

He climbed down, popping two fingers into his mouth. He reached for his mother's outstretched hand, but then turned back. "Tat tan help, Miss Wan-land."

Her brow furrowed. "Okay. I'll keep that in mind."

He disappeared down the hall with his mother.

She got up and moved to the screen that allowed them to view the toddler's room. "Are we sure we can see enough of the room?" she asked Stan, who was running sound checks at each station.

"I focused the camera mainly on the bed, like you said. So we can keep a close eye on the boy."

"The dark entity seems to come from the closet typically. I'm worried we won't see it coming."

Stan glanced at the screen. "Looks like his mom is tucking him in. You want me to go set up another camera?"

She twisted her hands together. "No, I don't want to scare him. Let's leave it. We'll just have to be careful."

Her crew already in place for the evening, she paced from one screen to the next.

Stan turned toward the living room, where Sterling lay on his side by the train track, examining a purple train engine with huge eyes and lengthy eyelashes on its painted face. "You want to go ahead and record your Confidential Corner now while we're just standing around waiting for the excitement to start?"

Sterling placed the train on the track and sat up. "Nah. I'll record a final rebuttal when we wrap. Let Kimberly have her night. She's flustered enough as it us."

"I am not flustered," she insisted.

He tipped his head at her. "If you say so." He stood, stretched, and joined her at the table.

Danielle finished reading a book to Drew and tucked him into bed. The young mom disappeared from one screen and reappeared in another, where she rocked Josh to sleep before easing him into the crib.

Sterling still watched Drew, who tossed and turned in his toddler bed. "Poor kid. I suffered from night terrors when I was little, too."

"He's not suffering night—" She stopped, remembering his interactions with Edna Miller's spirit the night before. "Do you still have them?"

"No, I . . . outgrew them."

She noticed his downcast eyes. "Did you?"

"Mostly." He shifted from foot to foot and cleared his throat. "Hope this little guy outgrows his."

"His night terror is going away tonight. I'll make sure of that. Tell me about yours."

"My night terrors? Nothing to tell. I was just a kid. My mom could probably tell you more than I can remember."

"Maybe someday I'll get to ask her. What can you remember?"

"I don't—just feeling like something was in the room with me, watching me, creeping closer to me. I'd wake up screaming. My mom said it was the worst thing she ever heard in her life."

"And you've completely outgrown them?"

The doubt in her voice prompted a hard stare from him. He studied her face, then softened. "I might still have one every now and again. But everyone has nightmares."

"Did it ever occur to you that maybe you detect presences? Like Drew feels the dark entity menacing him?"

"Don't be absurd. They're just very vivid, awful dreams. I'm sure that's true for Drew, too."

She knew better but had no proof with which to convince him. So she dropped the subject. She'd planted the idea.

She picked up her coffee cup from the table and circled the ring of screens, watching the family of four grow still as they dropped into sleep. Her heart twinged at the sight of Danielle and Stephen on opposite edges of the bed, backs to each other. Hopefully, with this disturbance settled, they would focus on repairing the marriage.

She lost track of time. Nothing happened in either bedroom as she finished her coffee and downed cup after cup of tea.

She grew dizzy and restless from parading round and round the table, fixated on the screens, the green night-vision images eventually blurring into nothing. Rubbing her eyes, she crossed to the living room and sat on the couch.

Sterling flopped beside her. "What if nothing happens tonight?"

She tamped down the growing anxiety prompted by the little voice in her head that currently asked the same thing. "Something will happen. It has to. It will."

"But what if—"

"She'll come. She's been searching for the kids while they've been at the hotel. She won't be able to resist."

"And you don't feel the slightest bit guilty using them as a bait?"

"I'm here. They're safe."

229

"Well, you know I don't think they were ever in any danger. As long as you're good with it, that's all that matters."

"I just need her to show up."

Several minutes ticked by. Sterling glanced at his watch. "So maybe she'll show at midnight? The Witching Hour?"

"Now that's a myth about spirits you can bust all you want."

"I knew it! It's really three a.m., isn't it?"

She eyed him. "And why do you think that?"

"Well, it's just . . . usually when I wake from a night terror, it's right after three in the morning."

So he did suspect more than just bad dreams. He just couldn't admit it to anyone. Not even himself.

"Interesting." Did she dare push the subject? "Every time?"

He nodded. "Usually 3:03 a.m."

"Huh." She mulled this over. "You should keep a diary. Write the date and time and the content of the dream as clearly as you can remember it. Keep the journal by your bed so you can record the entries immediately, when the memory is most vivid."

"A dream diary? How will that help?"

She hoped the journal would help him see a pattern. Perhaps even convince him to consider an outside influence at work rather than a nightmare. But she couldn't explain it to him in those words. "It could help you determine what's triggering them. Include what you ate that day. Indicate if you experienced any stressful events. Or if you noticed anything unusual or out of the ordinary."

"Anything unusual? You're still convinced it's a ghost." He seemed to ponder the idea. "You know what? I'll try it. But what do I do with my data once I've recorded it? Call you to come analyze it? My own personal investigation?"

Butterflies danced through her stomach at the intense heat in the look he pierced her with. But she didn't break eye contact. "I would. I would try to help if you asked."

His eyebrows rose. "Even at three in the morning?"

She nodded.

He leaned closer. "I'll be sure to keep your number in my favorite contacts, then."

She felt certain he intended to kiss her. Heart thumping, she sat perfectly still, realizing how much she hoped he would. Grateful the couch was around the corner from and out of sight of her crew, she closed her eyes. Then she came to her senses. This was not the time or the place. She couldn't allow anything to distract her tonight.

She opened her eyes and pulled away. "Anyway, the Witching Hour is a myth. Spiritual entities are not aware of or bound by our clocks. They appear at their own whim, whenever they can collect enough energy to manifest."

Sterling straightened in his seat. "Gather energy? From where?" She thought she detected disappointment in his eyes.

Before she could reply, she heard a soft, trembling voice from the hallway call, "Miss Wan-land? The Dark is here."

31

Kimberly jumped from the couch and dashed to the dining table. "Why isn't someone watching Drew's room?"

TJ, already on his feet and pulling his headphones off, waved her to his screen. "I heard the little guy, too, but there's nothing there. See for yourself."

She glanced at the screen. No movement. No images.

Stan, camera in hand recording the events, gestured to another screen. "Nothing on FLIR, either."

"That can't be. I knew we should've made sure the closet door was in the frame. Too late now."

Sterling joined her. "Maybe he had a nightmare. Or is unnerved and wants attention and comfort."

She shook her head. "The boy knows what he's talking about. If he says she's there, she's there."

Michael stood from his chair at the table. "You didn't feel the presence? But the boy could?"

She squirmed, embarrassed to admit she hadn't been paying attention, and glanced at Sterling. "I wasn't . . . Sterling and I were talking—"

A whimper diverted everyone's attention. "Miss Wanland."

Forgetting everyone else, she sprinted through the kitchen and rounded the corner into the boy's room. Light from the moon and streetlamps illuminated the room enough to make out shapes and shadows. His toddler bed sat in the corner of his room. The boy had pressed himself into the corner, his bear tucked under one arm, a threadbare blankie under the other, eyes squeezed shut.

"Drew," she whispered. "I'm here."

She felt the icy presence sweep over her but saw nothing. Something was different tonight. She calmed her breathing and attempted to pinpoint the location of the spirit. She stepped sideways toward Drew's bed. "Where is she?"

He popped his fingers out of his mouth and pointed toward the closet. But he didn't open his eyes.

The closet. Of course. Which explained why no one noticed anything on the cameras. The Dark hovered in the closet. *For now.*

Why?

"What are you doing?"

She jumped at the voice and turned to discover Sterling directly behind her, attempting to see into the room. Stan and TJ stood behind him, cameras in hand.

"Don't sneak up on me like that," she whispered. She clasped her crystal and breathed deeply in measured breaths.

"Just wondered what's happening. You okay?" he asked.

"Drew pointed to the closet. I'm attempting to ascertain the situation."

Michael pushed past the others. "Everything okay?"

"So far. Can everyone please be quiet and let me focus?"

"Just checking. Having the family in the house makes me nervous." He returned to the hallway.

Sterling, however, remained near her. "I'm not going anywhere. Someone needs to watch you for signs of another seizure."

"I don't have seizures."

Both cameramen followed her as she proceeded into the room, Sterling on her heels. She heard Michael giving directions.

"Elise, EMF?"

"Spiking. Almost as if the entity is feeding from a source."

She stopped moving halfway to the closet. "What source? We mapped all electrical sources before we started the investigation."

"The closet in this room contains the control box for the home security system, but it isn't armed. The Williamses said they couldn't afford the monitoring fees."

"Not armed is not the same as not powered. And if it's still powered, she could be drawing energy from it."

Sterling snorted. "Sure. Imaginary beings can do whatever you want them to do. Even eat electricity."

She crossed to the closet, ignoring Sterling's snark. "Stay by the boy."

"Careful, Kimmy," Michael cautioned.

She grabbed the doorknob and swung the door open half expecting an enormous, gaping maw ready to devour her. TJ raced to her side to catch the moment.

Nothing.

Drew whimpered.

"Kimmy? You have a reading?" Michael asked from the doorway.

"No visual." The Dark had to be somewhere. Drew, having spent the last few months terrorized by her, would know better than anyone.

Sterling appeared at her side. "Ready to admit the boy just had a bad dream?"

The frigid blast hit her, not a tidal wave crashing over her, but an iceberg, solid and powerful. And furious.

The icy shock took her breath away. She gasped.

The entity dropped from above and sailed past, blowing her hair behind her.

Strong, warm hands grasped her arms, intent on steadying her. She shook free as Drew screamed.

"I told you to stay with the boy!" She crossed the room in three steps and knelt beside the toddler bed.

Drew no longer sat in the corner.

"Kimmy? What's happening?" Michael called from the door.

"Just keep recording! She's here. She's powerful. Keep the cameras rolling."

Danielle's voice joined the fray. "What's wrong? Drew! What's happening?"

"Stay in your room," she commanded as forcefully as she could with lungs chilled by the dark entity. "Stay with your baby!"

Her fingers trembled as she searched the bed. Every square inch of the miniature thing. Her chilled hands were not so numb that they would miss a toddler's body. Where was he?

Frantic and scared, she lost control of her extrasensory perceptions. She stopped running her hands over the bed and held still. Clutching her crystal, she breathed deeply. Where was the entity? Where was the boy?

"Someone tell us what happened! My wife is freaking out!" Stephen yelled from the bedroom.

"Michael," she whispered.

"On it."

She heard his steps hurry down the hallway. She also heard Danielle's stifled whimpers. Michael's soothing voice calmed the young mom. No doubt he assured the woman that everything was under control.

It wasn't. The entity shunned her, denying all attempts to connect.

But she heard breathing. And . . . finger slurping?

Under the bed.

Of course. The boy had dove under the bed to hide during all the excitement. She lay on her stomach and peered underneath. Far too narrow for an adult, the tiny space accommodated the child.

And something else.

A pair of red eyes watched her from beside the boy.

"Drew?" she whispered. She heard him extricate fingers from his mouth.

"Hi, Miss Wan-land."

"You were smart to go under the bed," she praised.

"Tat!"

"Is Felix with you? Is that him?"

"Yes. Tat tan help!"

"Did he help you? Did Felix tell you to get under the bed?"

The boy didn't say anything, but she heard shuffling against the carpet that sounded like nodding.

She lifted her head. "TJ? Bring the FLIR. I think Felix is under the bed with Drew. Try to catch some images."

"Yes, ma'am!" The young cameraman dropped to the floor, camera pointed under the bed. "I see the boy's heat signature but nothing else. You sure about the cat?"

She frowned and leaned down for another look, swiveling her head left and right. Nothing. "I saw red eyes a moment before I called you."

"Sorry, Ms. Wantland. I don't see anything now."

"I don't, either. It's gone, I guess."

"Sorry, Miss Wan-land," Drew mimicked.

"That's okay, Drew. You didn't do anything wrong. You did great!" She noticed the frigid chill no longer filled her lungs or set her limbs quivering. "The Dark is gone, too. Why in the world would she just give up? I felt her clearly. She's completely amped tonight."

Sterling knelt beside her. "Dare I ask what amped means?"

TJ clicked his tongue and huffed. "Duh. Amped. Revved. Completely charged. Powered up."

"Whoa, pal. Power down. I just asked. I don't know your made-up jargon yet."

"Why bother now? You won't need it after tonight."

A moment of silence hung thickly in the air before Sterling answered. "No, I won't. You're right. Never hurts to learn something new, though."

Her heart ached at the sadness in his voice. Had she not been so consumed with where the entity disappeared to, she might have taken a moment to console him. But she had a feeling something terrible was about to happen.

She lay her head on the floor. "Drew, where did Felix go? Do you know?"

The wet smack of soggy fingers preceded his reply. "Fe-wix help baby Dosh."

"Baby Do—Baby Josh? Felix went to help Baby Josh?"

"Yes. Fe-wix will help."

"Why does Felix need to help Josh?" She sat up. Something clicked. "Oh no."

The rattle jingled in the crib. She jumped to her feet, a cold, sinking dread in the pit of her stomach. "This was a diversion. She's after the baby."

She bolted for the hallway just as Danielle's piercing cry called from the master bedroom.

"Oh, my God! Felix is in the baby's crib!"

32

Kimberly paused in the doorway long enough to whisper orders to Sterling. "Stay with Drew. Don't leave him alone."

She dashed down the hall and burst into the master bedroom. How could she be so naive not to see the baby was the intended victim all along? TJ's footsteps pounded behind her.

A night-light glowed in the corner, softly illuminating Danielle, who clutched the crib rail. "I know I saw him. He was here. In the crib."

Stephen stood behind her, a hand on her shoulder. "Shhh. Don't wake up Josh. There's nothing there. Come back to bed."

She went to Michael. "Did you see anything?"

He shook his head. "You know I never see anything. That's your job."

TJ spoke as he swung his camera side to side. "Nothing on the FLIR."

Danielle released her grip on the crib. "Ms. Wantland, I know I saw him. Please."

"I believe you. I saw him in Drew's room a moment ago."

"Drew, too? Is he okay?"

"He's fine. He showed no fear or concern toward Felix. He claimed the cat helped him hide from The Dark."

"Oh, my God. What is happening here?" Danielle sank against her husband's shoulder.

"Look," Stephen began, "you're upsetting her. You're not fixing anything. I want—"

The rattle jangled.

"Now you've done it," Stephen groused. "You woke the baby."

"No," TJ whispered. "The baby hasn't moved. I have the FLIR on the crib. I would've seen movement."

She crossed to TJ and looked inside. The infant's foot twitched once, and she noted the rhythmic rise and fall of consistent breathing. "Where's the rattle?"

TJ pointed to the far corner at the head of the crib. "Up there."

"The baby's nowhere near it."

"Nope. Couldn't have reached it."

"Maybe you rattled it," Sterling remarked from the doorway.

"I didn't rattle it. My hands are busy with the camera," TJ said.

"You could have bumped the crib."

"Why would I do that? It would show up as a shaky segment on the footage. You'll see. I wasn't close enough to touch it."

Stan entered the room, recording the interaction.

"Great." Stephen sighed. "My wife on national television in her pajamas. Just what I always wanted."

"Hush," Danielle said. "My pj's cover more than my Sunday dress. Who cares?"

"I care. Look around you. We're up in the middle of the night—again!—sleepless, about to be the laughingstock—"

"EMF is spiking again," Elise whispered. "One twenty. One thirty-eight. One forty-five."

TJ and Stan panned the room.

"I don't see anything," TJ said. "Not the cat, not the dark entity."

"Me, neither," Stan said.

"Kimmy, what's happening? Where is she?"

"Where is who?" Stephen demanded.

"The entity your son calls The Dark," she said.

Sterling offered his opinion. "Ms. Wantland believes you're being haunted by the ghost of the previous home owner. The schoolteacher."

"What? We heard they were a sweet old couple."

Sterling's voice indicated he enjoyed having another nonbeliever in the room. "Right? But now apparently she's here harassing you."

Michael finally interrupted. "Not now, Sterling."

She remained beside the crib, gripping her crystal, hoping for an opening to connect with the spiritual remains of Edna Miller. If she could connect, she should be able to guide the spirit, and hopefully convince her to cross over to the next plane of existence.

She rested a hand on the crib rail but yanked it away with a stifled cry of surprise.

"Kimmy? You okay?"

"The crib is hot again."

"EMF one sixty-seven," Elise said, "and continuing to climb. Pushing two hundred. I've never seen it so high. How is she doing this?"

"Kimmy, what's happening?"

"I don't know. She has to be here, but I can't detect her."

The hair on her arm stood on end. She felt a sensation she could only describe as a bucket of ice water dumped over her head. She gasped, her lungs struggling to process the suddenly cold air. She looked up.

The dark entity descended from the ceiling, features more clearly pronounced than she'd seen them yet, appearing almost corporeal. The face very much resembled the newspaper clipping photograph, but distorted, angry, somehow older, as if Edna Miller had continued to age after death. The wispy edges of the figure shimmered in the glow of the night-light as it drifted closer to the crib.

She took a deep breath and situated herself in front of the baby bed. "Get back," she gasped and pushed Stephen and Danielle backward. In her peripheral vision, she saw Stan and TJ maneuvering with their cameras.

Danielle and Stephen stumbled, clearly confused.

"Hey!" Stephen said. "What the heck?"

Danielle also sounded concerned. "What's happening, Ms. Wantland?"

"I'm not sure yet, and I want everyone back a safe distance. The Dark is in the room. I can see her. She's coming toward the crib."

"I want my baby!" Danielle moved to press past her.

"Stay back. I don't know what she's going to do." She spread her arms wide in an attempt to protect the infant.

Sterling stepped forward. "What are you doing? There is nothing in the room. You are terrifying these people for nothing."

"I told you to stay with the toddler. Go back to his room."

"He's fine. I'm more concerned about your fearmongering. Can you stop this charade and quit trying to convince these people you see some kind of spirit?"

"Listen to me. Please. I'm not pretending anything. I'm trying to protect the kids."

Danielle gasped. "Let me have my baby!"

"Ghosts don't exist. Nothing is endangering my family in this room except you." Stephen sounded at the end of his rope.

"EMF remaining stable at just under two hundred."

The Dark swooped in front of her. She could clearly make out facial features, twisted into a grimace. She reached out to connect but sensed only jealousy and loneliness. Ugly emotions that no doubt contorted the entity's face.

She stood her ground. "You cannot have this baby."

"What the hell?" Stephen demanded.

His wife wailed, "Let me have my baby!"

She heard tears in the young mom's voice.

"Kimmy?"

"She's right in front of me, Michael."

"I see her," TJ said, his voice hushed. "I see a shape on the FLIR. It's a heat signature."

"That's nothing," Sterling insisted. "A blip. Could be residual heat from Danielle or Stephen."

"No," TJ insisted. "It's blue. Cold. And it just showed up. This is freakin' awesome. First time I've seen live while taping."

"You want to see it, so you see it," Sterling countered. "I'm looking at it myself, unaffected by Ms. Wantland's histrionics, and I do not see a ghost."

"Dude, I keep telling you, you don't know what to look for—Ms. Wantland, be careful! It's, like, moving."

"Everyone, quiet."

The Dark drifted closer, one arm extended. Fingerlike extensions, longer and less opaque than real fingers, reached toward her.

She leaned backward to avoid contact but pressed into the scalding crib. With a cry, she stepped forward, closer to The Dark.

She glanced left and right, but if she moved at all she gave The Dark a straight opening to the baby. She saw Sterling attempt to cross to her, but Michael held him back.

Danielle once again moved toward the crib. "Let me have—" The young woman gasped.

"Danielle, what's wrong?" Stephen took two steps toward his wife before he, too, stopped in his tracks. "What the hell is going on? It's freezing over here."

"Kimmy? Cold spot?"

"Stay back, Michael," she said through chattering teeth. "Please. Let me handle it."

TJ laughed softly. "This is awesome. I see it on the FLIR. Big blue spot right in front of Ms. Wantland."

As she gulped lungful after lungful of icy air, the wispy tendrils closed around her throat and tightened. Her skin burned, and she couldn't breathe. She'd never encountered a spirit so determined or so strong.

She'd promised Danielle and Stephen help. She had insisted she could protect the family. And she'd truly believed it, never once doubted her ability. But she'd been wrong, she realized as her vision blurred. She couldn't breathe.

She wasn't aware of losing consciousness until she opened her eyes and discovered herself on the floor, Sterling cradling her head in his lap midrant.

"—told you she has seizures. Someone call a damned ambulance this time!"

Michael knelt beside her, patting her cheek. "Come on, Kimmy. Come back to us."

Danielle's and Stephen's worried faces swam into focus. They both bent over her. Danielle wrung her hands. The rest of her crew hovered around her, waiting for her to recover.

Her head hurt. She'd never felt so enervated. Sterling massaged her temples. She could get used to that. She closed

244

her eyes and allowed a moment of soothing massage before she opened them again. But what she saw behind the young parents roused her foggy brain better than a double shot of espresso.

The Dark hovered beside the crib, one arm reaching toward the baby.

She tried to warn them, to shift attention away from her to where it belonged. But her limbs wouldn't move, and her mouth wouldn't form words.

The rattle jangled, and a soft meow filled her with warmth and hope.

Danielle glanced around. "Felix?"

The young mother heard it, too. Drawing on her last reserve of strength, she pushed herself onto her elbows, then up into a sitting position.

"The baby," she managed through lips that felt thick, anesthetized.

Rosie raced to her side, the case of chakra stones in one hand, a mug of hot tea in the other.

"Not now," she gasped, forcing herself to her knees.

"You need to recharge." Rosie tried again.

She heard the baby gasp and work its infant mouth. The Dark leaned closer.

"No." She grabbed the crib, gritted her teeth as the wooden rail singed her hands, and dragged herself to her feet.

Sterling jumped up. "Are you insane? Michael, she's not in her right mind. Stop her! Call an ambulance."

He grabbed her arm, but she shook him off.

Another meow sounded through the room as she stood and peered into the crib. Felix crouched over the baby, back arched, fur on end.

The Dark's fingers curled around the infant's throat.

The baby didn't move.

245

Felix slashed at the entity's arm with unsheathed claws again and again. The cat turned its red eyes on her and hissed, fur on end. But now she understood. He wanted to help, not hurt. He crouched over Josh in an attempt to protect the baby, and he wanted her to intervene. She knew what she had to do.

"Michael," she gasped. "The Dark . . . is right by the crib. Try to get footage . . . before she drains the battery packs. Then don't reload. I have to . . . drain her."

"Kimmy, EMF is around two hundred. You can't drain that much energy onto yourself."

"I'll have to draw enough. Get the electronics out of here. As many as possible. Unplug everything."

The room faded into a blur. All the voices and noise in the room fell away from her. She grabbed her crystal, focused on The Dark, and drew a deep breath.

She plunged a hand into the dark entity, siphoning all the energy she could handle. Too much, and she'd risk psychic shock, a phenomenon comparable to electrocuting her spirit. If she overloaded her system, she risked permanent damage. But she had to save the baby.

The Dark turned to face her, the features a furious scowl.

"What the hell is going on?" Stephen asked. "What is she doing?"

"She's seizing again," Sterling answered. "Michael, do something!"

"No. Do not disturb her. She's fighting the spirit. In fact, everyone out of the room."

"Not without my baby!" Danielle cried.

She heard Rosie comfort the young mother as she led her from the room. "Your baby is in good hands. Let Kimberly do her job."

Kimberly shook uncontrollably and grabbed the crib rail to steady herself. The wooden slats no longer burned. The entity grew weaker as she drained it. Her plan was working. But she couldn't keep this up much longer. If she overloaded her system, she could lose consciousness. She couldn't allow that to happen before she knew the baby was safe.

Sterling's voice challenged Michael, strong as granite. "I'm not leaving her side. Someone needs to take care of her. Until I'm convinced she's in no harm, I'm staying right here."

His voice and concern strengthened her. But the entity seemed to grow stronger, as well. How was it doing this? The fingerlike projections still curled around the infant's throat.

"This is wild," TJ said, excitement in his voice. "I swear I can see the energy leaving the spirit and flowing into Ms. Wantland."

"TJ, your battery pack . . . you need to go," she said.

"But this is fantastic footage! Best we've ever caught."

"She's pulling more energy . . . from your batteries. Recharging while I drain."

"She said go!" Sterling's rough voice startled her. "Get out. Who cares about shooting now?"

From the corner of her eye, she saw him shove TJ roughly out the door.

The Dark snarled at her but remained focused on the baby. She closed her eyes and pulled more energy.

Felix let out a terrible shriek. She looked down in the crib. The infant's chest no longer rose and fell. She was running out of time.

"Felix, help me!"

"Michael, she's talking gibberish! If you won't call an ambulance, I will."

The cat spirit thrust both paws into The Dark's arm. The Dark opened its mouth as if to wail, but no sound resulted. The entity grew dimmer. She could see through it. Knowing she couldn't take much more, she gave one last push to drain energy away from the spirit. The room grew faint and distant, but she saw the spirit retract its appendage from the crib and dissipate.

She heard a desperate meow from the crib and knew what it meant. She fell into Sterling's arms. How did he always manage to catch her when she needed him most? "Call an ambulance," she instructed him as he cradled her. "The baby isn't breathing."

33

Kimberly opened her eyes and discovered herself lying on the couch again. The Williamses' couch had become her makeshift recovery bed. Her entire crew scattered around the living room. TJ and Stan stood nearby, shifting from foot to foot. Elise sat in a chair, nibbling nervously on a fingernail. Michael spoke quietly on his cell phone. Sterling paced the room.

Standing beside the couch, Rosie noticed she was awake before anyone else. "Hey, there. There she is. Thank goodness."

Sterling stopped pacing and dashed to her side. "Still think you need medical attention. But the infant took precedence, and Michael remains adamant you'll be fine if we just let Rosie tend to you. I would feel much better if you saw a doctor, though."

While he spoke, he curled his fingers around hers. Grateful for the concern, she squeezed his fingers. "Thank you. I'll be okay now."

She gathered the chakra stones from her energy centers and sat up. Her head pounded, the worst headache she'd ever experienced in her life. "How's the baby? What happened? Please tell me the baby is okay."

Michael hung up and sighed heavily. "The baby is okay. Everyone can relax. Danielle says the doctor wants to keep the baby under observation for a day or two, but they expect no complications. Very fortunate we were here tonight."

She saw everyone in the room breathe a sigh of relief. Stan crossed himself and held his hands to the ceiling, offering a prayer of gratitude. TJ murmured, "Thank goodness. Glad we didn't lose the little dude. That would've sucked big-time."

Michael crossed the living room and sat beside her on the couch. "You are okay, aren't you?"

She nodded, rubbing her temples. "Other than the worst headache I've ever had in my life, I think I'm fine, now I know the baby is okay."

"Danielle says the doctor has diagnosed this as SIDS. He says it's lucky the baby was discovered not breathing as quickly as he was, so they could resuscitate. Right now, they're predicting no brain damage or anything. You're a hero, Kimmy."

"I'm anything but. I promised you I'd keep this family safe. I can't believe I let the spirit get her hands on the baby. It was the most horrible thing I've ever seen in my life. She intended to choke that baby to death. Strangle it. I just can't imagine—" She shuddered, and a chill passed through her. She wrapped her arms around herself.

Rosie draped a blanket around her and pressed a warm mug into her hands. "Drink some tea. That always helps. You overloaded your chakra sources, and I had to drain some of the energy away. Since you were unconscious, it was difficult to know when to stop. I hope I didn't draw away too much."

"I'm okay. Or I will be once I clear Edna Miller from this house."

"What do you mean?" Michael asked. "You overpowered her. She's gone now, right?"

"No. She dissipated after I drained her, but she didn't leave. She's still here. So the disturbance isn't resolved. I have to convince her to go. For good."

Michael hung his head and pinched the bridge of his nose. "I thought we were done. And you're in no shape to wrangle with this again."

"I have to. This ends tonight. I can't risk the family returning home with her here waiting."

"What do you plan to do?" Rosie asked. "And how can I help?"

"You got your big finale," Sterling said. "There's no reason to continue the charade. The family isn't even here. You got your big standoff with the ghost. Lots of drama. You even get to end the show by telling your audience you saved a baby's life. I can't imagine a more compelling season finale than that. Why do you think you need to shoot more? You need to rest. And possibly go to a doctor. Let me drive you to the ER and get checked out instead of continuing on with this foolishness."

She really didn't have the strength to argue with him. And yet he had a knack for getting under her skin. "None of this has ever been a charade. I know, you won't believe me no matter what I say. But the baby was not a victim of SIDS. The spiritual remains of Edna Miller are still in this house. She never left. She's fixated on the children. Until she goes, the family won't be safe. She will try again when they return. When we aren't here to stop her."

"Spiritual remains?" Sterling said. "Ick. I think I prefer the term *ghost*."

"Okay, Ms. Miller's ghost is still in the house. And I need to help her translocate. I'm not quite sure how to convince her to come back and connect with me. The baby and toddler aren't here anymore." She thought for a moment. "Elise, what else did you learn during your research? About the Millers, I mean."

"Let me grab my folder." Elise bolted from the room.

Sterling shook his head. "You are stubborn as a pit bull, I'll give you that."

"Thank you."

"It wasn't really a compliment, but you're welcome. One last-ditch effort. Will you please let me drive you to the ER?"

"Later. After the disturbance is cleared."

He held up a little finger and crooked it at her. "Pinkie promise?"

"Um . . . here's Elise! What do you have, Elise?"

"Starting with the obvious, she liked teaching. So I think it's safe to assume she could respond to kids' school supplies like crayons—"

"Drew's drawings," she interrupted, snapping her fingers. "Drew's drawings of her."

Elise nodded. "Perfect. Let me see. Married to Dale Miller for sixty-two years. They asked her about her favorite things for the article. Favorite color, purple. Favorite food, chocolate milkshake, just like the soda jerk used to make. Favorite drink, vanilla Coke, just like the soda jerk used to make. Favorite pastime, crocheting baby blankets. She says, 'I sure wish I had some grandbabies to make them for. But I don't. And pretty soon arthritis will put an end to it anyway.'"

Rosie sniffed. "This is so sad."

"Then this will really get you," Elise continued. "Favorite song, 'It's Only a Paper Moon.' 'That was our wedding song. Dale used to sing it to me. And he told me life would always be grand as long as I believed in him. And it has been. We may only have a paper moon and a cardboard sea, but I believe in him, and he believes in me.'"

They all sat in silence until Sterling spoke.

"And you think the ghost of that sweet woman tried to kill a baby? Leave the medical diagnosis alone and let's wrap."

"She's confused and lonely and afraid. She's forgotten who she was. Her husband of over sixty years moved away, leaving her alone in an empty house. Don't you see? This is all the more reason to help." She looked at Rosie. "That's it. That's how to draw her out and get her to connect with me. And hopefully let me help her. I'm sure it will work. Sterling, you're a genius."

"What? What did I do? I didn't say anything about talking to a ghost."

"Rosie, bring all the lavender candles from the makeup trailer. Those are purple, her favorite color."

Sterling tried again. "Whatever idea you've had, it wasn't mine. I said leave it alone. Not talk to a ghost."

"Elise, we need the yarn again. And any crocheted blankets you can find."

Elise dashed to the hallway.

"Michael, I doubt you can find a milkshake or vanilla Coke at two in the morning. Can you gather Drew's drawings, crayons, any other art supplies you can find?"

"Sure thing!" He flashed a thumbs-up.

Sterling stared at her. "Want to let me in on the plan? Which is not my plan. Just saying. I mean, I don't even know what it is."

"I'll show you. Come with me. Let's see if your three a.m. charm helps today."

34

Kimberly sat cross-legged on the floor of the master bedroom. Lavender candles burned around her, soothing and relaxing. And purple. Crayons, safety scissors, coloring books, and Drew's drawings lay scattered about the floor. Skeins of yarn sat beside a few crocheted baby blankets on the bed. "It's Only a Paper Moon" played on loop from her cell phone. The newspaper article detailing Edna Miller's interview during her retirement party rested on the floor beside her.

She had drunk so much of Rosie's fortifying tea, she thought she might float away. Rosie had massaged aromatic oils into her skin. She breathed deeply and felt calm, collected, at ease with the world. She could do this.

Her crew arrayed behind her, ready to assist however possible. Stan and TJ stood on opposite sides of the room, cameras ready. A black box with coils hummed softly by the wall, electricity arcing from coil to coil with an occasional buzz.

Sterling sat on the bed facing her, watching her. Although his gaze prompted butterflies, she did her best to push aside the fluttery emotions and focus on only Edna Miller. At least Sterling maintained a positive attitude. She needed to prohibit all negativity tonight.

She breathed deeply and closed her eyes, one hand curled around her quartz crystal. She also wore blue turquoise and jade to help boost her communication and heart chakras. But the quartz remained most important. That one honed her psychic energy and focused it while connecting.

"Why do you grab that necklace?" Sterling asked. "Nervous habit?"

"No," she answered, eyes still closed. "It helps me focus my energy while I interact with spiritual entities. Gives my abilities a boost, as it were."

"How do you think that stone affects your energy? I'm pretty sure there's no science behind that."

"Shhhh. I need to focus right now."

"Right. Okay."

She heard him crack his knuckles but disregarded that, breathing in the soothing lavender scent surrounding her. She imagined herself floating and envisioned the energy of her chakras spinning and growing, traveling into the world around her. She thought she felt a nudge of a response but didn't push. She needed to allow Edna to come to her tonight.

"What is that thing?" Sterling asked.

She took another deep breath. "What thing?"

"That black boxy thing by the wall. With wires and gizmos sparking blue arcs periodically. Is it a giant lighter?"

"No, silly. That's the SEEPS. Stands for Spectral-Enhancing Energy Power Source. Think of it as a ghost charger. I drained Edna earlier to take control of the situation and save Josh. Now she's weak. I'm offering her a way to recharge quickly so I can communicate with her."

"I don't believe you interacted with a ghost at all. But in your scenario, you thought she managed to power herself before. Why can't she do that again?"

"Michael threw the breaker on the security system. No power to it. The SEEPS gives off a steady but lower-energy frequency. She won't be able to get out of control this time."

"You really believe this, don't you?"

She heard no hostility in the question, only curiosity. "Of course. It's true. Why wouldn't I believe it?"

"Electric-powered ghosts, huh? Eco-friendly?" He laughed at his own joke. "And how do you suppose that happens? They just absorb it and . . . ?"

She beamed at him. "You have the right idea. A strong power source draws residual entities. Without a body to protect, power, and nourish it, the spirit remains weak and helpless. A displaced spirit often feels vulnerable. And scared. Imagine how you'd feel if you were ripped suddenly from your body. But if a spirit can draw power from an energy source, it can manifest and potentially interact with the world around it again. Mrs. Miller has learned to do that. She can leave EVP, ruffle your hair, and unfortunately she's strong enough to choke me and attempt to strangle the baby."

"But when the body dies, that's it. There isn't anything else. When I die, I die. I will be gone."

She cocked her head at him. "Says the good Irish Catholic. What about your soul? Which is just another word for *spirit*, you know. Don't you believe you have a soul?"

"Sure. But that goes to heaven or wherever after death."

She pointed at him. "Aha. So you do believe in other worlds. Other planes of existence. We just call them different things."

"Whatever. If you want to believe that, go ahead. But I don't believe in ghosts. When we die, we die, and nothing remains behind."

"Except sometimes the process doesn't work quite right. That's when—"

The SEEPS crackled and beeped.

She snapped her head. "Here she is."

"EMF approaching one hundred," Elise said.

"Kimmy, we're detecting a cold spot forming to your right."

The conversation would have to wait. She closed her eyes again and cleared all thoughts but Edna Miller. The world around her melted to the background. Nothing mattered right now but clearing this house for the Williams family. The song began again, the upbeat rhythm drifting from her phone through the room.

Oh, it's only a paper moon . . .

She took a deep breath. "Mr. Wakefield, please come sit in front of me on the floor."

"On that candle? And burn my butt? I thought we'd arrived at a peace accord."

She suppressed the giggle but allowed the smile he prompted. They needed a light, jovial atmosphere tonight, and she appreciated his presence more than ever.

"Push the candle aside, of course," she directed him. "I'm not wishing injury on you. Just come join me on the floor, please."

"Okay, what is happening here?" Sterling asked. "What's with the weird voice? Is Kimberly possessed?"

"She's in a meditative state, Sterling," Michael answered, "so she can act as a medium for the spirit and help it transition to the next life. Please cooperate with her."

TJ clicked his tongue. "Dude, you are such a douche. I am so glad this is the last night we have to put up with you."

"TJ," she admonished, keeping her voice calm and even, "you know we cannot have any negativity in the room right now. We don't want to spook the spirit."

A ripple of laughter ran through the crew. "Spook the spirit," a few of them repeated.

"Wow. Ghost humor, huh?" Sterling said. "Feels like I'm on *Scooby-Doo*. Zoinks! Like, don't spook the spook, Scoob!"

The crew giggled again. She opened her eyes and caught Sterling smiling at his own cleverness. Her chest swelled with delight. She'd missed that smirk. She liked seeing him at ease on her show.

He pushed the candle aside and grunted as he situated himself cross-legged in front of her. "I'm getting too old to sit like this. Why am I down here?"

"I need you to be my second. My anchor."

He blinked and shook his head, brow furrowed. "Your what now?"

"If anything goes wrong—I don't expect it to, but if it does—I need someone to keep me tethered here. Will you do it?"

. . . but it wouldn't be make-believe if you believed in me.

Sterling's eyes glowed in the candlelight. He seemed to be choosing his words carefully. "I don't believe in other worlds or other dimensions or ghosts or spirits. But I know you do, and I'm honored you asked me to help you. Tell me what to do."

She scooted forward so their knees touched, then took his hands in hers. His warm hands dwarfed hers. Did she imagine the electric jolt when they touched? She squashed a fresh round of butterflies as they danced through her stomach. *Not the time.*

"Whatever happens, don't let go," she instructed him.

Michael spoke, his voice grave. "Cold spot is approaching you, Kimmy."

"I feel it." She nodded to Sterling and closed her eyes. "Come join us, Mrs. Miller."

The SEEPS beeped. Sterling jumped.

"It's okay," she said to reassure Mrs. Miller but also to let Sterling hear no fear in her voice. "We're here to help you. Come see what the children drew for you."

"EMF hovering around one twenty," Elise told her.

"She's powerful," she said. "But that shouldn't climb any higher now."

A gust of wind blew through the room, extinguishing the candles, plunging the room into darkness.

"Who did that?" Sterling asked. "Is that the kid? TJ?"

"That's our guest," she assured him, squeezing his hands. "She's looking around, trying to determine what's happening. We have her attention."

She opened her energy, inviting Mrs. Miller to focus on her, hoping to draw her attention. "Mrs. Miller, we know you got left alone when your husband, Dale, moved away. That must have been very scary for you. But I'm going to help you so you don't have to be alone anymore."

"Cold spot is by the crib, Kimmy."

"Drew and Josh aren't here, Mrs. Miller. I know you loved children, but you can't have these. They need to stay with their mother."

Another chilly gust set her hair blowing. The song continued to play. The yarn skeins shifted. One of them slowly unspooled, the blue yarn piling in a tangled mess on the floor.

"Do you remember crocheting?" she asked. "Remember making baby blankets?"

"How are you doing that?" Sterling asked. "Fishing line? Someone in the crew has the other end?"

"No, Mr. Wakefield. Nothing on my show is a cheap parlor trick or an illusion like your magic tricks. I know you normally debunk paranormal claims, but I'm telling you tonight you are encountering the real thing."

One of the folded baby blankets fell from the bed to the floor. The drawings fluttered. The volume increased on her phone until the song blared.

. . . but it wouldn't be make-believe if you believed in me.

She raised her voice to be heard over the music. "Do you remember Dale, Mrs. Miller? Think back to before. Before you got left behind. Do you remember your husband?"

The breeze died away. The drawings settled and remained still. The music softened, returning to the quiet background level she'd originally set it at.

No one spoke. The SEEPS crackled.

Sterling looked around the room. "Is that it? End of the show? Is she gone now?"

"No," she whispered. "She's here. I feel her."

"You think you feel a ghost—"

"Shhhh. She's thinking. Be still."

"Kimmy, cold spot forming again. Immediately beside you."

"It's okay. She's not angry. Let her come. This is what I hoped would happen."

"Image on the FLIR," TJ said. "This is awesome. I see her there."

She saw Stan move closer with his camera.

The SEEPS sizzled.

Edna Miller materialized beside her, hovering in a seated position at her level.

35

Kimberly caught her breath. "She's here. She's with me."

Sterling looked back and forth from her face to the area she saw Mrs. Miller. "I don't see anything at all. You're staring at empty space."

"No. She's here. I see her very clearly."

The spirit's face no longer possessed the hard, angry lines she'd seen previously. The countenance resembled the newspaper photograph.

She envisioned warm, soft light emanating from her heart, reaching out into the world, inviting the spirit to connect with her.

The spirit hesitated, perhaps shy or maybe simply scared.

"It's okay," she murmured. "I won't hurt you. Let me help."

She withdrew her right hand from Sterling's warm grasp. When he balked at releasing her fingers, she squeezed tighter with her left hand. "Hold on to this one. I'll be fine."

She picked up the newspaper article and held it toward the spirit. "Do you remember your retirement party? You taught school for sixty years. That's an incredible contribution. I know how much you loved children."

The facial features softened. A pale appendage drifted toward her and curled around her hand, turning the article as if to read it.

Images of chalkboards, coloring pages, primary-color alphabets, and children flashed through her mind—none of them her own thoughts or memories. She'd finally fully connected with Edna Miller.

"You spent so much of your life with Dale. Remember him?"

The images changed, focusing on Dale, first older as he must have been in their later years together, then drifting backward through time. Through birthdays and anniversaries, Edna Miller's memories of Dale aged in reverse. They clinked glasses over meals in restaurants. Dale held Edna as she wept, a doctor informing her she could never have children. They sat in a car at a drive-in movie. They shared a chocolate milkshake at a soda shop while a jukebox played. Dale's beaming face, barely more than a child, carefree and blissful, spinning Edna across a dance floor while "It's Only a Paper Moon" played. Their wedding.

The spirit's features relaxed again, appearing as young as Dale in the wedding-day memory. Sad eyes seemed to plead with her. The ethereal hand wrapped around hers grew cold. A dreadful loneliness and longing consumed her.

"I know you miss him. You can go join him again. You need to let go of this world and move on to the next."

The hand grew colder still, and she fought the urge to yank her own hand away.

"Yes, it's scary. Change is always scary. But Dale is there. He's waiting for you. I know he misses you. Wouldn't you rather go dance with him again than stay here without him?"

The SEEPS hissed and arced.

"EMF nudging higher," Elise warned her.

"She's drawing more power. I believe she wants to communicate."

"You're okay, Kimmy?"

"Yes. I'm making progress. Don't try to inhibit her."

Edna's spirit drifted closer. She could sense thoughts in addition to feelings and images. She voiced them for the camera to record what she heard.

"She's afraid. She remembers now but doesn't know how to cross over. She misses Dale and wants to reunite with him, but she's scared he won't be there if she leaves. She doesn't understand why she got left behind. And she doesn't want to forget her life again."

Michael stepped closer. "Can you help her transition?"

"Of course. That's why I'm here."

She closed her eyes. The spirit wanted to move on. That was the first step. She could offer comfort and support as the spirit crossed to the next world. Once they established the way. That was the tricky part.

Grasping her crystal, she focused all her energy to her violet chakra, reaching out, seeking the pathway the spirit would follow. The SEEPS sizzled and hissed. She opened her eyes as a blue arc of energy jumped from one coil to another. A bright-white oval appeared between the SEEPS and where she sat.

"That's it. That's where you need to go now." She smiled at Edna's spirit, nodding encouragement.

The spirit watched the opening for a moment before rising and drifting toward it.

"She's crossing," she announced to her crew.

Mrs. Miller's spirit stopped and looked back.

"It's okay. Go ahead. You'll be much happier."

The translucent entity hesitated, grasping her hand tighter.

Not good. "Let go, Mrs. Miller. You have to let go. I can't go with you. You have to cross alone, but then you'll find Dale waiting for you. One scary moment followed by an eternity with your love."

She felt Mrs. Miller attempt to disengage—to extricate from their connection. The fear told her the spirit wasn't letting go but trying to break off the transition. She'd worked too hard to lose her now.

"Mrs. Miller, stay with me. Don't run off." She tightened her spiritual hold as well as attempted to grasp the spectral hand clinging to her. She might as well have attempted to grab water. The tenuous connection held, but barely.

"Kimmy, what's happening?"

"She's scared and wants to bolt. She's trying to sever the connection. I don't know how long I can hold her."

Her head slumped forward as she gathered every ounce of remaining strength. She'd pay for this tomorrow but so be it. She shook with exertion. Her head snapped up and dropped back.

"Michael, she's seizing again. I cannot sit here and watch this happen to her. Do something!" Sterling's voice caught and he tried to scramble to his feet, loosening his grip on her hand. He let go and grabbed her shoulders, shaking gently.

She gasped and shuddered. Her spiritual energy tugged away from her body, ready to accompany Mrs. Miller to the next existence.

Mrs. Miller paused and turned to examine her closely, apparently aware of the change in energy weight. The specter pulled at her hand, seemingly pleased with this new development.

She drifted farther off center. No longer cold, no longer stressed, the lure of the next world gnawed at her soul. No more sleepless nights, no more worry about ratings, no more stalkers or tweets or Internet trolls. She allowed Mrs. Miller to coax her closer to the door to the great unknown. How long had she hoped for a glimpse of what lay beyond? Perhaps she would see her mother again. She watched the others as though outside her body.

"Michael, she's not breathing." Sterling cradled an arm around her, jostling her as his panicked voice sought help. "What do we do? Do you have a stick to pry her mouth open? Someone call nine-one-one!"

"You ass-hat!" TJ yelled. "You let go of her hand! You were her anchor."

"What?" Michael dropped the thermometer and fell to her side. "Kimmy? Kimmy?"

Elise raced to Sterling's side. "Take her hand! And convince her to stay. You can do it. That's why she chose you."

Rosie's voice chimed in. "Convince her to stay, Sterling. Give her something to live for."

Mrs. Miller pulled again. Kimberly felt the glow of the next world on her face. She squinted, desperate for a glimpse. Would her mother wait with open arms as she often imagined? She saw nothing and stretched closer.

A heavy weight engaged her left hand, jerking her spirit back toward her waiting body. She heard someone call her name as if through a deep pool of water.

Mrs. Miller realized her spiritual traveling partner no longer trailed behind her and yanked.

Sterling pulled in response, and she found herself in a tug-of-war between the two.

She stared at the bright light, the temporary portal to the next existence. She knew it wasn't her time, but the allure tantalized. No deadlines. No travel. No responsibilities. No hotel food.

But also, evidently, no Mom.

"Kimberly, please. Do not do this to me. If you die, the entire crew will believe it was because I let go of your hand. And they will blame me for your death. I'm here. I've got you. Don't let go."

And no Sterling.

She settled back into her body and gasped an enormous breath into her burning lungs.

The crew cheered as she rasped breath after breath.

But the struggle wasn't over.

"You guys, she's still got Ms. Wantland. I can see her on the FLIR."

Too weak now to sever the connection with Mrs. Miller, she clung helplessly to Sterling while the spirit continued to pull at her, pleading for help in translocating.

She attempted encouraging words to spur the spirit on, but her shredded lungs only wheezed.

Meow.

She snapped her head toward the portal. Felix stood before it, calling gently to Mrs. Miller. His eyes glowed their normal yellow now, as he cocked his head. He raised a pale paw, his stripes barely visible in ghost form.

The grip on her right hand lessened. She nodded to Mrs. Miller. *Go ahead. You can do it.*

"Come on, Edna. You sure as blazes took your sweet time." Dale Miller appeared in the portal, young and smiling, just as he'd looked in Mrs. Miller's memory of her wedding day. He stretched out one arm to his wife.

The music from the cell phone blared again.

Mrs. Miller seemed to forget everyone else. The spirit dropped her hand and drifted toward her husband's outstretched arm as if drawn by a magnet.

"I've been waiting for you." He curled his arm around her waist, took her hand, and danced her away to their wedding song.

Felix meowed one last time and leaped into the arms of a spirit Kimberly could only assume was once Danielle's grandmother. The spirit waved once, stroked Felix, and vanished.

The portal closed.

The SEEPS fell silent.

The phone battery died.

"It's over," TJ said with a sigh of relief. "No more activity."

"EMF dropped to ten. No signs of activity," Elise agreed.

Sterling clutched her head to his chest and rocked her gently. "Don't ever do that to me again."

She took breath after breath and reveled in the rocking before she answered. "No promises. It's kind of what I do."

36

Kimberly walked into the dining area for breakfast, no thought in her pounding head but how good the urn of coffee smelled. Recovering from Edna Miller's demanding transition would take days. Many of her crew lingered at tables, nursing cups of coffee or picking at plates of food. The usual post-investigation funk seemed to affect everyone. Sterling sat at a table alone but jumped to his feet as she walked by.

"Morning, Kimberly. Won't you join me?" He pulled back a seat at the table, where a still-steaming mug of coffee waited. "Just a splash of skim."

She dropped into the chair, curled her hands around the hot mug, and offered him her most grateful smile. "Thank you."

He returned to his seat. "How are you this morning?"

"I've been better," she admitted. "But I've probably also been worse. I'll be okay. Just need a few days to recover."

"And an appointment to see your doctor, right?"

"I'm fine. I don't need a doctor. I promise."

He opened his mouth to argue, but Michael interrupted.

"Good morning. How's my Kimmy?"

"I'll be fine. How are the Williamses? Have you heard?"

"I did. The baby is fine. He's been released from the hospital, and they're all back home."

"So we can wrap today?"

"If you feel up to it."

"I'm good. Let's close this one."

Michael rested a hand on her shoulder. "I'll go get things ready at the house."

The rest of the crew seemed to take their cue from the director. They likewise gathered up and left.

Rosie stopped at the table on her way out. "Did you see Sterling's tweet yet?"

"You know I didn't. I haven't even had coffee yet."

"You should see. So many likes, comments, and shares. He's drawing a lot of attention to the show."

"Ah, Rosie. Let her wake up," Sterling said, rubbing the back of his neck. "She doesn't care about that."

Rosie turned her phone.

@KWantland almost died last night. I saved her #hero #nooneelsecoulddoit #shepickedme #wantlandsavethedate

"Look at these comments. He's bringing you all kinds of publicity."

She nodded. "I know."

"I'm just saying, he's really good for the show."

"I got it. I'm glad he was here this week."

"Okay, well. I'll leave you two alone." Rosie raised her eyebrows before she turned and left.

She sipped her coffee. "Sorry about that. Rosie is a touch . . . colorful. But I love her."

"No, she's great. I love her, too." He cleared his throat. "So, it's over. You said we wrap today?"

"Right. We go back to the house, summarize the source of the haunting. I guess you'll record your rebuttal explanations. And we'll say good-bye to the family."

"I know we don't agree most of the time, and I know I irritated you a lot. I'm really sorry I was forced on you this week."

"I'm not sorry. Not at all." She rested a hand on his and smiled.

He smiled back. "I got something for you." He slid a box across the table in front of her.

"You didn't have to do that!"

"I want you to know how much I appreciate you putting up with me and trying to help save my show from cancellation. And it's not returnable, so I hope you like it."

She reached for the blue velvet box with a big white bow on it. She looked up to find him watching her, hope and trepidation in his eyes.

Amber stood behind him.

Kimberly shook her head. "Are you kidding me right now? Do you truly have no life?"

Startled, Sterling began to say something, then stopped when Amber rested a hand on his back.

"You're a sensation today," Amber purred.

Sterling pulled away from her. "What are you doing here, Amber?"

"Apparently, interrupting a moment." The young woman eyed the box. "Jewelry, huh? Doesn't seem like a gift you would get for someone you don't have feelings for. Or something you'd buy if you had to watch expenses because you're broke and jobless."

Sterling scowled, one hand curling into a fist. His jaw tightened. "My feelings for Kimberly are none of your business. My expenses are also none of your business. And how I choose to spend my money has nothing to do with you."

"Oh, but it does. I don't like my boyfriend giving other women jewelry."

Sterling shook his head. "You broke it off yesterday. You don't do canceled, remember?"

"I realized I acted in haste. You won't be down long. You'll have a new show soon. Or something else."

"That's very astute of you, but I'm getting really tired of telling you it's over. We are over. We are done. I have zero interest in continuing this relationship. Take your hands off me, turn around, and leave Kimberly and me alone."

The young woman narrowed her eyes, first at Sterling, then at her. "You've worked quite a number on him, haven't you? Well, I will never let him go. Never."

Kimberly didn't drop her gaze but met the fierce, burning eyes with an intensity of her own. "I think he's made it clear, Amber, that he is not yours to hold on to. I'm going to ask you nicely one time to please leave my friend alone. Then you will leave me no choice but to make you leave."

Amber threw her head back and laughed. "Make me leave? I'd like to see you try."

Kimberly pushed her chair back and stood. Reaching into her purse, she pulled out a bottle containing a concoction Rosie had brewed up for her and prayed this would work.

Amber scoffed. "And what do you have that you think will strike terror into my heart?"

"My own special recipe of succubus repellant."

Amber's self-satisfied smirk faded. "I don't know what you're talking about."

"I think you do. I figured you out the first time we met. You have two options right now. You can call me a crazy person and walk away and never bother Mr. Wakefield again. Or you can stand here and push the issue, and we will see how your skin reacts to a healthy dose of this." She held up the bottle of tan liquid.

Lara Bernhardt

Amber turned to Sterling. "Do you hear her? What is she talking about?"

"I don't know, and I don't care. I just want you to go. But this looks like it's about to get interesting." He leaned back and laced his fingers behind his head.

Amber threw her shoulders back. Her normally ghoulish pallor flushed pink. "I don't need this. I'm doing you a favor. You think I can't have anyone I want just like that?" The young woman snapped her fingers in his face.

"I believe you can. And I fear for your next victim."

Amber looked back and forth between the two of them. "Screw this. I don't have to put up with it. I can do way better than you. It's over, Sterling. Don't come crawling back to me." She spun on her heel and stalked away, head high.

Sterling watched her leave, sighed, and shook his head. "Sorry about that. I truly hope she's gone for good. Thanks for helping. Again."

She waved away the thank-you. "That's what friends do."

He smiled. His eyes crinkled at the corners in an endearing way she hadn't noticed before. "Friends? I like the sound of that. What do you have in that bottle anyway? Succubus repellant?"

She grinned, popped open the top, and took a big drink. "It's just tea. But I hoped she would fall for it. I don't think Amber is the brightest bulb in the box."

Sterling laughed, clapped a few times, and shook his head. "You are a brilliant woman, Kimberly Wantland, no denying that. Despite the belief in ghosts and magic rocks and all that rigmarole."

The fire in his eyes sent butterflies fluttering through her stomach. Wasn't she too old to get butterflies over a guy? And this warm, fuzzy feeling radiating through her? Apparently she wasn't. Who knew?

He cleared his throat. "You didn't open your present. I really hope you like it."

She slid the ribbon and bow off the box and rocked back the hinged lid. She caught her breath and her jaw dropped. "Sterling, this is . . . too much. This is just beautiful."

His face cracked into a smile. "If I'd known all it took to get you to use my first name was jewelry, I would've brought something the first day."

He leaned forward, eyes dancing as she marveled at his generosity. He looked very pleased with himself, but she didn't mind. He should be pleased with himself. She lifted the gold necklace draped inside the box. A quartz star merkaba pendant hung from the chain, looped by two gold rings. A quartz crystal point hung below the merkaba. Gems corresponding to all the chakras were spaced along the sides of the necklace.

"Do you see?" Sterling asked. "The stones make the rainbow you claim we all carry inside us. The woman who made this said the pendant is called a merkaba, and that it carries lots of mumbo-jumbo powers. But I asked her to add this plain quartz at the bottom because you always grab your quartz pendant. And the merkaba looked way too big and bulky to wrap your hand around. This way you still have quartz to grab. That seemed important. And now you can wear all the stones at once. In my humble opinion, it turned out to be a pretty cool necklace I designed, even if you don't believe in magic rocks, which I don't. But I thought you might like it." He finally stopped talking and watched her carefully.

She cradled the necklace in her hands, palming the merkaba, struck by the weight and power of it. He'd designed a magnificent piece of equipment for her. And the jeweler who crafted it knew what she was doing. "I love it. It's the nicest thing anyone has ever given me." She dabbed the corners of her eyes. He would likely never fully appreciate how much this

273

meant to her. "This is a very thoughtful and generous gift, and I will wear it every day. Will you help me put it on?"

He jumped up from his seat. "Sure!" He draped the necklace in front of her, his arms circling her. The clasp gave him some trouble, but he managed it eventually. He brushed against her neck as he smoothed her hair back into place. She shivered at his touch. "The clasp is a little tricky."

She tried to admire the necklace without a mirror. "This will be even more powerful now because it's charged with friendship." She sipped her coffee to hide her blushing face as he returned to his seat. She watched his eyes admire his gift on her and couldn't help noticing his gaze lingered on her chest. "Well, what do you think? How does it look?"

"Very nice." His voice, husky and rough, caught on the words. He cleared his throat and stood. "I guess we better get to the house so we can wrap this up. Right? We wrap up today? And then the show is over?"

She swore she saw disappointment in his eyes. "Yes, that's right. We wrap it all up today. But would you mind sitting back down for just another minute?"

His brow furrowed, but he sat.

She fiddled with the coffee cup. "I don't have a present for you exactly." She wrapped her hand around the quartz point hanging from her new necklace.

He held up his hands. "No, no! Don't even think about it. This is a thank-you for letting me be on your show this week. I didn't give it expecting a gift in return."

"I understand. But I did this not expecting a gift in return, too. And it took a little effort, so I hope you like my gift as much as I love yours." She took a deep breath and squeezed her coffee mug before plowing ahead. "Since *SpookBusters* didn't get renewed and since we seem to be a hit team, I wondered if you'd consider staying on permanently as my cohost."

Sterling's face didn't change. He sat motionless and still. Then he blinked and looked around the empty room. "You have a camera hidden somewhere? Am I being Punk'd?"

She laughed. "No. To both questions."

"You're serious about this?" He sat forward and clasped his hands.

"Completely serious." Her heart thumped. She expected him to jump at the offer.

"You're not saying this because you feel sorry for me, are you? 'Cuz I don't need anyone's—"

"I don't feel sorry for you. I think it's a good idea."

"What if we tank? What if I alienate all your devout fans, and the ratings plummet?"

"You're kidding, right? With your social media presence and natural charm? Rosie told me we're blowing up the Internet together."

"You think I'm charming?" He cocked one eyebrow.

His grin disarmed her. "Well, I . . . apparently some people do. Look, the truth is my ratings slipped this season. Your fans alone could compensate. And who knows how many more new viewers you'll lure in with your tweets and vines and blips—"

"Blips?"

"Whatever. You know what I mean. And then if we do tank despite all that, well, we tank together. And I had a fantastic ride."

He raised his eyebrows, and too late she heard the double entendre. She shook her head. "You're incorrigible."

"You're the one who said it. Not me."

"That's not what I meant, and you know it." Yet images of him standing shirtless, wrapped in a towel in her hotel room, flashed through her mind. She resisted the urge to fan herself when she flushed.

He fidgeted in his seat. "What about Michael? And Hoffmeier? They're bound to take some convincing."

"I already talked to them both. They're excited to make this happen. RandMeier is waiting to hear if you're on board and then will move forward with your formal offer and contract."

"You did all that for me? I thought you hated me."

"I thought I did, too."

"For the record, I never hated you. Even when I was kinda being a jerk."

"Rosie also told me that. You fooled me, but not her."

"Rosie's pretty damned smart."

"I know. So? Are we doing this?" He still hadn't said yes. Surely he wasn't leading her on just to turn her down.

"I'd be a fool to say no. And I'm pretty damned smart, too."

37

Kimberly, Michael, and Sterling sat at the Williamses' dining table facing Danielle and Stephen.

Danielle, cradling Josh, blinked. "So The Dark, the real root of the problem, was the sweet, elderly lady who lived here before us?"

Stephen rolled his eyes at Sterling. "The Realtor told us they were quiet, gentle people. Why would you think one of them stayed here to menace us?"

She watched Sterling, expecting him to pounce on his opening. But he gestured to her.

She smiled at him before continuing. "We originally dismissed the Millers for the same reason. But Edna revealed her identity to me. Her spirit, however, wandered confused and lonely and had forgotten her identity in her previous life. All her life she'd longed for a child but never had one. She became fixated on your children. Her desire was so intense she was able to manifest at a remarkable level and exhibit strength we rarely see."

Stephen narrowed his eyes at her. "And you truly believe this ghost attempted to strangle our son?"

Lara Bernhardt

This time she hesitated. Danielle clutched the baby tighter. Kimberly wanted to reassure the mother, not leave her with images of an invisible entity choking her infant son as he slept.

Sterling answered. "Look, she says the ghost was involved, the doctor said SIDS. Bottom line, your son is alive and well because Kimberly was here to intervene."

She could have kissed him. Supportive Sterling was a pretty nice guy to have around.

Stephen cocked an eyebrow at Sterling. "So you believe this explanation of hers? I thought you were here to bust her ghost theories."

Sterling held up a hand. "I'm here to offer objective evidence from my own observations. And I didn't see a thing I couldn't explain. The yarn? I saw no ghost cat. She manipulated the yarn herself. Ghostly images? Blurs and smudges. My ruffled hair? Could've been either some wind or a vent. The alleged voice telling us to get out? I believe it was added to the footage. Or it could have been background noise that only sounds like 'Get out' after they suggest it. I saw nothing I couldn't explain. As for Kimberly's fits, her conjecture the crib became hot enough to burn her, her belief she hears, sees, and interacts with spiritual entities. Well, she's the only one who sees, hears, and feels these experiences. I can't corroborate or disprove what's only in someone's mind." He looked her square in the eye. "I don't think it's a scam. I think she truly believes in these experiences. Or maybe she's a touch unstable. Who knows?" He grinned.

And just like that, she wanted to strangle him again. Why had she agreed to let him out of the Corner? She shook her head and took a deep breath. "But the spiritual disturbances are resolved now. That's the important thing." She scowled at Sterling.

278

"What about Felix?" Danielle asked, shifting Josh to her shoulder and patting his back.

"He's also gone. He only wanted to help. I think perhaps your grandmother sent him."

Danielle's eyes misted. "He really was a wonderful, wonderful cat. Now I wish he'd stayed here with us."

Stephen pressed his hands against his forehead. "Oh, for the love of . . . are you kidding me? After all these months of sleepless nights—"

"And cut," Michael called. "Okay, all that's left is the closing sequence. Kimmy and Sterling, let's bring you into the living room and centered on the fireplace. Just find a place around the train track."

She stood and shook hands with Danielle and Stephen. "Thank you for letting us come to your home. This has been a great week. You have a beautiful family, and now life can get back to normal."

"I can't thank you enough," Danielle replied. "I don't know what we would've done without you. Oops. Stephen, I think Josh threw up down my back. Can you get that?"

Kimberly shuddered and backed away as Stephen scrubbed at the curdled white mess. A tug on her sleeve stopped her retreat. Drew stood beside her, two fingers in his mouth, holding a piece of paper, which he handed her.

She squatted in front of him. "Did you draw this for me?"

The toddler nodded.

He'd drawn four stick figures with oversize heads and smiling faces—two taller figures with a smaller figure between them and a baby stick figure on the arm of one of the taller figures.

"Is this your family?"

The boy nodded again.

She noticed two figures at the top of the page, above the stick figure family. "Is this Mrs. Miller? The Dark?"

He nodded and popped his fingers out of his mouth. "Dat's Dale," he said, pointing at the second floating figure.

Her eyes teared as she hugged Drew. "That's right. She's with Dale now." She knew the boy was gifted. She hoped he developed his gifts in the future and never feared them.

"Kimmy? Let's close."

She ruffled Drew's hair. "Take care, little guy."

Picking a path around the wooden track, she joined Michael, stood beside Sterling, and passed the drawing to Elise for safekeeping.

"Okay, let's have you two stand back to back."

She groaned. "Really, Michael? Back to back?"

He gave her the look, and she fell into place, leaning against Sterling, arms crossed.

Stan focused the camera on them. Michael counted them in.

"This was an intense investigation and I'm glad Sterling was here to assist. In fact, I've invited him to join me permanently as cohost. And he's accepted."

Rosie quietly clapped and did a little happy dance. Michael gave her a thumbs-up. TJ muttered, "Aw, man. I hate that guy."

She turned over her shoulder to smile up at her new partner. His return smile sent a warm rush through her.

"Thanks, Kimberly. I'm excited to be here and can't wait for the next case." He turned back to the camera. "I hope you'll join us again."

She faced the camera, as well. "Yes. Come back next season for more *Wantland Files*."

Acknowledgments

Many thanks to Kindle Press and my editor, Robin, for bringing this book to fruition.

Thank you, Bill, for your tireless willingness to read this book as it developed as well as for the helpful suggestions and critiques along the way—and for listening whenever I bubbled over with excitement telling you about the latest twist. I've learned so much about writing from you and am forever grateful.

Thank you David, Beth, Kadey, Madeline, and Alan for being my first cheerleaders and for encouraging me to carve out the necessary writing time to complete this book. You always believed some day I would be published and encouraged me to keep going on days I wanted to give up.

Thank you to my writing group Betty Ridge, Faith Wiley, and Elton Williams. I'm so glad for your continuing support.

Thank you to my cover designers Maria and Victoria at BeauteBooks for crafting just the cover I wanted. I appreciate your patience and diligence as I figured out exactly what I wanted. I smile every time I look at it.

Lara Bernhardt

About the Author

Lara Bernhardt is a writer, editor, and audiobook narrator. She has written two novels, contributed the novella *Cassandra* to the Shine series, and narrated over a dozen audiobooks. She is the Editor-in-Chief of the Balkan Press and also publishes a biannual literary magazine, Conclave. Lara lives in Oklahoma with her husband, author William Bernhardt, and their family.

CPSIA information can be obtained
at www.ICGtesting.com
Printed in the USA
LVOW11s1451220217
525092LV00002B/234/P